CHRISTOPHER BUSH
THE CASE OF THE EXTRA MAN

CHRISTOPHER BUSH was born Charlie Christmas Bush in Norfolk in 1885. His father was a farm labourer and his mother a milliner. In the early years of his childhood he lived with his aunt and uncle in London before returning to Norfolk aged seven, later winning a scholarship to Thetford Grammar School.

As an adult, Bush worked as a schoolmaster for 27 years, pausing only to fight in World War One, until retiring aged 46 in 1931 to be a full-time novelist. His first novel featuring the eccentric Ludovic Travers was published in 1926, and was followed by 62 additional Travers mysteries. These are all to be republished by Dean Street Press.

Christopher Bush fought again in World War Two, and was elected a member of the prestigious Detection Club. He died in 1973.

CHRISTOPHER BUSH

THE CASE OF THE EXTRA MAN

With an introduction
by Curtis Evans

DEAN STREET PRESS

INTRODUCTION

Ring out the Old, Ring in the New
Christopher Bush and Mystery Fiction in the Fifties

"Mr. Bush has an urbane and intelligent way of dealing with mystery which makes his work much more attractive than the stampeding sensationalism of some of his rivals."

—Rupert Crofts-Cooke (acclaimed author of the Leo Bruce detective novels)

New fashions in mystery fiction were decidedly afoot in the 1950s, as authors increasingly turned to sensationalistic tales of international espionage, hard-boiled sex and violence, and psychological suspense. Yet there indubitably remained, seemingly imperishable and eternal, what Anthony Boucher, dean of American mystery reviewers, dubbed the "conventional type of British detective story." This more modestly decorous but still intriguing and enticing mystery fare was most famously and lucratively embodied by Crime Queen Agatha Christie, who rang in the new decade and her Golden Jubilee as a published author with the classic detective novel that was promoted as her fiftieth mystery: *A Murder Is Announced* (although this was in fact a misleading claim, as this tally also included her short story collections). Also representing the traditional British detective story during the 1950s were such crime fiction stalwarts (all of them Christie contemporaries and, like the Queen of Crime, longtime members of the Detection Club) as Edith Caroline Rivett (E.C.R Lorac and Carol Carnac), E.R. Punshon, Cecil John Charles Street (John Rhode and Miles Burton) and Christopher Bush. Punshon and Rivett passed away in the Fifties, pens still brandished in their hands, if you will, but Street and Bush, apparently indefatigable, kept at crime throughout the decade, typically publishing in both the United Kingdom and the United States two books a year (Street with both of his pseudonyms).

Not to be outdone even by Agatha Christie, Bush would celebrate his own Golden Jubilee with his fiftieth mystery, *The Case of the Russian Cross*, in 1957—and this was done, in contrast with Christie, without his publishers having to resort to any creative accounting. *Cross* is the fiftieth Christopher Bush Ludovic Travers detective novel reprinted by Dean Street Press in this, the Spring of 2020, the hundredth anniversary of the dawning of the Golden Age of detective fiction, following, in this latest installment, *The Case of the Counterfeit Colonel* (1952), *The Case of the Burnt Bohemian* (1953), *The Case of The Silken Petticoat* (1953), *The Case of the Red Brunette* (1954), *The Case of the Three Lost Letters* (1954), *The Case of the Benevolent Bookie* (1955), *The Case of the Amateur Actor* (1955), *The Case of the Extra Man* (1956) and *The Case of the Flowery Corpse* (1956).

Not surprisingly, given its being the occasion of Christopher Bush's Golden Jubilee, *The Case of the Russian Cross* met with a favorable reception from reviewers, who found the author's wry dedication especially ingratiating: "The author, having discovered that this is his fiftieth novel of detection, dedicates it in sheer astonishment to HIMSELF." Writing as Francis Iles, the name under which he reviewed crime fiction, Bush's Detection Club colleague Anthony Berkeley, himself one of the great Golden Age innovators in the genre, commented, "I share Mr. Bush's own surprise that *The Case of the Russian Cross* should be his fiftieth book; not so much at the fact itself as at the freshness both of plot and writing which is still as notable with fifty up as it was in in his opening overs. There must be many readers who still enjoy a straightforward, honest-to-goodness puzzle, and here it is." The late crime writer Anthony Lejeune, who would be admitted to the Detection Club in 1963, for his part cheered, "Hats off to Christopher Bush....[L]ike his detective, [he] is unostentatious but always absolutely reliable." Alan Hunter, who recently had published his first George Gently mystery and at the time was being lauded as the "British Simenon," offered similarly praiseful words, pronouncing of *The*

Case of the Russian Cross that Bush's sleuth Ludovic Travers "continues to be a wholly satisfying creation, the characters are intriguing and the plot full of virility. . . . the only trace of long-service lies in the maturity of the treatment."

The high praise for Bush's fiftieth detective novel only confirmed (if resoundingly) what had become clear from reviews of earlier novels from the decade: that in Britain Christopher Bush, who had turned sixty-five in 1950, had become a Grand Old Man of Mystery, an Elder Statesman of Murder. Bush's *The Case of the Three Lost Letters*, for example, was praised by Anthony Berkeley as "a model detective story on classical lines: an original central idea, with a complicated plot to clothe it, plenty of sound, straightforward detection by a mellowed Ludovic Travers and never a word that is not strictly relevant to the story"; while reviewer "Christopher Pym" (English journalist and author Cyril Rotenberg) found the same novel a "beautifully quiet, close-knit problem in deduction very fairly presented and impeccably solved." Berkeley also highly praised Bush's *The Case of the Burnt Bohemian*, pronouncing it "yet another sound piece of work . . . in that, alas!, almost extinct genre, the real detective story, with Ludovic Travers in his very best form."

In the United States Bush was especially praised in smaller newspapers across the country, where, one suspects, traditional detection most strongly still held sway. "Bush is one of the soundest of the English craftsmen in this field," declared Ben B. Johnston, an editor at the *Richmond Times Dispatch*, in his review of *The Case of the Burnt Bohemian*, while Lucy Templeton, doyenne of the *Knoxville Sentinel* (the first female staffer at that Tennessee newspaper, Templeton, a freshly minted graduate of the University of Tennessee, had been hired as a proofreader back in 1904), enthusiastically avowed, in her review of *The Case of the Flowery Corpse*, that the novel was "the best mystery novel I have read in the last six months." Bush "has always told a good story with interesting backgrounds and rich characterization," she added admiringly. Another southern reviewer, one "M." of the *Montgomery Advertiser*, deemed *The Case of the Amateur Actor* "another Travers mystery to delight the most critical of a reader audience," concluding in inimitable American lingo, "it's a swell story." Even Anthony Boucher, who in the Fifties hardly could be termed an unalloyed admirer of conventional British detection, from his prestigious post at the *New York Times Books Review* afforded words of praise to a number of Christopher Bush mysteries from the decade, including the cases of the *Benevolent Bookie* ("a provocative puzzle"), the *Amateur Actor* ("solid detective interest"), the *Flowery Corpse* ("many small ingenuities of detection") and, but naturally, the *Russian Cross* ("a pretty puzzle"). In his own self-effacing fashion, it seems that Ludovic Travers had entered the pantheon of Great Detectives, as another American commentator suggested in a review of Bush's *The Case of The Silken Petticoat*:

> Although Ludovic Travers does not possess the esoteric learning of Van Dine's Philo Vance, the rough and ready punch of Mickey Spillane's Mike Hammer, the Parisian [sic!] touch of Agatha Christie's Hercule Poirot, the appetite and orchids of Rex Stout's Nero Wolfe, the suave coolness of The Falcon or the eerie laugh and invisibility of The Shadow, he does have good qualities—especially the ability to note and interpret clues and a dogged persistence in remembering and following up an episode he could not understand. These paid off in his solution of *The Case of The Silken Petticoat.*

In some ways Christopher Bush, his traditionalism notwithstanding, attempted with his Fifties Ludovic Travers mysteries to keep up with the tenor of rapidly changing times. As owner of the controlling interest in the Broad Street Detective Agency, Ludovic Travers increasingly comes to resemble an American private investigator rather than the gentleman amateur detective he had been in the 1930s; and the novels in which he appears reflect some of the jaded cynicism of post-World War Two American hard-boiled crime fiction. *The Case of the Red Brunette,* one of my favorite examples from this batch of Bushes, looks at civic corruption in provincial England in a case concerning a town counsellor who dies in an apparent "badger game" or "honey trap" gone fatally wrong ("a web of mystery skillfully spun" noted Pat McDermott of Iowa's *Quad City Times*), while in *The Case of the Three Lost Letters*, Travers finds himself having to explain to his phlegmatic wife Bernice the pink lipstick strains on his collar (incurred strictly in the line of duty, of course). Travers also pays homage to the popular, genre altering Inspector Maigret novels of Georges Simenon in *The Case of Red Brunette*, when he decides that he will "try to get a feel of the city [of Mainford]: make a Maigret-like tour and achieve some kind of background. . . ."

Christopher Bush finally decided that Travers could manage entirely without his longtime partner in crime solving, the wily and calculatingly avuncular Chief Superintendent George Wharton, whom at times Travers, in the tradition of American hard-boiled crime fiction, appears positively to dislike. "I generally admire and respect Wharton, but there are times when he annoys me almost beyond measure," Travers confides in *The Case of the Amateur Actor*. "There are even moments, as when he assumes that cheap and leering superiority, when I can suddenly hate him." George Wharton appropriately makes his final, brief appearance in the Bush oeuvre in *The Case of the Russian Cross*, where Travers allows that despite their differences, the "Old General" is "the man who'd become in most ways my oldest friend."

"Ring out the old, ring in the new" may have been the motto of many when it came to mid-century mystery fiction, but as another saying goes, what once was old eventually becomes sparklingly new again. The truth of the latter adage is proven by this shining new set of Christopher Bush reissues. "Just like old crimes," vintage mystery fans may sigh contentedly, as once again they peruse the pages of a Bush, pursuing murderous malefactors in the ever pleasant company of Ludovic Travers, all the while armed with the happy knowledge that a butcher's dozen of thirteen of Travers' investigations yet remains to be reissued.

Curtis Evans

PART I
THE BOSFORD CASE

1

DORIS BOSFORD

IT'S ONLY rarely that anything interesting turns up when Norris, my manager, happens to be out and I do a turn of duty at the Broad Street Detective Agency. Usually Norris mentions certain contingencies and suggests how to cope with them, or he leaves me accounts to check or reports to compile—just enough work, in fact, to fill in the gaps between a couple of crosswords, with, of course, a break for morning coffee. But that particular morning something happened that was out of the rut. It was a long way out of it, and in half a dozen ways.

It was exactly ten o'clock when Bertha Munney rang through on her private extension.

"A Mrs. Bosford would like to see you, sir. Something to do with her husband."

I think I smiled at that—heaven knew why, unless it was that I was a husband myself.

"Nothing to do with divorce, Bertha?"

"Oh no, sir!" Bertha sounded almost horrified. "Just a missing husband."

"And what's she like?"

"Well, sir, to coin a phrase, she's not exactly off the top shelf. Quite pleasant though, and cheerful. She says she knows you."

"Knows *me*! What's her full name and address?"

"Mrs. Doris Bosford, 'Pinewood', 18 Malmsey Avenue, Harringay."

"Never heard of her," I said. "Perhaps she's trying to force an entry with malicious intent. Any guns or hand-grenades on her?"

"How you do talk, sir!" Bertha told me archly. "I think she's all right. Shall I show her in?"

"Might as well," I said, and knocked out my pipe and lowered a window to let out the accumulated smoke. Then I hastily closed it again. It was a raw morning of late November, and there was quite a deal of fog.

Doris Bosford came in. I was certain I'd never seen her in my life. She was a blonde of about thirty; tallish, and with a figure slightly on the plump side, pleasant-faced and perfectly self-possessed. That was rare in itself. Most clients look nervously about them. She looked only at me. Perhaps it was because I was holding out a hand.

"How d'you do, Mrs. Bosford. Won't you sit down? And did I understand that you and I have met before?"

She was most attractive-looking when she smiled. I was to think, as the talk progressed, that there was much of the gamine about her—shrewdness, pertness, frankness and a philosophy that had optimism as its main constituent.

"I don't expect you'd remember," she said, and mentioned an enquiry of ours in one of the big London stores. She'd been—and still was—assistant buyer in the millinery department where a certain curious case of pilfering had happened to come our way.

"Of course, I was dressed differently from now," she said, "and I hadn't a hat on. Only, when this happened about Andy and I happened to think back I knew it'd be all right if I came and consulted you."

"Andy?"

"Yes, Andy. Andrew, of course." She smiled. "That's what's on the marriage lines. He's my husband. He's been gone now for over a fortnight and I'd like to know where he is. I haven't even had a word from him."

Her accent was slightly cockney. The voice was perky; perky as the little hat that contrived—heaven knew how—to cling to the side of her head. I rather liked her. She struck me as the heart-of-gold type—someone you could trust in a crisis. Or was there just a little too much on the surface?

"Let's get it all down formally," I said. "But not so formally that we can't have a cigarette. You smoke?"

She did. A couple of minutes and we got down to essentials. Andrew Bosford, now aged thirty-six, was her husband, and she'd been married for three years.

Don't imagine that everything came out in chronological order. You can rarely pin clients down to that. In the intervals of talking you try to steer them to this and that and hope, out of a great deal of irrelevance, to establish essential facts. The facts in this case were that Andrew Bosford's father had had a jeweller's shop in Clerkenwell and that the son had been brought up to the business. Then he'd become a crooner and had worked with various bands. Doris had met him at a certain palais de danse. A year after their marriage—which made it two years ago—some infection or other had ruined his throat. I didn't say so but it seemed to me that to qualify as a crooner one's throat had to be in pretty bad shape from the outset.

"And what did he do then?" I said.

"I don't know," she told me frankly. "I know that he met an old friend. He let that much out, but he didn't tell me his name, and after that he was always pretty busy. He used to make quite a lot of money. I don't know what he kept for himself but he gave me some to keep. It's in a box under the bed."

"You never tried to worm out of him what he was doing?"

She moistened her lips. She took her time about stubbing out the cigarette. When she looked up there was a wariness in her eyes.

"Suppose you tell *me* something," she said. "Is anyone ever going to know about all this? What we're talking about?"

"No one," I said. "A firm like this couldn't exist for five minutes if that sort of thing happened. Everything said between you and me, Mrs. Bosford, is as confidential as if you were in your doctor's surgery."

"Well then, I didn't ask him," she said. "Andy was madly in love with me, but he wouldn't trust me with that. What he was doing, I mean. I'm not the nagging sort, either. All I knew was that he was making good money and he was trusting me with it and he wasn't worried himself."

That was when her look changed. She added an important something.

"Not till about three weeks ago."

I didn't interrupt.

"I never thought it was anything—not then," she went on. "He was at home, you see, and I had my own job, so I never saw him really till evenings, and often not then. Then that week he was at home. I sort of kidded him about having a holiday, but he wasn't in the kidding mood. Then he said he might have to be away three or four days. That wasn't anything unusual. He was often away for that long. It was the way he said it, as if this time it'd be different. Then when I got home that night—a fortnight ago, that'd be—I just found a note to say he'd gone. I brought it with me."

She had another look at it before she handed it to me. Her face flushed slightly as she explained that chicken was one of his terms of endearment.

> *Off for three or four days, chicken. Don't go sitting*
> *with strangers in the long grass.*
> *Cheerio.*
>
> ANDY.

I gave the note back.

"Not much information there," I said. "Any ideas yourself as to where he'd gone?"

This time she took out one of her own cigarettes and she didn't hurry over lighting it.

"Perhaps," she said. "I'm not a fool. I mean I can put two and two together."

"Not keeping two homes going?"

The smile was more of a sneer. It gave her face a hardness I hadn't seen before.

"Not that," she said. "You can always tell. Andy was a one-woman man. He wouldn't look at another woman."

"I don't blame him," I said casually. "You're an attractive woman, Mrs. Bosford."

"I don't know about that," she told me, "but I know enough to hold a man once I've got him. If he's worth while."

I couldn't find a rider to that. I asked how she knew where he'd gone. Or might have gone.

"Well, I guessed he'd been near the seaside," she said. "Occasionally he'd bring back a lobster or a couple of crabs. And I was pretty sure he'd been to France. He'd bring back bottles of French brandy and liqueurs and little things for me. You know—personal things."

"Did he speak French?"

"Ever so well," she said. "His mother was French. His father was in the 'fourteen-'eighteen war and met her out there, and she came to England soon after it began, and they were married."

"You know his parents?" That wasn't so irrelevant a question as it might seem. What I was trying to do was establish a background.

"Oh no," she said. "They were killed in the blitz. The shop was blown up, too. Andy got compensation later on, and then he worked as a salesman for someone else, and then he went in for crooning, like I told you."

"I see," I said, if only to make time. "And you had no idea where he went to when he left the house of a morning?"

"I knew that he had a sort of office. In Clerkenwell."

"You did?"

"Yes," she said. "A regular little detective—that's what I was. How it happened was that a Gladys Mitton—she's one of our saleswomen—happened to see Andy going into a place called Sharman House. That's in Clerkenwell. She knew Andy—see. I didn't say anything to him, but when he was home that week I told you about, three weeks ago, he went out on the Saturday afternoon and left his keys behind, and there was a Yale key that wasn't like the one to our front door, so I slipped round to that ironmonger's where they cut keys while you wait and had one cut for myself. Then as soon as Andy had gone—a fortnight ago, I mean—I went along to this Sharman House to see what I could see, if you know what I mean. And there it was on the first floor. One room with

A. BOSFORD

IMPORTER

on it in black. So I let myself in when no one was looking and shut the door. All there was was a desk and that was locked, so that wasn't any good to me. And about a dozen wooden boxes stacked up against the wall. Little boxes. About so big."

So big seemed about a foot wide.

"And what then?" I said.

"Well, nothing. I just went out again."

"Nothing else in the room?"

"Not really. An electric fire. And a chair. Two chairs. Just ordinary office chairs."

"No telephone?"

"Oh yes. There was a telephone. It stood on top of the desk. One of those yellow-looking, roll-top desks."

I frowned for a moment or two in thought.

"You've been back there? Before you came here, for instance?"

"No," she said. "It wouldn't have been any good. I hadn't a key to his desk. There were all sorts of keys on that chain of his, but all I took was the door key. The office door."

That seemed about all. I leaned back in my chair.

"Well, you've been frank with me, Mrs. Bosford, which is how it should be. But one important question. In fact it's a question I've been wanting to put to you for the last few minutes."

I leaned forward and just wagged the pencil idly at her.

"Just why haven't you been to the police about all this?"

Her face flushed. She took the cigarette-case from her bag again.

"Well," she said slowly, "perhaps I had an idea that Andy wouldn't like to have the police mixed up with his affairs."

"But why not? The police are the natural people to trace a missing husband. They have resources and powers that we here can't command."

She didn't say anything. I leaned back in the chair.

"Look, Mrs. Bosford," I said, "you've told me a lot and I also can put two and two together. I've assured you that everything said here is in strict confidence, so why not go the rest of the way? *Why didn't you go to the police?*"

"Very well," she said, "I'll tell you. I've thought for a long time that if Andy was strictly on the level with whatever he was doing for a living he'd have told me about it himself."

"Right," I said. "What we've both got to assume is that what he was doing wasn't strictly within the law. That word 'importer' on his office door, for instance, might cover a multitude of transactions. There's also that matter of his holiday three weeks ago. He might have been keeping away from his office because he was afraid to go there. By the way, if you've that key with you would you mind letting me have it? I'll see it's returned to you by post."

She made no bones about giving it to me. I told her what our terms were, and she pulled out a wad of notes from her bag. Five minutes later we'd signed the contract forms and she'd seen me put my copy in the safe.

"You're on the telephone?" I asked her.

She gave me the number and I said I'd keep in touch. Six-thirty at night or not later than eight in the morning, she said, were the best times to reach her.

"Just a last question or two. One always thinks of last questions; but had your husband any relatives?"

"None," she said. "He'd only his father and mother, and I told you they were killed in that blitz."

"Any friends that used to come round to the house?"

"None," she said. "I used to think that was queer. Before he got that new job, whatever it was, one or two friends from his crooning days used to drop in sometimes on a Sunday. Then they sort of dropped out. I did tell him once that he ought to make some new friends and bring them round, but he said he liked his house to himself what little time he had in it. He said he knew a friend who'd gone off with another friend's wife." She smiled. "I think he was pulling my leg. Not that he didn't like his home to himself. And me. And his television."

"And just one more question. Absolutely the last. You were as fond of him as he was of you?"

She slowly moistened her lips.

"I guess perhaps I wasn't. I was always straight with him, mind you. Never looked at another man."

She had said that almost fiercely. Then she shook her head.

"Andy was a bit too fond of me. You can get tired of that. But I reckon you wouldn't understand."

"Maybe I do," I told her. "Life can't be a perpetual honeymoon. All the same, there's something I can't quite understand. Let's put it bluntly. Things had begun to pall with you a bit. Yet you're so anxious to get him back that you come to us."

The lips clamped together. They widened slowly to an ironic smile, that same smile that suddenly made the face hard and almost calculating.

"There's that money under the bed," she told me. "If anything's happened to him, then it's mine. If nothing's happened to him, then it's still his. I want to know *whose* it is. Hadn't we better leave it like that?"

"You're the client," I told her gently. "Unless you'd like to tell me just how much there is under the bed."

She smiled again—the pert smile or the knowing one.

"Perhaps I don't know myself," she told me, and went towards the door.

That was when I remembered something else, something I should have done long before. I could tell myself that I was definitely losing my touch.

"Did we mention a photograph?" I asked at the very door. "You have one?"

She did have one in her bag. You'd have thought the forgetfulness was hers, for she apologised for not giving it to me. She also told me a whole lot of things that she'd never have told anyone else.

As for the photograph, it was about two years old, taken while Andy Bosford was still crooning. As far as she knew he'd had no photographs taken since then. I said it didn't matter so long as it was still a good likeness.

"It is and it isn't," she told me. "It was before he grew his moustache."

You see what a flibbertigibbet kind of brain I have. Far too hurried and sketchy. Had Norris been in that morning he would have wormed his way laboriously into all sorts of things—things that I was then trying anxiously to summon as in need of answers.

"What sort of moustache?" I said.

"Just ordinary," she told me. "Not one of those streaks like some crooners and band-leaders have. A real moustache. Rather like yours, only not so close-clipped."

That gave me a chance to take a forgotten description. Bosford was five feet ten, black-haired and brown-eyed. The rest was on the photograph. She said he had no special distinguishing marks. Another minute after her telling me that I was seeing her through the door and Bertha was taking over.

As soon as the door had closed I could console myself with one satisfying idea. I'd been so unmethodical over that talk with Doris Bosford because I'd had ideas. I'd had them before she'd been ten minutes in that room, and from then on I'd been bursting to get to work on them. That, as I said, shows the kind of mind I have. All the same, I couldn't get to work till the afternoon, when Norris would be back.

Sometimes I wonder what has happened to my brain since all those years ago when I began working with George—Chief Superintendent—Wharton as an unofficial expert at the Yard. Once, and I say it myself, I'd had a good, solid, reliable sort of brain. As an economist I wasn't a city editor or a George Schwartz, but I did have a capacity for methodical thinking, and a logical restraint that never got me out of hand. Then, with detective work, a rot set in. Sudden confrontations with what might or might not be evidence meant too rapid decisions. You couldn't always add two and two and expect the answer to be four. You weren't working with figures but with ideas: shadowy stuff like human behaviour, reactions to this and that and the impact of motives; and when you deal with that kind of material and think you're holding silver in your hand, as like as not it turns out to be moonshine.

You may wonder what the point is in this jeremiad. It is this—that after a forty-minute interview with Doris Bosford, a woman I'd never before seen to the best of my knowledge, I had so run ahead with a formulation of theories that I could seriously ask myself if her husband was dead and if she had killed him. In that case, of course, her visit to us of that morning had been merely a bluff. She might have been trying to establish some devious alibi or to lead us—and subsequently the police—astray by a series of carefully strewn false trails.

Doris Bosford, I had told myself, was two women. One had a pert sort of smile. She was the self-possessed, confident and optimistic Doris—the one who was still holding down that assist-ant-buyer's job, popular with the staff and nice, as one said, with the clientèle. Underneath that woman was someone harder, the one that had that other smile—a hard-bitten kind of smile that gave a glimpse of something calculating and even predatory.

As to facts, based on my belief in what she had told me, she had tired of that uxorious husband of hers. Life no longer centred round him but round a box beneath a bed. She might say that she wanted to know if her husband were alive, but my deduction was that she would be far more relieved to know him dead—if he weren't dead already. Against that was the frankness with which she had admitted certain things—that, for instance, she had tired of him and that she suspected he was engaged in some kind of racket. And there, after a deal of verbiage, was the vital question. Was that frankness bluff? Was her husband dead, and did she know it? If so, precisely why had she come to us?

I'd had lunch brought in, and it was not long afterwards that Norris arrived. Naturally he wasn't excited over a small-time job like the one I had to outline, even if his reactions were even quicker than my own. Bosford, he said, had skipped with some other woman, probably French. All that uxoriousness had been merely a calculated screen. And if Bosford were really a shady character, then Norris—an ex-chief inspector at the Yard and now managing director of a staid and reputable detective agency—would have preferred that Doris Bosford should take her custom elsewhere.

"I'll look into it myself," I told him. "In any case there's nobody we can really spare. If there's anything fishy about the whole thing I'll drop it like a hot potato."

"What's this Bosford been up to?" Norris said in his slow, careful way. "Looks to me as if he was in the watch-smuggling racket."

That was stealing my thunder—something I thought I'd worked out rather cunningly. Still, I supposed it did stick out a mile, when I came to think of it.

"Maybe," I said. "I might be able to get a line on that. If there's nothing else you have in mind I think I'll push off."

Norris gave his dour smile.

"The fact of the matter is, sir, if anyone had come here about a lost kitten you'd have jumped at the job."

I had to own he was right. When I'm at a loose end in intervals of working with George Wharton I'm prepared to do practically anything to kill time. But Andy Bosford, I could tell myself, wasn't a lost kitten, and looking for him would be a long way from killing time, or that's what the contract said which I'd locked in the safe. And all that, I should add, took place not in November of 1954 but in November 1953. That was to turn out to be a matter of considerable importance.

Just round the corner I hopped a bus for Clerkenwell, that district which for well over a hundred years has been a centre for the watch and jewellery trade. A passing postman directed me to Sharman House.

It was a building both grimy and remote—side-tracked, as it were, into the narrow confines of Mobbs Lane. Once it had been a dwelling-house, but now its three storeys were offices, most of them one-room affairs. The tenancy board just inside the open door said that "A. Bosford, Importer" was on the first floor. On the landing the click of typewriters was coming from one or two rooms, but Bosford's room, when I listened at the door, was utterly quiet. I slipped the key into the lock and went in, and even before I turned I was wondering if I should see on the floor the body of Andy Bosford. When I did turn I saw that the room was empty. It had a damp kind of emptiness—the emptiness, say, of a long-deserted and deteriorating house.

It was a room some twelve feet by ten. The desk was still there, and the two chairs and the electric fire, but those boxes that Doris Bosford had seen had gone. The room had no other door, and only the one window that looked across the narrowness of Mobbs Lane. The electric fire stood in what had once been a used fireplace, and on each side was a shelved, built-in cupboard. The shelves were bare, but here and there a comparative freedom from dust showed where objects had stood. Some of them seemed to have been the kind of boxes that Doris Bosford had seen piled against a wall.

The desk that should have been locked came open when my fingers tried the flap. Its small drawers and pigeon-holes were empty. It was, as Doris Bosford had said, a second-hand affair that was worth a fiver at the most. With my gloved hands I opened the three long drawers. There was something in the bottom one, away in its far corner—a *Bradshaw* of a couple of years ago. I slipped it into my pocket. I looked under the desk; I looked in the cupboards again. I pried, in fact, into every corner of that room and found not even the smallest scrap of paper. Obviously, and since the visit of Doris Bosford, that room had been carefully emptied. And the only person who had emptied it was presumably her husband. In that case it looked superficially as if Norris had been right. Andy Bosford had skipped, and the odds were that it was with some other woman. But what Norris hadn't taken into account was that money in the box under the bed. Bosford wouldn't have skipped without that.

And yet somehow I was far from sure. I could even tell myself that that almost gutted room was what I should have expected. That was why, in a couple of minutes, I was tapping at the frosted window of G. Gormer and Son, Wholesale Jewellers.

2

THE MISSING HUSBAND

G. GORMER and Sons were just across the landing. The room I entered was occupied by a couple of typists. Both of them took a look at me but only one kept on looking. I told her my name was Travers and I'd like to see one of the principals. She thought someone named Mr. Ernest was in. She buzzed through, and he was. He was opening the door almost at once.

I asked if there was somewhere we could talk privately. He'd raised his eyebrows at the business card I'd given him, but he motioned me through the door. Gormer and Sons didn't seem to be doing too badly. They had another and larger room with display cases and more typists, and Ernest Gormer himself had an office. He was a short, tubby man of about sixty, bald except for a greying fringe round his hair-stuffed ears.

"Take a seat," he said. "What can I do for you?" He had another look at that card I'd given him. "Nothing wrong here, I hope."

I told him frankly that the Broad Street Detective Agency had been asked to find an Andrew Bosford who'd been missing for a fortnight. His wife had heard no word and she was worried.

"This is a photograph of him. He grew a moustache since it was taken, but you'll see I pencilled one in. You've seen him from time to time?"

He did a good deal of frowning before he said he thought he'd just caught sight of him once or twice.

"What about his actual business? Was there plenty going on?"

"Not that I ever saw," he said. "But a lot of these places are only a front. Somewhere you can get your mail and answer it. Mind you, I can't guarantee what went on when we weren't here. We close at five."

"Well, he's gone," I said. "Everything cleared from the room except a second-hand desk and two office chairs. The telephone's still there but not a directory."

He shrugged his shoulders.

"Who're the lessors of this building?" I asked him. "Maybe they'll know something."

"Ah, them," he said. "Wyvis and Gride. Farnum Street. Just behind the Mansion House."

"I'll call there straight away," I said. "One other thing, though. Could I possibly question your staff?"

He shot a suspicious look at me.

"Just to ask if they've seen Bosford," I told him. "Or anything going on at his office."

He said he'd do it himself and give me a ring later. I couldn't have expected him to do more, so I thanked him and left. I turned quickly at the head of the landing, almost expecting him to be watching me from his door.

I knew Farnum Street. It was a brisk afternoon and I walked there. Wyvis and Gride had the ground floor of a two-storeyed building. The usual display of offices and premises to let, lease or sell ran right across the one front window. This time I didn't trouble about principals. The suave-looking man in city black on duty at the enquiry desk looked good enough. I handed him my card. He gave me a glance, then read it a second time. I told him why I was there.

"Bosford," he said. "Sharman House. I'll enquire, sir."

He disappeared through a door just beyond the handsome mahogany desk. Hardly before I'd had time to look round he was back with a slim file.

"Here we are, sir."

He adjusted a pair of reading glasses with tortoise-shell rims, almost as thick as my own. The premises, he read, had been taken on the 30th of May 1953, on a six months' basis with option of renewal at a yearly rental of eighty pounds. The premises had now been relinquished. This was—he glanced up at the wall calendar—the 17th of November, so the tenant had actually renounced only a fortnight.

"Might I see the letter?"

He hesitated for a moment, then turned the file round towards me. That letter had been typed. It had the Sharman

House heading and the date was Saturday, the 6th of November. I think I gave a grunt.

"The key was returned?"

He pointed a nicely manicured finger at the word "key" at the foot of the letter. It had a tick against it.

I always carry a magnifying glass. I have done for years. It has a folding handle and fits snugly into a waistcoat pocket. To tell the truth, I use it more in antique shops than on the affairs of either the Yard or the agency. A long, long time ago I got badly swindled over a set of silver date marks and it taught me a lesson.

Bosford's signature didn't tell me much. It was legible, I'll say that for it, but the letters were so carefully formed that the whole thing lacked character.

"I wonder if you'd let me do something," I said. "What's your name, by the way?"

It was Wallace, and Wallace was pretty dubious about letting me do what I wanted to do. I gave my avuncular smile.

"Look, my dear fellow, this isn't some carefully organised scheme to forge Bosford's name to a document. All I want is a photostat of this letter so that I can compare his signature with one I know to be genuine."

"You mean this isn't genuine!"

"There's only one chance in a thousand that it isn't," I told him. "But I've got to be sure. Keep this to yourself, but Bosford presumably left London on the night of the third. And yet on the sixth he writes from Sharman House relinquishing his tenancy or whatever you call it."

I let my eyes screw up to a quizzical smile.

"Your firm wouldn't like to be mixed up in anything shady?"

"Most certainly not," he told me earnestly.

Snobbery and intellectual arrogance are, in my judgment, two of the deadliest of sins, but there are times when you have to throw your weight about. I quoted half a dozen impressive references and invited him to try them, and finally I induced him to ring the office, check up on me with Norris and then hand me the telephone.

"Travers here, Norris. I want you to get Abe Geldermann at once and get him to come himself or send someone in double-quick time to Wyvis and Gride of 12 Farnum Street. I want a photostat of a document. Tell him to come by taxi."

I told Wallace I'd wait outside. Abe arrived in ten minutes—his place is in Cheapside. And to cut the story short, he took a couple of shots of the letter and I signed a chit the prudent Wallace had drawn up for me saying what it was all about. At Abe's studio I got him to take a shot of the Bosford photograph with a moustache more carefully drawn in. He said he'd have everything at the office by the morning.

I walked the few hundred yards to Broad Street because I wanted to think. Frankly I didn't like the way things were beginning to turn out. Take that typewritten letter, for instance. Doris Bosford had seen no typewriter in that office, and it was something she'd hardly have missed.

I thought of the sequence of events as far as I remembered them.

Wed., 3rd Nov.—Bosford leaves his home.

Fri., 5th Nov.—His wife goes to his office.

Sat., 6th Nov.—Bosford writes letter to house agents.

With those dates clearly in my mind I could see that I had jumped a bit ahead. Bosford might have gone to Sharman House at any time on that Wednesday—his wife was out—and have taken the typewriter away. If it was in good condition it was probably the most valuable thing in that room. But he didn't remove the boxes that had been stacked against the wall. He didn't remove those, and clear the desk and shelves, till after his wife's surreptitious visit on the Friday during her lunch hour.

If he had removed the typewriter before that, then he must also have typed the letter beforehand. When it had been posted I had no means of finding out, since the envelope had naturally not been kept by Wyvis and Gride. And all I could say about the whole thing was that it was uncommonly curious. But for that money in the box under a bed I would have said it was a certainty that Bosford had skipped the country and would never be heard of again.

When I got back to the office Norris had a message for me from Gormer. He'd said his staff knew no more than himself about Bosford. They'd caught sight of him from time to time, but no more. I went out to Bertha's room and used her telephone to try to get hold of Tom Holberg.

Tom runs the biggest and best-known theatrical agency in town. He and I have had a lot of dealings together, and he'll always stretch a point for me or spare a minute. But Tom's secretary, Miriam Levy, said he was busy, so I left the message with her. I wanted to have confidential information about a crooner named Andy Bosford who'd dropped out of the business a couple of years before: what bands he'd sung with, and so on. I said I'd be grateful if someone would ring me any time that night at my private address.

Outdoors there wasn't a fog but there was quite a mist. I took a bus for Charing Cross, and as I sat down I felt something in my pocket. It was that oldish *Bradshaw* I'd found in a corner of a desk drawer in Bosford's office. I didn't see at that moment what it might tell me, and I preferred to save it for after tea and a cosy chair by the fire while waiting for Tom Holberg's call. Also I was thinking of all sorts of things connected with a case that had as yet scarcely begun. One, at least, was almost incongruous. Doris Bosford had spoken of her husband as a crooner. Wasn't that rather derogatory? Shouldn't she have called him a singer? Not that it mattered. If it was proof of anything, it was that he'd ceased to be the glamour boy she'd married. And as I made my way along the crowded early-evening pavements towards home I was wondering something else—just how much money there really was in that box beneath the bed.

After tea, as I'd promised myself, I tackled that *Bradshaw*. First I had to discover if there was any slip of paper between the leaves, and that meant turning each leaf separately. It was while I was doing that, towards the end, that I noticed a marginal pencil mark. It was alongside the trains connected with Seahurst, that popular seaside resort on the south coast. Not only was there the marginal line but one particular train was underlined—the one that left Charing Cross at 4.20 p.m. and reached Seahurst at 6.15.

I turned over the rest of the leaves of that book and found no more annotations. As a clue it consisted entirely of that underlining of one special train, so I re-stoked my pipe and stretched out my long legs to the fire and tried to puzzle out the significance of that one train. I looked at the *Bradshaw* again. It was the edition that covered all adjustments for late autumn and winter services, and it was two years old. So Bosford, it appeared, had bought himself a *Bradshaw* in order to be able to look up the times of trains, but one train only had interested him. But I thought I'd better check up on that, so I went right through that book again.

There were definitely no other markings, so there seemed only one thing to do: risk the loss of Tom Holberg's call and ring ENQUIRIES at Charing Cross.

"The four-twenty to Seahurst," I said. "Could you tell me how long it's been running?"

"That's a tall order," the clerk told me. "I do know it's been running for at least ten years."

"That's capital," I said. "Just what I wanted to know. And it's still running?"

"Oh yes. It's still running."

I thanked him, and that was that. Bosford, if I was working it out correctly, had had reason to take that train. Then he had discovered, as I had, that it was one of the unaltered regulars and no new *Bradshaw* had been needed. *If that was the only train he ever took.*

I spread the net of deduction still wider. Doris Bosford had thought her husband had gone to the seaside and to France. Was it to the seaside and *thence* to France? Newhaven was not far from Seahurst, and from Newhaven he could have gone to Dieppe. But if he had had Newhaven in mind, why hadn't he gone there direct? I turned to Newhaven in the *Bradshaw*, but nothing had been noted against the name.

That was when the telephone went. It was Miriam, Tom Holberg's secretary, on the line, apologising for Tom's not speaking himself. She asked me if I had pencil and paper handy.

It was a comprehensive statement. Bosford was small fry, and there must have been some deep digging to unearth what I took down. He had started with small local combinations—the sort that took engagements for club and gala dances, and at first had doubled, as they say, on vocals and drums. Then he got a job as singer with Jimmy Coot's band, which had engagements at small suburban dance halls. He moved on to Ted Skipper and his Crewcuts, who were a little higher in the palais-de-danse brackets. His last engagement—the one apparently when something happened to his throat—was at the Silver Boat Club, a restaurant and dance club run by a man named Marler. Bosford was then working for Joe Arliss and his Music, as the band was grandiloquently styled. Bosford had made only two recordings, neither of which had sold well. He had never broadcast. His speciality had been songs made popular by French artists like Jean Sablon.

That, considering Bosford's status in the dance-band world, was pretty comprehensive, as I said, but it wasn't much immediate help. That was why I shifted to the implications in his wife's story, and with the hope of tying something up with what I had learnt from that *Bradshaw*. What it all got back to, of course, was that smuggling racket. I'd thought I'd been rather clever in spotting it, but Norris had fastened on to it from the word go.

Not that the obvious can always be trusted. If things were as easy at that, brains in the detecting business would go rusty for lack of deduction. But that Bosford business did seem made, as it were, to measure. Bosford was brought up in the jewellery trade and later he had worked as a salesman. He knew the technical side and he had connections. So when his voice had become impossible, even for crooning, he'd gone back to something connected with his old trade. But his years as a crooner had had a certain tawdry glamour, and, as I saw it, work at the bench or as a salesman would have been unthinkable. So would the money. Like most of us, he would want easy money and plenty of it.

All the available evidence connected him with a jewellery or watch-smuggling racket. There was his French and the fact that his wife as good as knew he had been to France. As for the secrecy which kept him from telling even her what his new job was, that seemed to suggest that he was a member of a gang. If so, he was a fairly high-up in that small gang, for not only did he assist in operations at the French end but he also ran that office at Sharman House as a distributing centre. All that, again, was confirmed by the fact that he was making a lot of money.

My own problem was to know just where to begin. I did know that in the morning I would run down to Seahurst and try to discover if anything was known of Bosford there, but in the meantime I had an itch to be working. And the best place to call at seemed to be that Silver Boat Club where Bosford last worked, so I looked for it in the telephone directory, but it just wasn't there.

All the same, I guessed it wouldn't cost me anything to question a taxi-driver, so I went out to the traffic lights at the Haymarket and waited till the queue began to form. One cab was empty and I told the driver to take me to the Silver Boat Club.

"They don't call it that now, sir," he said. "It's the Pink Moon. Still want to go there?"

I did. We finally ended up at Walling Street, bang in front of the doors. It looked a fairly large place, quiet and well conducted. Off the smallish foyer was a cloakroom and a bar.

I made for the bar and had a gin and tonic. The price wasn't exorbitant.

It was the quietish spell before dinner. The barman even had time for me.

"I've been away for some time," I told him, "and I really dropped in to see Marler. They tell me he doesn't have the place now. Or does he?"

"Been gone a couple of years," he said. "He still drops in occasionally, though."

"I suppose you've no idea where he lives?"

"Not the faintest," he told me.

"Remember a crooner who was here about two years ago? Name of Andy Bosford. Worked with Joe Arliss's band."

"Can't say I do," he said. "Might have heard the name, though. Crooners are five a penny round here, unless they get to the top."

"And you've no idea where Joe Arliss is working now?"

"One of Benny Carter's boys might tell you," he said. "Go right through the restaurant. One of the waiters will show you."

I gave him a tip. The restaurant was a big room, with tables round it and a fairish space for dancing. I was directed through to a dressing-room alongside the kitchen. Only two of the band had arrived, and it was the bass-fiddler who thought that Joe Arliss was at the Ledisham Palais de Danse. He said I could check on the telephone. I checked. Joe was there.

I walked the few yards to Cambridge Circus and found a taxi. It took us half an hour to get to Ledisham. Maybe that was as well. Arliss had just arrived. He and his boys were warming up in a large room on the first floor, just behind the snack-bar. He told me he had plenty of time. I said I'd want no more than ten minutes of it. What I learned in that ten minutes was this. I give it in Joe's words—more or less.

He was a man of about fifty, fattish and slightly bald. He was soft-spoken and had a slight lisp, all of which is by the way. He told me that Andy Bosford was quite a nice boy and it was a pity about that throat infection. Not that he'd ever have got very far. Joe certainly hadn't been to Eton himself, but he spoke of Andy as someone on whom you always had to work. There'd been, for instance, an old number revived: something to do with a Tyrolean hat, and could Andy pronounce that word as Tyro-lè-an? Not a bit of it. You'd get him pronunciation perfect, and then when he sang the number, out it came as Ty-ròl-ean, which, as Joe succinctly put it, bitched the whole thing up.

"He wasn't a bad boy, though," Joe said. "Not too bright, but a good-looker. Any idea what he's doing now?"

I said that that was what I wanted to know myself.

"Well, give him my regards if you run across him," Joe said, and that was the end of the interview. Except for something I tried as we shook hands.

"Did you know his wife?"

"Well, yes," Joe said. "She used to follow him around after he was first married. Keeping an eye on him, I guess. A blonde, wasn't she?"

I confirmed it. Then I asked about Marler. Joe had to be reminded that it was at the Silver Boat he'd been working when he'd had to find another vocalist. What he told me was what I knew—that Marler had sold the place and it had changed its name. He didn't know Marler's private address.

I didn't want to hunt the telephone directories from there, so I took a taxi to my club. The only F. Marler I could find was at Grafton Gardens, S.E., which looked as if it might be a block of flats. I rang my wife to say I couldn't get in to dinner and hailed another taxi. Grafton Gardens turned out to be reasonably handy, and it was a block of flats. They were not in the top class but good enough. Quite a few big cars were parked in the open space before the main entrance. At the enquiry desk I asked for the number of Marler's flat.

"Did you want to see him?" I was asked. "I'm afraid he isn't in. He hasn't been in for some days."

"How do you know?" I said.

"Well, these are service flats," I was told. "His bed hasn't been slept in and he hasn't been in to meals."

"Any idea when he's likely to be back?"

The receptionist said he'd no idea. Marler had never been away so long before. Sometimes he was away for two or three days on business but never longer. I asked if I could see the manager.

Five minutes went by before I saw him in his office. He couldn't help me. Marler, he said, had been gone about a fortnight. He was a considerate tenant, and he'd mentioned at the desk that he'd be away about two days.

"What about his wife?" I said. "Is he married?"

"Not to my knowledge," he told me with a slight reproof. "We never enquire into the private affairs of tenants."

"He couldn't have had an attack of some kind and be ill or dead in his flat?"

That didn't shake him in the least. Only that morning he had been in the flat—a furnished one, by the way. Everything was in order and as if awaiting Marler's return. After that there was nothing else I could ask him, except one thing, and to that I didn't expect an answer.

"I want to see Mr. Marler in connection with the disappearance of a man called Bosford," I said. "He might possibly throw some light on it."

I described Bosford, but the manager had no knowledge of him. If he was a friend of Marler, then, as he pointed out, there'd have been no need to go to the desk. So that was all. I thanked him, wrote a brief note to be given to Marler on his return, and went out into the misty November night. It wasn't bad walking, and in twenty minutes I was back at my own flat. Bernice—my wife—had finished her meal, but I had something sent up. Then I settled down by the fire to another bout of thinking.

I wasn't sure, of course, that there was any connection whatever between Marler and Bosford. The only, and very tenuous connection was that it was while Joe Arliss's band had been playing at the Silver Boat that Andy Bosford had caught that throat infection that had cut short his singing career. And yet it was odd. It was very odd. Bosford had been missing for about a fortnight and so had Marler.

I tried from the little I knew to put the two men side by side, but I had far from enough data. Bosford had presumably been living in a Harringay villa and Marler at a flat which had cost him about four-fifty a year—without meals and extras. What was he doing now he had sold the Silver Boat? Or was he living on capital? I didn't know. I didn't know anything except, as I said, that it was while working at that club of Marler's that Bosford had caught the throat infection; and I knew, of course, that both men had been missing—and inexplicably—for the same period of time.

So I decided to leave Marler out of things and to concentrate on Bosford. My knowledge of him had been somewhat added to by Arliss. I saw him as far as concerned the world beyond his original job, as a good-looking moron who had discovered in himself, and to a certain extent exploited, a talent for making those extraordinary noises so beloved of the jungle-minded—the off-beat rhythm, the slurred notes, the catch in the throat and all that imitatively acquired, emetical technique of the crooner's trade. Doris Bosford had tired of that amiable, uxorious moron for whom perhaps she had once ambitiously had considerable hopes. Now I knew, as surely as I was sitting in that chair, that the only thing worrying her was the uncertainty—not so much as to whether he were dead or alive but as to the legal ownership of what was in that box beneath the bed.

But why shouldn't I ring her? No sooner did I think of that than I was doing it. It was well after the evening time she had given me, and I thought she might be out, but she wasn't.

"Mrs. Bosford?" I said. "This is Travers, whom you saw this morning. We've been working on a certain matter and wonder now if you could help us a little. Do you, for instance, know a man named Marler?"

She didn't answer for a moment. Then she was having trouble in clearing her throat.

"What name did you say?"

I spelt it out for her. The answer came pat. She knew nobody named Marler.

"Then did you ever know your husband mention Seahurst?"

"How do you mean?"

"In connection with any business of his being there. I don't mean mentioning it directly. Letting it slip, shall we say."

"No," she said slowly. "I never had even an idea."

"I see," I said. "I had an idea he might have done some business there. But about the enquiry. I have something I'd like you to see. Would it be convenient for you to come to the office tomorrow evening? Or one of our people could come to you?"

"Well, perhaps I'd rather you came here. What is it about?"

"I'm not in a position to tell you yet, but it's rather important. Shall we say at about half-past seven?"

She said that would be suitable. There was just one other thing to add.

"I wonder if I might give you a bit of advice—unsolicited advice? It's about a certain box. You know what I mean?"

"I think so."

"Well, why not deposit the contents? You have a banking account?"

"Only the Post Office."

"Well, do something about it," I told her. "You're out all day, you know. And there're such things as burglars."

She laughed.

"They wouldn't scare me. Besides, I've got a gun."

"The devil you have!" I said. "Got a permit for it?"

"Permit? What sort of a permit?"

I had to laugh myself, if only at the naïveté.

"Let's forget it," I said. "I'll explain it tomorrow night."

But as I hung up I wasn't even smiling. Doris Bosford knew Marler—to that I'd have been prepared to swear. That question about him, the very mention of his name, had taken her so by surprise that she'd had to play for time before giving me an answer. And if I could assume that she did know him, then that was exasperating. One doesn't like clients who flagrantly conceal what might be urgent evidence. For all I knew I might be uncovering other things which she would attempt to deny or conceal. And I'd told Norris that if I had suspicions about anything fishy, then I'd drop the whole thing.

Not that I'd got to that state yet. If there's one thing with which I'm endowed or cursed it's with an overwhelming and shameless curiosity. That's why I knew I should still be going to Seahurst in the morning.

3
DEAD MEN

I GOT to the office at about nine. Abe, as usual, had been as good as his word, and the photographs were there. The photostat of the letter to Wyvis and Gride was exceptionally clear, and on the picture of Andy Bosford the added moustache might have been the real thing.

At Charing Cross I caught the nine-fifty for Seahurst. When I got there I went straight to police headquarters. They knew me there and, for that matter, I knew them. We'd had a couple of cases connected with Seahurst, and—I say it with all the modesty I can muster—we'd done them a couple of remarkably good turns. Grainger, the Chief Constable, I knew very well. On private affairs, so to speak, we were pretty good friends. When it came to professional matters things were not so good.

It's curious the only partially concealed hostility the professionals have for us amateurs. It's a kind of intellectual arrogance. Their attitude is that which Job put so neatly to his supposed comforters—*Ye are the people and wisdom shall die with you.* They, as the modern term has it, know it all, and the rest of us are necessarily bunglers, and interfering at that. One admits that they have the means and the tried and true methods, but there's still room for both of us. I've never said this, mind you, but if their methods weren't so tried, true and hidebound, then at times they might go farther and far more quickly. If—let's quote a modest example—they recognised the existence of a hunch.

Grainger wasn't in at the moment, but I did see his C.I.D. man, Inspector Padman. We also knew each other pretty well. We shook hands warmly enough, but there was a something in his manner which told me he was wondering if once more I was a bird of ill omen. But he wasn't all that busy. He rang down for coffee and we yarned for a bit over our pipes. Then I told him just so much about the Bosford affair.

"Never heard of him," he said. "Still, I might be wrong."

He rang through to his sergeant for the files to be checked. The sergeant rang back to say there was no mention of any such name.

"That's a dead end, then," I admitted, and I told him about the *Bradshaw*. He didn't say so but I guessed he was thinking that private agencies made easy money taking trips to here and there on the strength of a pencil mark. And just then Grainger came in. His face fell at the first sight of me, but our greetings were most friendly. Padman rang for more coffee and Grainger was told all about it.

"I don't know where you can go for information," he said. "We know nothing. The hotels might. That'd be a long and expensive job. I don't know whether your client would stand for it."

I ruled it out. We just hadn't the available men.

"Supposing there's something in that idea of a smuggling racket. Do you think the Customs people would open out?"

Grainger doubted it. They might co-operate with the authorities but not with a private agency. He admitted that smuggling was going on, and on a pretty big scale. Those behind it were well organised, and Preventive Men were far too few.

"What I'll do is keep my eyes and ears open," he told me, "and if I do hear anything I'll give you a ring. But those rackets aren't usually my pigeon. I've got quite enough to do handling my area without worrying about the Customs and Excise."

His *was* a pretty big area. In terms of population it wasn't so great, but his jurisdiction, so to speak, ran well back into the county and as far west as Maverton and east to Happton.

Maverton, because of its cliffs, is just an unspoilt fishing village. Happton, as you may know, was once that kind of village. Now it is a kind of bungalow resort where one gets little for one's money but fresh air and cheaper living than in Seahurst itself. I'd only been there once, and the sight of it had made me decide to stay in my car.

I had it on the tip of my tongue to mention Marler's name, then I decided against it. I did ask Grainger to lunch with me at the Royal and he said he'd be delighted to. We had quite a good meal and it so mellowed him that over coffee and a fine old port he volunteered a something.

"Wouldn't do any harm if I rang the Customs people," he suddenly said. "If it comes from me they might loosen up, if there's anything to loosen up about. What did you say this chap Bosford was like?"

Five minutes later he returned from the phone booth. The Customs people had nothing on anyone named Bosford.

"Mind you," he said, "he might be operating on a false name. That's easy now rationing and identity cards and all that are over. I'll still keep my ears open and let you know if anything turns up."

That was all I got for my trip to Seahurst. I took the two-forty back to town. After that there seemed nothing worth the starting till I'd seen Doris Bosford.

Her house was what I'd expected: a semi-detached villa in a long street of similar villas. That street was quiet and rather a cut above the average: it had the as yet unpollarded plane trees, for instance, which justified its name of avenue. No. 18 had the usual paved path to its front door, flanked by two formal flower-beds, in the centre of each a standard rose-tree.

The sound of my knock had scarcely time to reverberate before Doris Bosford was opening the door. The dark skirt and tight-fitting jumper concealed the incipient bulges, and she was looking even younger than her years.

"Hallo," she said in that perky voice of hers. "I hoped it would be you. I hate meeting strangers."

We went into a front room that I could describe only as lush. I don't suppose it was more than fourteen feet by twelve, but it had everything, and most of them the things that my own queer tastes detest. The walls had gilt-framed oils that had probably been bought at a local auction; the carpet was deep-piled but highly coloured; the two spacious chairs and the settee were in maroon plush; a radio cabinet was wedged in a corner and there was a television set and something that was soon to be identified as a cocktail cabinet. I'd have been prepared to bet it was the only one in Malmsey Avenue.

"Will you have a drink?" she said. "There's some very nice brandy. Or Andy said it was. I don't drink much myself. It does things to your figure."

She pressed a button and that cabinet opened. It seemed to be holding a nice assortment of everything. She had a glass of port. The brandy was first-class, even when drunk from an ordinary glass. It had a famous French label.

I told her what had so far been done, but I didn't mention Marler or the photostat. I produced that after I'd refused a second brandy. She was positively staggered.

"But how could he! How could he have been there on the Saturday!"

Then she gave a little gasp.

"Yes?" I said.

Her smile was a bit rueful.

"But if he *was* still in London, then he might have caught me when I went to his office. Then there might have been a fine old to-do."

"It's all very puzzling," I told her. "But about this signature. You're sure it's your husband's?"

She said she was positive. I thought that was hardly enough proof. Did she have any document that bore his signature? She licked her lips as she thought.

"There's his will," she said. "I know where it is if you don't mind me looking."

I didn't hear her feet on the stairs—maybe the carpet was too thick—but I did hear her in the room above me. I strained my ears but I heard only slight movements, though I guessed she was getting out that box from under the bed. When she came back she was holding a foolscap envelope. She didn't let me open it, or read what was in it. After a quick look she showed me the signature—*Andrew Bosford*. I compared it with the photostat and it looked the same to me.

"Andy got the milkman and the daily woman to witness it," she told me. "It leaves everything to me. All you could expect, really. We're a couple of orphans, so to speak. And was that what you particularly wanted to see me about?"

"That was it," I said. "And you can't throw any light on the mystery—why he was supposed to be away and in London nevertheless? He cleared out that office of his since you saw it and wrote that letter."

She moistened her lips again.

"I can't think of anything—unless he was afraid of the police."

I had to say there was something in that. Certainly he'd dissociated himself entirely from that office and removed every clue as to what his business there might have been. And that, as I said, still left the main problem. Where was he now? And why hadn't he telephoned?

"Search me," she said. "That's why I came to you."

I'd left Marler till the last. As I mentioned him I was watching her as closely as if trying to discern the first wrinkle. She was ready for me, though that didn't keep the faint flush from her face.

"Could Marler have been the friend for whom your husband was working?" I said.

"I don't know," she said. "I didn't know anyone called Marler."

"But, surely!" I said, and smiled. "He owned the Silver Boat. Your husband was working there with Joe Arliss when he caught that throat infection. Didn't you ever hear him mention Marler? Didn't you go to the Silver Boat ever yourself?"

You could almost see her brain working. Reluctantly she let a slow recognition dawn. She gave an exasperated click of the tongue.

"How silly I am! You'll think I'm an awful fool but I didn't connect anyone with *that* Marler."

"It's easy to forget," I told her. "But did he show any special interest in your husband?"

"No," she said slowly. "Not really. Not more than anyone else. But he did like those French songs Andy used to sing."

"What songs were those?"

"Well," she broke off to smile, "no harm now in telling you the tricks of the trade, as they say, but Andy used to buy all sorts of records of Maurice Chevalier and Jean Sablon and so on—there's stacks of them in that sideboard drawer—and then he'd play them over and over till he had them by heart. That'd be mostly in the daytime. I wasn't here, thank God! It'd have driven me crackers."

"But I thought you said he spoke French well."

"So he did," she said patiently. "Just like a Frenchman. But don't you see? What he did was really imitations. He had to get the style and little tricks and everything."

There, strange as it may seem, I left things. I didn't tell her about Marler's disappearance and note her reactions. I just gave the usual assurances, said the polite goodbyes and left. You see, we're not choosy about clients, even if the bulk of our income is from contract work and we're practically independent of them. What we don't like is a client who wants to hide all his disreputable little secrets and expects us to grub like moles in the dark. That's the kind who's likely to get you involved with the law and make trouble all round. Not that I expected trouble from Doris Bosford.

All I knew was that something was telling me to let that matter of a missing husband taper quietly off, as it were. We wouldn't make any money out of it, but we'd get out with no chance of bad publicity. What sort of bad publicity it would be I didn't know; what I did know was that Doris Bosford had lied about Marler. I guessed she had had an affair with him, and that might mean that her whole idea in coming to the Broad Street Detective Agency was a roundabout way of getting evidence for a divorce. It might be even more serious than that. It might be some craftily calculated scheme to cover up a murder. I never did like missing people. Far too often we've found them dead.

That was what I put up to Norris the following morning. He agreed. The best thing to do was to notify Mrs. Bosford that we were unable to proceed further and to advise her to go to the police. It was while we were actually discussing the wording of the letter that the telephone went. Who should be on the line but Grainger, the Chief Constable of Seahurst.

"A body's just been discovered at Maverton," he said. "On the rocks there. Probably a million to one against it being your man, but I thought I'd let you know. I'm just going along there myself."

"I'll come down at once," I said.

"Better come straight to the mortuary," he told me. "We ought to have him there by then."

The train would be quicker than a car and I just had time to make it. It was eleven o'clock when I got to Seahurst. Grainger was in his room.

"Sorry you've had a journey for nothing," he said. "The man's named Marler. There was full identification on him."

Something was telling me that for once I'd better open out.

"That's curious," I said. "I've an idea that my missing man Bosford had a connection with someone named Marler."

"Really! Well, this is a Frank Marler. Town address—Grafton Gardens. Local address—The Dunes, Happton."

"It's my Marler," I said. "He lived at Grafton Gardens. I went there and was told he'd been away unexpectedly for a fortnight."

"It fits in," he told me. "This chap's been dead about a fortnight."

"Foul play?"

"Don't think so," he said. "Like to have a look at him?"

We went downstairs and along a passage to the mortuary. The uncovered body lay on the slab and the air had the sickly smell of formaldehyde. The police surgeon was already at work. I hate that side of my job. I've always hated it, but this time I had to look. It was a pretty ghastly sight. The body was bloated and the face no more than a bulbous grey mass in which features were scarcely discernible.

"That ought to have identified him, if nothing else did," Grainger said, and pointed to the body. What he meant was the still recognisable tattoo. Once it had been a hovering bird—an eagle probably—holding something in its claws.

"What about the lungs, doc?" Grainger was asking.

"Everything O.K."

"Stomach content?"

"Haven't got to that yet," the doctor told him, and waved an indifferent hand at a something on the marble-topped side table. "Most of it's been dissipated. Still, I'll do what I can."

Grainger gave me a nod and we moved off.

"I'm running out to Happton now," he told me. "Thought I'd save it till you got here, just in case."

His man was ready in the police garage, and we set out at once. It took us a quarter of an hour to get to Happton, and we didn't do much talking. I didn't feel in a talking mood. I wanted to get out of my mind the horrible, bloated thing that had been on that mortuary slab. Even in the clear air of that morning I still had somehow the smell of disinfectant in my nostrils.

"Here we are," Grainger said, and drew the car to a halt in the car park of the Golden Lion. "Padman ought to be somewhere about. I sent him on ahead an hour and more ago."

I liked Happton even less than when I had seen it first. The whole place was a tetter of pink-and-red-tiled bungalows, with only here and there a larger house. Grainger had told me that the only thing that had kept it from being a seaside resort on its own was the fact that the currents were treacherous and that the narrow beach shelved suddenly and deeply. But there was a little quay and plenty of boats riding at anchor. Fishermen were standing about or tending their nets. It would have been picturesque enough if one hadn't had to look at the bungalows.

Grainger was clicking his tongue impatiently at the non-appearance of Padman. Then we walked along to a fisherman who was gathering in his dried nets. The Dunes, he said, was the last bungalow if we kept straight on. So we kept on. The beach road curved slightly, and when we had rounded it we caught sight of Padman's car. Then we saw him at the opened door and he came to meet us.

"Find anything?" Grainger said.

"Plenty," Padman told him. "You'll see for yourself, sir, soon as you get inside."

It was a brick-built bungalow with an asbestos-tiled roof. It looked, and was, the usual four-roomed type, but it had in addition a built-on brick garage which turned out to have been used also as a workshop-store. The front garden, of sand and marram grass, had never been dug, neither had a larger garden at the back.

"Two bedrooms, as you'll see, sir," Padman said as soon as we were through the door. "And occupied from time to time, I'd say, by two men."

Each of the small bedrooms was scantily furnished; the tiled floors each had only a mat alongside the camp bed, and the beds—one unmade—had no sheets but only blankets. Each room had only a modern chest of drawers and a bed-side table with reading lamp. The window curtains were thick and would obscure all light from the windows.

"Both chests have only spare clothes," Padman said, and opened a drawer or two. "Thick stuff, mostly, like jerkins and pullovers and long stockings. The sort of stuff you'd use on a boat. This is Marler's own room, by the way."

"How d'you know?" Grainger asked him quickly. "Find something of his in it?"

"In a way—yes, sir."

He opened a small, top drawer. In it, on top of some hand-kerchiefs, was a worn wallet. Padman opened it with his gloved fingers and drew out a couple of envelopes. Each was addressed to Marler at Grafton Gardens, and each was a bill—one from a tailor and the other from a wireless store in Tottenham Court Road.

"Now look in here, sir," Padman said, and opened a door to a small bathroom-lavatory. "On that glass shelf, sir. Two separate sets of shaving tackle."

"Yes," Grainger said. "And what else?"

"Through here, sir."

The far door led to the second bedroom. On top of the chest of drawers were various objects: a bunch of keys, a benzedrine inhaler, a fountain-pen, some loose change and again some letters—this time three of them. Padman's hand went to pick one up, then the hand hovered as he gave me a look.

"Like to guess whose these are, sir?"

I thought I knew, but I let him have his moment.

"The one you were asking about yesterday," he told me triumphantly. "A Mr. Andrew Bosford."

A few minutes later Padman had gone to fetch a fisherman named Spooner. Grainger and I were in the bungalow living-room, and we were talking about a dead man, and possibly two. Marler's garments had been drying when I'd been in the mortuary and so I hadn't seen them, but Grainger said they were just the kit a man would wear when going out to sea on a blustery night.

"It was pretty choppy here that week-end," he said. "Mind you, we don't know what actual night he was drowned, but a week-end ought to cover it."

I said I'd put the actual drowning on the Saturday night—the 6th. That was the date of the letter Bosford had written to the house agents, and it was by then that he had cleaned out his room. Grainger spotted something which I'd hoped he'd miss.

"One thing I can't quite fathom," he said. "Let's assume this Marler and Bosford were smuggling. We'll guess more about that after we've seen this chap Spooner, but let's assume it. Very well then. Bosford closes down his office which presumably he's used for disposing of whatever it was he was bringing in illicitly. That looks as if Marler and Bosford were getting out. And yet they put to sea again for another haul of whatever it was! That doesn't fit in."

"Early yet," I said. "The more you know, the better the pieces will fit in."

Padman arrived with the fisherman. He'd also brought a hacksaw for cutting through the stout padlock on the garage door. There was an entry door to the garage from the living-room. Marler, we were to learn, had had it specially made. But it was locked from the inside. Through the window we'd been able to see that there was no car.

We both shook hands with Harry Spooner, a fresh-complex-ioned, dark-haired man of about fifty in the usual high boots and blue trousers and jersey.

"Sit down, Harry," Grainger said. "Don't know if the rumour's got around here yet but we fished Marler, the owner of this place, out of the sea at Maverton this morning. He'd been dead a good time. You know anything about him here? His life and what he did and so on?"

"Can't say as I ever saw much of him," Spooner said in his deliberate way. "He weren't down here much."

"What was he like?"

"Hard to say. About my height"—that'd be about five feet ten—"and looking a bit of a toff."

"What about his hair?" I said.

"Dark, far as I remember." Then he did remember. "That's right. Dark hair. Black, if you like. I see him working on that boat of his about three weeks or a month ago. He'd got his shirt off. 'Nice to see someone working, sir,' I say, and he laughed."

"Notice anything on his chest?"

Harry gave him a look.

"Thought for a minute you was pulling my leg. I see he was tattooed on his chest if that's what you mean. Couldn't see what it was exactly."

"That's fine," Grainger said. "And what about that boat of his?"

Harry said it was like a small naval launch, probably picked up at some government sale. It was painted dark blue. Name—*Dainty*, painted each side of the bows in light blue. Marler used to take it out at night, mostly. He had a small trawl net and some lobster-pots.

Padman had the padlock sawn through, and he was opening the door through to where we sat. We had a look in that garage. It wasn't too wide, but it was long. At the far end that trawl net hung across the wall. Half a dozen lobster-pots were under a bench on which were various tools.

"What sort of a car did he have?" Grainger wanted to know.

"One o' them station-wagons," Harry said. "Something like a small truck. Painted a sort of yellow."

"And that boat of his—was it seaworthy?"

Harry gave him another look. Maybe Grainger's terms weren't quite right. I wouldn't have known.

"Sturdy enough," he said. "I reckon he could've gone most places with it. Depends on the weather."

"Across the Channel?"

Harry shrugged his shoulders. He said it all depended.

"Well, we think he went out with it—or her—on the Saturday night," Grainger said. "But before we get to that, did you ever see another man with him?"

"Once I did. He was about a hundred yards out and I see there was two in her. Too far out to see who the other one was."

"Ever see anyone with him by daylight?"

Harry shook his head. Not that he remembered. But about that going out on the Saturday night. Grainger was wrong. It was on the Thursday—the night before Guy Fawkes Day—that Marler went out.

"How do you know?"

"Well, I heard a sort of pop and I thought them young devils of boys was setting off fireworks through someone's letter-box or something like that, but it wasn't. It was Mr. Marler's boat. I couldn't see her, mind you, but I knew the sound of her engine. And next morning she weren't here. And she hain't been here since. I thought he'd taken her somewhere to berth her for the winter."

"What sort of a night was it?"

"Well," he said reflectively, "that was about eight o'clock and pitch-black. A bit choppy then, but nothing much. Blew harder towards morning."

"Well, we're much obliged to you, Harry," Grainger told him. "May want you at the inquest, but we'll let you know."

Grainger and Padman and I went back to the living-room. Grainger was looking puzzled.

"Can't fit things in again," he said. "If it was on the Thursday night they had that disaster to the boat, then who cleaned out Bosford's room—the one you were telling me about, the one in town?"

"There's one simple solution," I said. "It may sound too simple. Marler and Bosford weren't all the gang. There was a third."

"That's it!" he said. "You're right. That makes it all much simpler. Marler and Bosford did the smuggling and Bosford had the office in his name, though another member of the gang disposed of the stuff."

He got to his feet. Padman was to use a couple of the local men and pick up everything they could about Marler, and possibly Bosford. I parted with one of my Bosford photographs.

"I'll see the Customs people," Grainger said. "They're always nosing about. They may know something. Like to drop in at the station and hear the latest?"

I said I would. But I didn't have to go to that mortuary again. Grainger rang down from his room and what I learned was that Marler's death was definitely from drowning. The doctor still couldn't narrow the time down from a fortnight.

I said goodbye to Grainger and he promised to let me have any news there was. It mightn't be for a day or two, but he'd definitely keep me informed, especially if Bosford's body came ashore.

"That likely?" I asked him.

He shrugged his shoulders. He said the experiences of Channel swimmers was proof enough of the strength and eccentricity of the currents. Marler had come ashore at Maverton. Bosford might land up anywhere. He might never be washed up at all.

4

THE THIRD MAN?

IT WAS almost two o'clock when I left Grainger and I just had time for a pint and a snack at a pub and to catch the two-forty back to town. When I got to the office Norris and I talked things over. What we were hoping was that Bosford's body wouldn't come ashore immediately, because we weren't sure that Grainger, in that case, wouldn't make us appear at the inquest. That wouldn't have been quite the right kind of publicity.

"What're we going to tell Mrs. Bosford?" Norris wanted to know. "She'll see about Marler in the paper, and you think she knew Marler pretty well."

I said I didn't think she was one to read a newspaper. We might string her along for a day or so on the off-chance that her husband's body came ashore. Besides, we weren't dead sure that Bosford had been engaged in anything illicit. We wouldn't know about that till Grainger told us what he'd learned—if anything— from the Customs people. What Grainger told us would affect the kind of information we gave to Doris Bosford. She, for instance, wouldn't want the wrong kind of publicity. It wouldn't do her any good in her job if it were known that her husband had been actively engaged in smuggling.

As an argument, that was all rather woolly. I may own the agency, but I never interfere with Norris. But there are times when I have to use devious ways to make him see things through my eyes. What he didn't know was that that insatiable curiosity of mine was making me want to know all the ins and outs of the Marler-Bosford story; and if Doris Bosford was still our client then I had at least an excuse to poke and pry. But just when we'd agreed to do nothing at the moment in the matter of Doris Bosford Bertha buzzed through to say that there was a call for me. I picked up the receiver.

"That you, Travers?"

It was George Wharton.

"In the flesh, George," I said. "How are you?"

"Can't grumble," he told me laconically. "I'd like to see you, by the way. Can you come over at once?"

"Business or pleasure?" I asked him flippantly.

"Business. To do with Seahurst. That satisfy you?"

"Yes and no," I said. "But I'll be over. In about a quarter of an hour."

It was all fairly obvious. Grainger wanted information at the London end and he'd rung the Yard. His requests had come in front of George for scrutiny and he'd seen my name. And that was just what it turned out to be.

George wasn't stuffy, though I couldn't say the same for that room of his. If anything he was quite amiable. He didn't even slip in a sneer about private detective agencies. He asked after Bernice, and seemed almost solicitous about my own health. Then he came to the point.

"This isn't a murder case," I said. "I can only tell you about my client if it's in strict confidence."

"Of course it's in confidence," he said, and the snort blew that moustache of his till it must have ruffled his nose. "You've seen Grainger and he's asked us to try and get certain information. You can help us. You appear to know more than he does."

George may be devious, secretive and a score of other exasperating things, but you can trust his given word. So I told him everything I knew, including my impressions of what had happened that morning at Seahurst. He had brought in a stenographer and it was all taken down though I didn't have to sign it.

"Just what we wanted," he said. "I'll issue extracts and then we can get to work."

"Anything discovered since I left Seahurst?"

"Don't know," he said. "Did you know about the Customs people? They'd had ideas about Marler. They actually intercepted his boat one night, but there was nothing on it. Mind you"—he wagged an admonitory finger—"when I say they had ideas, they have them about everybody. They even check up on the fishermen sometimes. The trouble is, they've too few men and too big an area to cover."

"What might he have been smuggling?"

George shrugged his massive shoulders.

"Can't say. Watches, jewellery—even dope. There's big money in it in any case. By the way, did your client mention anything about her husband earning big money?"

I lied unblushingly.

"The only thing that concerned us, George, was if she could pay the retaining fee and look good for the rest. She has quite a fair job of her own, you know."

"Bloodsuckers," he said, and had the grace to give an ersatz chuckle. Then he was getting up, and a couple of minutes later I was out. I had a quick verification of the time. It was a quarter-past six, so I made for the nearest telephone booth and decided to risk it. It was Doris Bosford who answered me. She said she had only just got in.

"I think we're getting on with things," I said, "but I want to give you a word of warning. I have an idea the police are on to what your husband was doing. They may be along soon to question you—"

She was trying to cut in, but I told her to listen.

"You know nothing about your husband's activities. You've got that? Not a word about that key and going to his office. And, above all, not a word about that box under the bed. He just gave you house-keeping money and nothing else. Got that?"

She said she had it. I asked her to give me a ring if the police did happen to come and I gave her my private number. That was all. I went home and spent a peaceful night. Doris Bosford didn't ring.

The next morning I was picking up my two newspapers as soon as they were pushed through the letter-box. Each carried the Marler story but only to the extent of a longish paragraph. Naturally there was no hint of smuggling, nor of a possible second victim of the disaster. Then, in a few minutes—just after eight o'clock—the telephone went. Doris Bosford seemed agitated.

"Have you seen the *Daily Picture*?," she was asking almost breathlessly. "About that Frank Marler being drowned?"

"Oh yes," I said airily. "But you hardly knew the man. How could what happened concern your husband?"

She didn't speak for a moment. Then I could practically hear her smile.

"Of course not," she said. "I just wondered—that's all. And you will let me know if there should happen to be anything?"

"Just leave it to us," I told her. "Nobody called last night?"

Nobody had called. I said I was pretty sure they'd be along, and probably that evening. I reminded her about certain pieces of advice.

Nothing happened during that day. At just after six o'clock—it was sheer luck that I happened to be at Broad Street—Grainger rang. He hadn't much news, but what he had was interesting. Contact had been made with Marler's widow.

"I never even suspected him of being married," I said.

"Well, he was," he told me. "They've been separated unofficially for quite a time and she hasn't seen him for over a year. By the way, I don't suppose it interests you but the inquest's the day after tomorrow. Eleven o'clock. Room 6 at the Town Hall."

"Thanks," I said. "I might be there and I might not. Anything else new?"

"Yes," he said. "The Yard's traced Marler's car. And you know what? He sold it about a week before this affair to a firm not far from that flat of his. Where he got his petrol."

I merely gave a Whartonian grunt. It was for him to comment, and he did.

"You see?" he said. "That office was given up and now we know the car was sold. Didn't that mean winding up the business?"

"Looks like it."

"And yet they went off on another trip!"

"It's still easy," I said. "I don't say it's right but mightn't both that car and that office have become too hot?"

"Yes," he said. "There may have been that."

There was nothing else except that the Yard was trying to get news of the Marler-Bosford operations at the French end. I didn't comment on that, and in a minute or so was hanging up. The next thing that happened was at the flat. Doris Bosford rang soon after our evening meal.

As soon as she spoke I knew something had happened. Her voice had a conspiratorial hush.

"They've been," she said. "I told them just what you said and I only had to sign a statement."

"That's fine," I said. "I don't expect you'll be bothered any more. There wasn't any mention of your going to Seahurst for the inquest on Marler tomorrow morning?"

"No, nothing about that. You're going to it yourself?"

"I'm not interested in Marler," I told her, "except in so far as he concerns your husband."

"Yes," she said, and hesitated. I'd had an idea that she was working up to something, and suddenly it came.

"Mr. Travers, was there any truth in what they were hinting? About Andy being on that boat?"

"I'm afraid it looks like it," I said.

"You mean . . . he's dead?"

"A bit too early to presume that. All I can say is that all the evidence points that way. But let's leave it like that, shall we? We'll be writing you some time tomorrow. That all right?"

"Quite all right." It was as if she were licking her lips. My guess was that she'd be going straight upstairs and hauling out that box and counting once more what was in it.

When I woke in the morning I knew, in spite of what I'd told Doris Bosford, that I'd be going to that inquest. So I got the car from the garage and was at the office early. One of the operatives, a man called Jackson, was reporting after the end of an assignment. Bertha didn't know of anything immediate, so I told her to tell Norris that he'd be with me. I expected to be back in the early afternoon.

The train would have got us in too late for that eleven-o'clock inquest. The car got us there with a quarter of an hour to spare. We parked the car behind the Town Hall, and it was then that I knew why the actual inquest was there. The Town Hall and police headquarters virtually adjoined. All that the jury would have to do in order to view the body was to walk across the concrete way some forty yards to the mortuary.

It was because I didn't know if the body had already been viewed that I went towards the mortuary myself, intending to ask someone on duty. I went through a door and there I was in the tiled hall from which ran the corridor to the mortuary. A uniformed constable was having an argument with someone. I stayed where I was. Their backs were towards me and I couldn't help listening.

"Depends what you want to go in for," the constable was saying. "This isn't a circus, you know."

The other man was of medium height. As he turned sideways, almost cringingly, the light caught his hooked nose and seemed to prolong it upwards to the whiteness of his bald head. His lips were full, and when he spoke there was the trace of a lisp.

"I know, officer, I know. But I think I knew someone named Marler."

"All right, sir. In that case you can go in. You must sign this book first."

I drew quietly back and went out to the yard again. An idea had come. One might call it a preposterous idea, very much of a leaping ahead. It arose out of that theory I'd put up to Grainger—that there'd been a third man. Could that man who was so anxious to see Marler's body be that third member of the gang? Mind you, I knew the idea was absurd. Things couldn't just happen like that, and yet something was telling me to find out more.

Jackson was still in the car and I joined him. I was just in time. A collection of people were making for the mortuary and it was obvious they were the jury.

"A job for you," I told Jackson. "There was a man, medium height and about fifty, who was anxious to see the corpse. He had to sign a book. There's a constable on duty, but you ought to be able to get the name and address. In fact you've got to get it and I don't mind how. Then stay on somewhere nice and handy and take note of anyone else who's anxious to see that corpse. I shall be in the inquest-room and then I'll come back here. There's the man now! Take a good look at him."

He was well enough dressed in darkish clothes. The black felt hat hid the baldness and he walked with a slight shuffle. He looked neither to right nor left but went straight ahead to where I guessed that inquest-room would be. Just as he was out of sight the jury emerged. I didn't think they looked particularly animated. I wouldn't have been surprised if there'd been a casualty or two. I'd have given a good deal to have avoided another look at what had been lying on that tray.

A minute or two and I went to Room 6. There weren't more than a score of people there. I sat at the back and the unknown man sat in the same row but farther along. The verdict ultimately brought in was "death by drowning". The rest doesn't matter, and most of it you've heard. What I *was* interested in was the evidence of Marler's widow.

She was a remarkably handsome woman. The dark-grey costume probably added to her age, but my guess was that she was about thirty. She was a slim, tallish brunette, her eyes very dark and curiously intense. In the artificial light her face looked very pale, but there was still a touch of colour in the cheeks. Her voice was low-pitched and as attractive as herself—the sort of voice that, heard from another room, would make you want somehow to take a look at its owner.

The coroner dealt very gently with her. Doubtless she had been questioned beforehand and the leading questions suitably arranged. She was a mannequin, she said, but the name of her employers was not asked for. She had married Marler five years ago but had been separated from him for the last two years. It was over a year since she had even seen him, and she had had no idea what he had been engaged in during those two years. She received no allowance from him and wanted none. She had never relinquished her job and was able to support herself.

The only sign of distress she showed was when she said she had identified the body. She had no doubt whatever that it was her husband. That was all. Grainger himself took her gently by the arm and helped her to a chair behind the Press box. I slipped out to the car. Jackson saw me and joined me.

"This should be what you want, sir."

On a page from his note-book was a name and address:

> T. Robinson,
> 177 Temple St.,
> London, E.10.

"Right," I said. "Slip round to the main door and pick him up when he comes out. Stick with him wherever he goes. Report back to the office when you're satisfied."

I sat on, wondering if I ought to have a word with Grainger, who'd doubtless seen me in court. It was lucky that I did. Mrs. Marler suddenly appeared at the far end of that car park. I nipped out of the car and craned up from my full six-foot-three to watch her. A uniformed chauffeur appeared as from nowhere and touched his cap to her. Then the parked cars hid what happened, but almost at once a superb and shiny Rolls drew out and, before I could make even an attempt to get its number, it was out of sight behind the far wing of the Town Hall.

I think I let out a breath. So unexpected was that connection between the woman I had seen in court and that six thousand pounds'-worth of grace and speed, that it was almost like something out of the Arabian Nights. And straight on the heels of all that came the ideas. Bosford and Marler partners in a lucrative racket. Doris Bosford had that box beneath the bed. Mrs. Marler had a chauffeur and a sleek new Rolls. Or was that right? Maybe it was the Rolls of some friend. A woman as young and handsome as she might have quite a lot of friends—male friends. Not that it was any concern of mine. That, I admit, I added reluctantly. Then I got out of the car and went to have a word with Grainger.

He wasn't in his office, but I saw Redman. He told me there were no new developments but they were hoping—they and the Customs people. Grainger, he said, had been particularly keen on that idea of a third member of the gang. He added—and I thought irreverently that he sounded like something out of a crime comic—that the gang couldn't be considered broken up while that third man was loose. I hypocritically agreed, and that was that. I left my regards for Grainger and went in search of lunch. Just before dusk I was back at the office. Jackson, I was told, hadn't come in yet.

Norris left and I stayed on. It was just after six o'clock when Jackson turned up. He looked a bit rueful.

"Sorry, sir, but I lost him," he began.

"It's happened before," I told him consolingly. "Start at the beginning."

Robinson, he said, had taken a stroll along the front after leaving the inquest-room. Then he'd entered a smallish restaurant in Bank Street and Jackson had picked him up about an hour later. He went straight to the railway station and took the two-forty to town. At London Bridge he took a bus and went inside. Jackson went on top and kept a lookout at the stops. At Aldgate he thought he might take a peep inside, but when he came down Robinson wasn't there. The conductor thought he'd got off at the traffic lights at Harland Street.

Jackson did the next-best thing. He went to the main E.10 post office and asked for the whereabouts of Temple Street. There was no such street. The only one in the whole East End was at West Ham, which was E.13. Jackson made his way there. Temple Street was merely a cut between two other streets. It hadn't a 177. It didn't have anything beyond a 45.

The whole thing was my fault. That man had looked the last person to be called Robinson and I should have guessed that both name and address were false. So that again was that. I went home, and on the way I posted our official letter to Doris Bosford. It said that we could proceed no further in the matter, and that the enclosed statement of accounts showed that the retaining fee just covered expenses. We thanked her for her patronage and added that we were hers faithfully, The Broad Street Detective Agency. In other words, the Bosford Case was over, and I could tell myself that I was glad of it. That's why I had had a postscript added—that any future communications should be sent to the office. I hated the thought somehow of Doris Bosford's ringing me at my private number again.

One thing I will admit. Until I got it out of my mind that case still intrigued me, and I would lie thinking of it when I was on the borderland of sleep. I knew it was the kind of thing I'd like to be turned loose on, by some munificent client, perhaps, who'd give me carte blanche. And as, waiting for sleep, I wandered in the ramifications of that Bosford affair, new ideas would present themselves. I wondered if Bosford were really dead, and if he had been responsible for the death of Marler. I'd have liked to know a good deal about the man who'd signed his name as Robinson. I'd have liked to know a lot more about the owner-ship of a certain Rolls-Royce. I'd have liked to know just how much was in that box beneath Doris Bosford's bed.

But, as I said, that case went gradually from my mind. Not that there weren't a couple of reverberations. A few weeks after it was all over I happened to hear from George Wharton that the French Narcotics Bureau had been interested in an English-man who closely resembled Bosford. In Paris he had posed as a Frenchman and had travelled, apparently, under a false pass-port. I mentioned to George the queer business of the man Robinson, but he didn't seem interested. If he did anything about it, then I never knew.

The other echo was in early spring. The body of an unknown man was washed up on the coast of Cornwall. As a matter of fact there was little that came ashore but bones and rags. There was something about it in the newspapers because it was supposed he was one of the victims of an air crash in the Bay of Biscay, but identity was never established. The queer thing is that Doris Bosford rang me about it one April evening, using my private number. She said she was sure the body was that of her husband.

I hope I was polite, and I know I prevaricated. I said she might be right, though I knew the chances were that she was wrong. I asked her what she was going to do about it.

"That would be telling," she told me pertly, and, except for the final goodbye, that was the last I heard of her. It was the last I was to hear of the Bosford Case or so I thought.

PART II
INTERLUDE

5
THE BURGLARY

THE bulk of our work, as I've already said, comes from regular clients. We have retainers from two London stores and three in the provinces, augmenting their own detectives during sales and investigating any possible leakages. We also work for two big insurance companies. Take the matter of a fire, for instance. As soon as a company's notified it sends its assessor, who assesses the damage and the value of any salvage. If everything's in order, then the company pays the policy-holder. If it isn't absolutely in order, then we may be called in to make a confidential report. Hallows, our senior operative, is reckoned to be about the best man in the business. What he doesn't know about arson isn't worth the knowing.

If you're interested, what happens next is this. The company receives our report and, on the strength of it, will perhaps refuse to pay. That leaves the onus on the insured person to sue for the money. If he does, then the company communicates with the police, who have our report as a basis for their own investigations.

But arson is only one of the methods by which the dishonest seek to make money out of insurance companies. All sorts of accidents may need investigation. The death certificates issued by doctors and verdicts at coroner's courts are important, too. Then there are robberies, from smallish thefts to the big-scale affairs. The assessors check them all, and we may follow in their trail.

United Assurance is one of our clients. It was almost exactly a year after the ending of that Bosford Case that I was rung one morning by John Hill, their secretary. He wanted me to call at the earliest convenient moment. It was myself he wanted to see instead of Norris, because in the apportioning of duties United Assurance happens to be my affair, and principally because Hill is a personal friend.

It was about ten o'clock that morning when I was shown into his room at the company's head offices in Fenchurch Street. As soon as the usual greetings were over he asked if we were prepared to get to work at once. Then he rang through to his secretary for an appointment to be made with a Sergeant Fraser at Morniment Mansions at eleven o'clock.

"That'll give you plenty of time," he told me. "It's to do with a robbery. You know Morniment Mansions?"

I said I thought they were somewhere near Hyde Park.

"That's right," he said. "They overlook the park from the north. Some of the best flats in town. The one in question is at a rental of twelve hundred pounds."

I rather raised my eyebrows.

"They're fine flats," he said. "Virtually as good as a town house, without the disadvantages. I needn't tell you that this is in confidence, but the lessee is Edward Cortin, chairman of Cortin Aircraft Limited. He's a wealthy man but level-headed, and personally I like him. He's only about forty. A Rugger blue at Cambridge. Plays a good game of golf, too, so I'm told. And wonderful war service. I'm telling you all this so that you'll know the kind of man you'll be dealing with.

"His first wife died a few years ago as the result of a car accident and he married again about a year ago. I haven't met the second Mrs. Cortin, but I'm told she's an exceedingly attractive woman. They have also a place at Tyefield in Sussex, called the Manor. It's near a good golf course and handy for the sea. A married couple look after it and the Cortins spend most weekends there. You've got all that?"

I said I had.

"Then we'll come to the actual robbery," he said. "It took place presumably the night before last at the town flat. Jewellery, insured with us for about eighteen thousand pounds, was taken and one or two oddments that don't matter so much. Silver mostly. I have a list for you of the jewellery items, all of them presents, by the way, from Cortin to his wife. On the face of it the thief simply let himself in, took the jewellery out of a smallish safe, and walked out again. As far as can be ascertained, he wasn't seen."

"Sounds routine," I said. "What's the snag?"

"We won't describe it as that just yet," he told me dryly. "But these seem to be the facts: Cortin was in Paris on business. That was on the Wednesday. The same night his wife went to Covent Garden to hear a performance of *Rigoletto*. She wore some of the jewels which had been brought for the occasion from the bank where they were usually kept. On returning she locked them in the safe, and the following morning went down to Tyefield. That same night the burglary took place."

He gave me a look.

"Any comments on that?"

"I don't know," I said. "You fired the question a bit too quickly. But you can't call Thursday part of a normal week-end."

"A good point," he said. "She explains it by saying that as her husband was away she preferred to be at Tyefield. And her husband was joining her there. He'll be there actually this morning."

"Any reason why she didn't leave the jewellery in the keeping of the management at those flats?"

"Well," he said, "the safe was there. And it was her husband who always returned the jewellery to the bank."

"There doesn't seem much wrong about that," I said. "Suppose you tell me why I'm here."

He smiled.

"That's one good thing about you, Ludovic. You're always so direct. But the trouble is that there isn't any trouble. Everything, on the face of it, explains itself. And yet I've got a hunch. Mrs. Cortin, for instance, was away at an unusual time. I gather that she made up her mind at the last moment to go to Tyefield on the Thursday afternoon. And yet the burglar knew the flat would be empty. How did he know? The management say there was no leakage at their end. No one enquired at the bureau, for instance. Besides, it isn't customary for the tenants to notify the bureau when they're going to be absent. They're virtually self-contained flats. I admit that Mrs. Cortin was seen leaving and she was carrying just a small bag. Naturally she has everything she needs at Tyefield as well as in town. She went by car, also as usual."

"And the actual robbery?"

"That was reported at once to Mrs. Cortin by the management," he said. "The maid—one of the staff—wasn't aware that Mrs. Cortin was away and she brought early morning tea as usual. She let herself in, and as she went through to the bedroom she saw the safe open. She notified the management and they got in touch with Mrs. Cortin. She said the police should be notified and she was coming to town at once. And she did. The detective-sergeant—Fraser—was already there, with a man of his. They found no strange prints."

"What sort of safe?"

"A Harley-Morrison, opening with a key. There were signs of tampering with the lock."

"Then there shouldn't have been," I said. "A burglar who took any pride in his job would have had his own keys."

"Well, there you are," he said. "You can see Fraser and hear what the police think. Then I'd like you to run down to Tyefield this afternoon and see the Cortins. I needn't tell you that all you'll need is your usual urbanity. No suggestion of our not paying up. Just a routine check."

"Right," I said. "I'll see what can be done. Eighteen thousand pounds is quite a useful sum of money. Any special reason why the Cortins mustn't be antagonised?"

"We carry fairly heavy insurance on both of them," he said. "He's an uncommonly useful client."

"Right," I said again. "I'll use what's left of what you described as 'the usual urbanity'. No hurry for a report?"

"I'd like it within two or three days." Then he remembered something. "I'll let the Cortins know you're coming. What time do you think?"

I suggested three o'clock. With luck that should mean a free tea. I like teas in Manors. Cinnamon toast, perhaps, and plenty of cakes; beautiful china and Georgian silver; nice loungey chairs and the smell of potpourri, and a beautiful fire in a handsome grate. I told myself I'd make it nearer half-past. Maybe the Cortins had tea at four.

I met Sergeant Fraser in the elaborate entrance hall of Morniment Mansions. He said he'd seen me somewhere before. As soon as I mentioned George Wharton's name he remembered. That made everything friendly from the start. He got the key from the bureau and we walked up the thickly carpeted stairs to the first floor.

It was a magnificent flat. I could go into rhapsodies, but I'll leave it at that. The outer door had a Yale lock. There was never a scratch round it. There didn't need to be. When you know the trick you can work such a lock in a matter of seconds. Fraser—I think he was in a showing-off mood—did it in five seconds dead with a tiny sliver of celluloid and a tiny metal gadget he didn't let me see.

We went through to a smallish cloakroom. To get to Mrs. Cortin's bedroom direct, Fraser explained, you had to go through the drawing-room. It was a kind of short cut, the one the maid always took with the early tea. We went through to the large, lofty drawing-room. It was beautifully furnished. I could go into rhapsodies about that, too. All I'll say is that the Chinese carpet wouldn't have been dear at five hundred guineas. As for the safe, that was skilfully concealed in what seemed the base of a large television set. To get at it you had to open the lower mahogany door of the television cabinet.

"Neither the door nor the safe was properly closed," Fraser told me. "And tell me this, sir: would you ever have suspected that that safe was in there? Wouldn't it have been the last place you'd have looked? And another thing: would you have expected both doors to be left open? They ought to have been closed—then the robbery wouldn't have been discovered for three or four days. And," he went on, "you can't say he was disturbed or in a hurry. It doesn't take a tick to shut these two doors."

"In other words, you mean—what?" I asked.

"An amateur job," he told me, and with a moue of what looked like disgust. "Have a look at the lock of the safe."

I had a look at it through my glass. There were scratches round it but none actually inside the keyhole.

"Curious," I said. "Why the scratches? What was he trying to do? Pick the lock in some way? If so, why can't we see any scratches inside?"

"Yes, sir," he said. "It's mighty curious. You any ideas about it?"

"Not that I can prove. But if I were a suspicious sort of character I'd be inclined to wonder if the door wasn't opened with a key and the scratches made to give the idea it'd been picked."

"Exactly!" He said the word as if he were pronouncing a benediction. "And tell me something else, sir. That suspicious mind of yours couldn't think no-how that it was an inside job?"

"That's asking," I said warily. "All I'm here for is to note the facts. But you've made enquiries?"

"Tentatively, yes," he said. "You have to go carefully in this kind of case. Still, we have hopes. Someone sometime or other must have been able to make a duplicate of that safe key. And it was someone who knew where the safe was. That stands to reason."

"What was Mrs. Cortin like when you saw her?"

"Very upset, sir. She said all that jewellery had a sentimental value as well as its actual value. A very nice lady, sir."

"So I believe." I was not going to be outdone in knowledge of the wealthy. "And could she throw any light on things?"

"Not a bit, sir. 'Sergeant,' she said, 'I'm just as much at a loss as you are. I simply can't believe it. You hear about it happening to other people but you can't imagine it happening to yourself.' Mind you, sir, I did throw out a gentle hint about the maid and the management staff, but she wouldn't hear of it. She said she knew everyone personally and she'd vouch for them, so to speak."

"And you thought that was a touching faith in human nature," I told him roguishly. Then I held out my hand. "Afraid I have to be going. Thanks for all you've done for me. And good luck in the enquiry. You *are* going on with the enquiry, I take it?"

He said he certainly was. I think he'd have told me the law never forgot and its arm was long if I hadn't given a farewell wave of the hand and made my way out.

You may think that inspection most casual, but it wasn't. It was no business of ours to find a criminal. All we were concerned with was the question as to whether or not that robbery had been genuine. Besides, we could always find out, or Hill could, what the considered verdict of the police might ultimately be. The usual reward had already been offered in the Press, and it might or might not produce evidence on which the police would work. Also, if I wanted to inspect again the scene of the robbery I was able to do so. But I'd seen enough for the moment—that is, until I'd talked with the two Cortins.

One or two other factors had to be considered. If it were we who recovered the jewellery, then we received a useful bonus. But the police were in charge and we couldn't cut across their enquiries. Also two days had gone by, and that jewellery was probably broken up and melted down, whether the job had been an inside one or an outside one. Thieves, professional or amateur, are conversant enough with what happens after a jewel robbery—the notification and description to every known dealer and pawnbroker. It consisted, by the way, of two diamond and platinum rings, a bracelet, rivière and tiara. It had been bought as a complete set—if that's the term—by Edward Cortin and given to his second wife just after their marriage, and the jewellers who'd supplied it were in a position to furnish a complete description and the weight and shape of all the stones.

I went straight to the club when I left Fraser and hunted the reference books to get a line on Edward Cortin. His father had founded the firm which now specialised in the manufacture of freight aircraft. It wasn't a large firm compared with some. Its capital was just over two millions, but its financial position was said to be exceptionally strong. Edward Cortin the elder had been killed in an air crash in 1949.

The son had had a career which could only be described as distinguished. His school was Harrow, and at Cambridge he had specialised in physics. I imagined the term included aero-dynamics and whatever else was essential to a thorough knowledge of everything connected with the work with which he would later be concerned. After leaving Cambridge he entered the firm's works at Coventry. He had a pilot's licence, and on the outbreak of war was called up at once; he ended as squadron leader, with a D.S.O. and bar, and a D.F.C. After the end of the war he went back to the works and took over at his father's death.

Who's Who gave the name of the first wife as Alicia Mary, daughter of Charles and the Hon. Mrs. Price, of Shafton Court, Warwickshire. There were no children. The second marriage was not mentioned, which meant that Cortin hadn't bothered to bring the entry up to date. The firm's headquarters were naturally in Coventry, but I noticed that there was also a London office in Leadenhall Street. To all that data, which might be either useful or so much lumber, could be added John Hill's statement that Cortin was a wealthy man, and a rider to the effect that he was remarkably generous to his wife. And that indicated, to put it crudely, that neither should have an interest in faking a robbery.

So much for that. I lunched at the club, went back for my car and set out for Tyefield. It was a clear November day with a cold wind, and while that wind lasted there would be no fog. In other words, there'd be no need of hurry to get back to town. At Tyefield I didn't need to be told the whereabouts of the Manor, because I passed something that looked like it just before I was entering the village. I backed the car and found I was right.

The Manor was a half-timbered house, and larger than most. The usual type is what I might call "two reception and three to four bed". This place looked as if it might have up to six good bedrooms, and either its reception rooms were uncommonly large or it had more of them. Its timbering was exceptionally fine, as were the two chimneys. There was quite a drive to it, but all the time it was full in view; the whole place had an uncanny neatness and it reeked of money. The lawns, in a time of dead leaves, were smooth and green as in summer. Borders had their full colour from dahlias and michaelmas daisies, and roses were still blooming lavishly in the beds. Behind the house was a tiled barn, old as the house itself, and a fork of the drive swept round to it. I felt faintly presumptuous in parking my oldish car in front of the door. In fact I moved it on a bit, and alongside what I was to learn was the dining-room window.

I pushed the bell. It was quite a time before I heard a sound, and then it was the barking of a dog. To have pushed that bell twice would have been something like lèse-majesté, and when the heavy oak door was opened it was by a middle-aged woman in a grey dress and white apron—the wife, as I thought, of the married couple. I was ushered in as soon as I mentioned my name. I just had time to have a look round the entrance hall and its oak furniture while I was taking off my overcoat and then I was shown into a room on the right. It was a very large lounge or drawing-room. Before I'd taken a couple of steps forward a cocker spaniel bitch was frisking towards me. Cortin—he'd been standing with his back to the fire—called her back. He moved forward, holding out a hand.

"So you're Travers," he said. "I'm Edward Cortin. John Hill rang me about you. He tells me you were at Cambridge."

We weren't at the same college, but it was rather more than a point of contact. In a couple of minutes we were yarning away, our comfortable chairs facing each other in front of the open fireplace. I'd never have thought of him as the man he was. He had the look of a country squire. His hair was fair and his cheeks red, and he wore a most untidy fair moustache. His tweeds were good, but the jacket was worn and the trousers baggy. He was the friendliest and most unassuming person you could ever hope to meet. If anything he was on the plump side and he had the happiest of smiles. His shoulders were immense and made him look less than his height—which was just over six feet.

I hadn't been in his company five minutes before I was liking him enormously. He hadn't a one-track mind: in fact, I knew him widely informed. Shallowness can always be discerned, and his mind was far from shallow. I knew that, because somehow or other we'd got to discussing economics, which had once been my job, and as we sat there talking I had all at once a kind of perception. It was a curious thought. Edward Cortin was a kind of embodiment of all schoolboy heroes: brawn, brain, courage and a supreme leavening of modesty. A man's man, too. The kind of man you'd be proud to have as a friend.

All at once he was drawing in his long legs from the fire and getting to his feet. He was still remarkably agile for his weight.

"What about tea. I'm sure you must be dying for some."

He pushed the bell that was just beneath the great beam that ran across the open fireplace, and he stood there as I'd seen him first, back to the fire, hands behind him to the warmth of it.

"I'm sorry, by the way, that you won't be able to see my wife. She hasn't been too well lately. Headaches. Practically migraine. She's down with a particularly bad one at the moment."

"I know," I said. "My wife has them occasionally."

He smiled. It was a different sort of smile.

"Between ourselves, this is rather unusual. We're hoping— we're not sure, mind you—that it's . . . well, that there may be a third in the family. Or did that sound too Victorian?"

"It sounded pretty good," I said. "You're hoping it will be a boy?"

"Don't know," he said, and laughed. "I was an only son and I don't think I'd like that. We'd both like a family—say three or four."

The housekeeper—I call her that for want of a better term— came in with a tea-tray. There was no cinnamon toast, but there was what I call a man's cake.

"I don't go in for tea much myself," Cortin told me. "Just a cup of tea and a slice of cake. Would you like something more?"

Then he was calling to the housekeeper just as she reached the door.

"Alice, what about Mr. Harry? Is he about?"

She said she thought he was at the garage.

"Don't disturb him, then," he said. "If he wants tea he can have it later."

He explained to me: Henry Calvert was his wife's brother. He'd been a flying-officer during the war and had been shot down over Holland, losing a leg and then having a particularly bad time in a prison camp.

"When he came back," he said, "he was really a psychiatric case. But he's all right now. He lives here and just takes things steady. Or we try to get him to."

He didn't add to that last cryptic remark.

"Suppose we talk about why you're here," he said. "Do you mind? I don't quite see where you fit in, and John Hill was rather elusive."

I explained. I prevaricated to the extent of making it appear that the Broad Street Detective Agency was the victim of its contracts—that automatically we had to run an eye over all claims. The whole thing was routine and, in this particular case, with the police already at work, something of a nuisance.

He looked at me rather quizzically.

"Somehow I can't think of you as a private detective. If I had any preconceived ideas, you certainly don't conform."

"What about yourself?" I said. "Do you look like the chairman of an important aircraft company?"

"Ah," he said. "You should see me when I'm sitting at a board table. I'm a vastly different fellow."

I told him how the agency worked and the modestly active part I played in it, and he seemed very impressed. Or maybe that was just his perfect manners. I didn't have time to judge, for the door suddenly opened and a man came in. Cortin got to his feet and I followed suit, my mouth full of cake.

"Come along in, Harry," Cortin said. "I'll ring for another cup. This is Mr. Ludovic Travers. He's called on behalf of the insurance people to bring us up to date about that robbery."

It seemed almost reluctantly that the newcomer came towards us. He was tallish, dark-haired and thin, and he walked with a slight limp. That, I guessed, would be the artificial leg. His cheeks were rather sunken and his eyes uncommonly dark. He was wearing an old tweed coat and grey flannel bags that looked as if due for a dry clean. He held out his hand to me and his smile was thin and dry. I put his age at the middle thirties.

"How are you?" he said.

Cortin was drawing up another chair. Alice came in with a wholly new tray, and on it was a plate of buttered toast. Calvert had the tray to himself. He tackled that toast as if he was pretty ravenous. I don't say he was crude but he was certainly taciturn. Cortin was aware of it. He kept making attempts to draw him into the conversation.

"Harry's a first-class mechanic," he said. "He'd rather like me to back some scheme for a new British racing car."

"Why not?" Harry said laconically. "It'd pay you in prestige." The dark eyes were suddenly switched to me. "You interested in cars, Mr. Travers?"

I said I was, though I was almost certainly only the rawest of amateurs compared with himself. But we did get to talking about cars, even if he was soon away over my head. He'd bought an oldish Mercedes, it appeared, and was doing some experimental work. Then, with talk of that still somewhat in the air, he was pushing his plate away and getting to his feet. "Think I'll get back to the garage," he began.

"I can count on you for billiards tonight?" Cortin said. "The Admiral and Penelope are coming in."

"Sorry, Ted, but I can't." There seemed a genuine regret in the shake of his head. "I promised to see a chap about that new suspension."

I just caught the click of Cortin's tongue.

"What a fellow you are! Why don't you ease up a bit? There's all the time in the world."

"Sorry," Calvert told him dourly. He hesitated for a moment. "Could you see me for a moment outside?"

It was Cortin's turn to hesitate. Before he could move Calvert was addressing me again.

"Has anything happened about that affair in town?"

"If you mean, have the police caught the thief, then I'm afraid not," I said.

"You think they've a chance?"

I could only smile and shrug my shoulders.

UNEXPLAINED MYSTERY

WHILE the two were away I had a look round that room. There was the devil of a lot of money in it, from the rugs on the polished oak floor to the two Cotmans, a Cox and a superb Clarkson Stanfield on the walls. There were a couple of Adam mirrors and some fine period walnut. There was a breath-taking apple-green Worcester tea-service in a corner cabinet, and on the bracket above the main beam two pre-Marcolini Dresden groups flanking an eighteenth-century French clock. The collector in me was telling me it was a room I must try sometime to burgle.

The little roan cocker bitch hadn't gone out with her master. Maybe she was a mistress's dog. I didn't know, but when I sat down after that quick inspection of the room she half raised her head and I guessed she could hear Cortin coming back. And practically at once he was back, and alone.

"Sorry about all that," he said. "I do hope you don't mind."

I'm always wondering why people confide in me. I admit I'm a good listener, if only because in my job it's the other person whom you want to hear talk. Maybe, too, there's something artless about me: something the French call a *sentiment sympathique* that makes them suddenly decide to let me share their private troubles.

"You're thinking seriously of backing your brother-in-law in that racing-car matter?" was how it began.

"Good lord, no!" he said. "I haven't that kind of money. If it has to be done at all it should be government-sponsored. No"—and he gave himself a nod as he settled in his chair again—"that's something I'm definitely not paying out for."

There was silence for a moment or two and the room so quiet you could hear the little bitch give a tiny whimper that was part of a dream. Then Cortin stirred in the chair.

"I wonder if I might trespass on your kindness? You're an older man than myself, or so I judge. Certainly more experienced in the ways of the world. And there's this agency that you run, and your connections with Scotland Yard. It made me wonder something."

"Yes?" I said, gently urging him on.

"It's Harry," he said. "He's a real good fellow and he's had a bad time. He and my wife are extraordinarily fond of each other; maybe because they lost their parents when young and were brought up by relatives. I told you about his health and how he's recovered now, but he's got this mania about racing cars. He's a magnificent mechanic, by the way. If he had the enormous sums that sort of thing costs I honestly think he'd produce something remarkable. I hope you'll take this in the right way and not set me up as anything special, but I make him quite a good allowance. All the same, he's a bit of a drain on me. Not to an extent I can't afford, I suppose, but—" He broke off and gave himself a queer, bewildered shake of the head. "The fact is he doesn't get value for his money. And he has to have money. For instance, he's managed to make contact with someone he calls an old friend who's now connected with the Mercedes works and he wants to put in a month in Germany. But where's it all leading to?"

"A difficult question," I said.

"I know. And I shouldn't be bothering you with it. But what I was coming to is something particularly confidential. Tell me something. What control have the police over gambling places in London?"

"Strictly by law, there aren't any," I told him. "If the police get wind of any, through informers or by observation, then they're raided."

"I see," he said, and once more stirred a bit uneasily in his chair. "Why I asked is this: a month or so back Harry wanted money and he tried to get it the easy way. What he did was lose what he had and a couple of thousand pounds. I didn't want to raise any stink, so I paid."

"What proof had you that you were actually paying a gambling debt?"

"Only his word," he said. "But I've never known him tell me a lie. He's always absolutely open and frank. So much so that he's almost naïve. He's so . . . well, so irresponsible financially and so above-board that you feel you'd be an absolute curmudgeon and a heel if you refused him anything."

"You know where he lost the money?"

"No. He wouldn't tell me."

"You're sure he handed it over?"

"Dead sure. He wanted it in cash, and he was hard up himself again within a week. And I'm pretty sure he had no expenses."

"Nothing can be done, then," I said. "There is, of course, one thing I could suggest, but I don't think you'd like it."

"I'm open to hear anything," he said.

"Well, if he should land himself in any similar mess again we might be able to handle it. Possibly we could trace the establishment where he lost the money, provided, of course, we were let know in time."

"A damn sensible idea," he said. "I'll certainly do that. The trouble is that he promised me it should never occur again."

There was another silence. The little bitch woke up, yawned and came across to him. He fondled her ears, but he wasn't smiling.

"If you people are open to do business with us," he said, "I think we might make use of you from time to time. We're not without trouble occasionally at the works. Minor sabotage and that sort of thing."

"We'd be happy to handle it," I told him. "Maybe some time you'll let us talk it over."

"Fine," he said. "We'll leave it like that. But Harry—what am I to do about him?"

"Your wife would be upset if you kept him strictly to his allowance?"

"Don't know," he said. "It's something I've kept to myself. I'm pretty sure he's never gone to her for money."

"It's a problem," I said. "The only thing I can suggest is that you should buy him a good, profit-making garage somewhere. A manager could handle staff and so on, and your brother-in-law could use the profits for his experiments. The trouble is it might mean a big initial outlay. You yourself could retain some control."

He didn't seem to think it so impossible a scheme. He said he'd certainly think it over. Then we got back to the business that had brought me there—that robbery at the town flat. He, too, wouldn't believe that it was an inside job. I didn't ask any awkward questions. What I told him finally was that in due course the insurance company would almost certainly pay.

The housekeeper came in belatedly to take the trays. We stood up, and once more my eyes went covetously round that room. I apologised, saying that it was unpardonable of me but I was always doing it. I was a schizophrenic, and what he was seeing was the collector in me. He laughed.

"But you've got a wonderful place here," I said. "And it's been beautifully restored."

"The dining-room's our show-piece," he said. "Like to see it?"

In the hall we stopped for a minute while I admired the staircase. It was the original, and the barley-sugar twists of the balusters had a patina that was like old lacquer. We went through the opposite door and he switched on the lights. It was a large and lovely room, its original panelling intact. The ceiling beams were exquisitely carved, and the great beam across the open fireplace carried a date—1613—and a couple of flanking heraldic shields.

The furniture was in keeping—a handsome, bulbous-legged table and oak chairs whose seats were softened by cushions in fine embroidery. There was a noble court cupboard, a Jacobean corner-cupboard, and a long sideboard or serving table inlaid with ivory and ebony. The polished floor was the original and it carried only strip rugs round the actual table.

"I suppose one really ought to have Tudor or Jacobean portraits hung here," he told me, "and pass them off as my ancestors. All I've got, as you see, are these Dutch School landscapes. No great value. That's a Hobbema. Not one of his best. I doubt if it's worth four figures."

"But that isn't Dutch," I said, and waved a hand at a portrait in oils that hung above the sideboard. "It looks modern."

"Modern it is," he said. "You know Georges Pellot, the couturier?"

"I'm a married man," I told him, and he laughed.

"Well, my wife used to work with him, and his brother is Henri Pellot, the painter. He was always wanting to paint her portrait—that was before we were married, of course—so later on I got him to do this. I made him keep it to the size of the actual panelling. Rather like the ideal Carmen, don't you think? That's what he said he had in mind."

The black hair was piled high and a jewelled comb was in it. The dark eyes had something haughty about them, and the lips had an ironic curl. Had it been a full-length portrait it would have been with swirling skirt and hands on hips. Carmen, about to dance for Don José.

"You like it?"

"It's superb," I said. "The colouring, the bravura—"

Then I stopped. I moved slightly till that portrait was less in the glare from the light.

"It's fine," I said. "Your wife must be a very handsome woman."

Then I was smiling sheepishly.

"Sorry. That was a curious thing to say."

"But why?" he said, and his eyes were on that picture again. "She *is* what that picture says she is. It doesn't flatter her. I'm sure you'll like her. We must really arrange to meet some time."

I said, stiltedly no doubt, that it would be a pleasure to which to look forward. But I didn't tell him we'd met already. Not socially, of course: just myself sitting at the back of a coroner's court, and she giving evidence about a dead husband.

I set off back to town some very few minutes later, and I drove slowly. Before I reached the suburbs I wanted to do a whole lot of thinking. And yet, when I really got down to it, there was practically no thinking to do. Certain things were now explained, of course—that Rolls and its chauffeur that had brought her to and taken her back from Seahurst. It was obviously one of Cortin's cars. Since he had married her shortly after her husband's death, he must have known her well beforehand. I wondered why there had not been a divorce. After all, the Marlers hadn't lived together for about two years.

As for the brother, Henry Calvert, he was something far more shadowy in my mind. I hadn't spent more than a very few minutes in his company and I hardly knew what to make of him. I hadn't seen any signs of lack of mental balance, but if what Cortin had told me was correct—and it had to be—then there was definitely a queer streak still in him. For that matter, I could tell myself, there's a queer streak in quite a lot of us. His was that *idée fixe* about restoring British prestige in the car-racing world: not as a driver—his game leg would be too great a handicap—but as a designer. And when I tried to see the whole thing in an unbiased way, I couldn't for the life of me see any great abnormality about that. Nor, for that matter, in that attempt of his to be independent for once of his brother-in-law's financial help by having a private flutter. I might have done the same thing, except that when I'd lost my capital I shouldn't have gone on playing on tick.

I let the whole thing slide from my mind while I drove through the suburbs. The next day was a Sunday and a day when I rarely let business worry me. And it didn't. The only echo of my visit to Tyefield was that portrait of Helen Cortin which would keep coming back to my mind. I wasn't staggered, so to speak, by the coincidence of seeing it, for in my view what one calls coincidence is something we're inclined to magnify out of all proportion. Life is bound to be shot through with the unexpected.

But that night as I lay waiting for sleep I did do some thinking. Because of it I got into touch with Sergeant Fraser first thing in the morning. He told me no progress had been made in the case, unless it was that he himself was now of the opinion that no member of the staff had been directly concerned.

"That doesn't mean," he said, "that one of 'em mightn't have passed on the tip that the flat'd be empty. But then against that is the fact that they've never had that sort of robbery there before. They're all wealthy people in those flats and they must have thousands of pounds'-worth of jewellery, and this is the first time anything serious has been taken. You know what I mean, sir—anything beyond petty larceny."

I thanked him and then went to Broad Street. Norris was given an outline of what I proposed to do. If he had other ideas, then he didn't express them. After that I made an appointment with John Hill for eleven o'clock that morning.

When I walked into his office Hill almost held out a hand for the report.

"No report," I told him. "There're certain curious features about this business that I'd like to put up to you."

He looked a bit perturbed as he pushed the silver cigarette box towards me.

"Not anything serious, I hope?"

"It's up to you to judge," I told him. "I will say this, that it's so confidential that I didn't like to entrust it to a report."

I told him what I'd done, where I'd been and what I'd learned. I said nothing about Helen Cortin, as late Marler, *née* Calvert, except that she'd been down with an attack of migraine and I hadn't been able to see her. To Hill she was just Cortin's wife. But what made him prick up his ears was what I had to say about her brother.

"You were right," he said. "It's fishy. Remarkably so. You think this Henry Calvert may have made himself a duplicate key to that safe and helped himself?"

I shrugged my shoulders. It was for him to judge. I could present only facts and impressions.

"He would certainly know where that safe was," I said. "He would almost as certainly be able to make an impression of the key. He may have been in urgent need of money. Also he's going to Germany in the immediate future. And it shouldn't be impossible for you to arrange a sort of routine search of him and his baggage at the port."

He was all of a fluster. If you knew John Hill you'd know why. To a high-up executive like himself, and dealing with a high-up client like Edward Cortin, there was something almost vulgar in my hints.

"If you like to leave it to us we'll handle it," I said.

"No, no, no." He waved an agitated hand. "It wants a lot of thinking about."

"Don't let that Customs search worry you," I said to him. "That can be fixed."

"No, no," he said again. "You may be wrong. Then think what fools we'd look."

"Of course I may be wrong," I said. "But tell me something, John. What's Edward Cortin worth to you that makes eighteen thousand pounds look like odd change?"

It was he who did the shoulder-shrugging.

"I resent that remark," he told me. "You can't run things on those lines."

"Look," I said patiently. "You and I have always trusted each other. Why the squeamishness now?"

"Well, he's a valuable client," he said, and almost pettishly. "He's thinking of transferring some really big business to us."

"Then why didn't you say so?" I told him bluntly. Then I got up. "You'd still like a report? Or would you rather leave things as they are?"

"For the moment, as they are."

"And we're to take no further action?"

"Well, perhaps not."

"Right," I said, "we're under your orders. So long as you're satisfied so far, that's good enough."

He was suddenly most effusive. He was more than satisfied. We'd handled everything with the utmost discretion.

"That's fine," I said. "I was only wondering if a contract was going to be sacrificed on the altar of Edward Cortin."

"My dear fellow, how ridiculous! We're more than satisfied with what you do for us. We always have been, and I'm sure we always shall be."

He was consulting his diary.

"Look, my dear fellow, have lunch with me. Say the day after tomorrow. I'll just tell you officially then what's been decided."

*

I did have lunch with him, and at his club. We kept off business till the coffee and liqueurs.

"Calvert left for Germany yesterday morning," he told me. "We did arrange that search. Nothing on him."

"What a humbug you are!" I told him. "The last time I saw you it was something you wouldn't have touched with a ten-foot pole."

"Well, it was rather taken out of my hands," he said. "It was all very discreet. Calvert knew other people were being searched. And it'd have been discreet if anything had been found on him. We were ready to get into touch with Cortin at once."

"And they say money doesn't talk nowadays," I said. "But what about paying up?"

"We shall settle," he said. "I don't think there's any doubt about that. Oh, and I was to convey to you an appreciation of the way you handled everything."

Never, I thought, had so much gratitude been shown for so very little. And I'd also had a first-class club lunch. And I was intending to have one of the club's fine old ports.

"You liked Edward Cortin?" Hill was adding.

I said I'd liked him enormously. By the time I left Hill that early afternoon I was prepared to like everybody enormously. I liked Hill and I liked his club, even if in less ample moments I think it more snooty than my own. I liked, above all, United Assurance who'd soon be paying our account without the vestige of a tremor. I even liked Ludovic Travers. I took him out for the rest of the afternoon to see a highly praised French picture at the Melodeon. I took him to tea afterwards at Fuller's, but he wasn't so pleased with life by then. I think something was on his mind. It might have been that he hadn't telephoned his wife.

We heard no more about that theft of the Cortin jewels. If the thief had been caught I should have read about it in the papers. A Case, too, is a Case. They come and they go. But I was rung up one day by Cortin, who said he would be in town and would I lunch with him. We had an indifferent meal at a highly expensive restaurant where only the wine was good. In the course of the hour and a half we were together I asked after his wife and he said she was fine. Only an occasional headache.

"And your brother-in-law?"

"He's still having a great time in Germany," he said. "I hope it won't fill his head with ideas when he gets home."

But what he had wanted to talk over with me was a job of work. There'd been another definite case of sabotage and there might have been a nasty accident if it hadn't been discovered. The police had been informed, but he was wondering if we couldn't plant a man or two in the works.

I said we certainly could, but it would be expensive. They'd be specialists, and two men for maybe some weeks couldn't come cheap. It didn't worry him in the least. We arranged for Norris to see his works manager in Coventry.

We did that job, though it meant using an outside operative. Hallows was the other. And, believe it or not, we cracked that case in just over a fortnight. It had nothing to do with Communism as had been thought—it was just a matter of personal hostility between a mechanic and one of the firm's pilots, and a woman was at the root of it all. Cortin was delighted. Later he rang twice to get my wife and me to lunch with his wife and himself in town. The second time I accepted, even though Bernice wasn't there.

You know how women are. Or don't you? They say they don't want to meet other women, and then when they've met them they rave about it for days. Bernice had things done to her hair the day before, and bought a new hat. She was certainly looking fine when we walked into the lounge of that restaurant. Helen Cortin was looking something special, and it wasn't the clothes she wore. I suppose she could have been wearing mink, but she wasn't. It was just a black coat with an astrakhan collar and hat to match, and a red blouse peeping out beneath. To me it looked just a nice coat. Bernice told me afterwards that it was probably one of Georges Pellot's and had almost certainly cost the best part of a hundred guineas.

It was a good lunch and our women got on well. When I was introduced to Helen Cortin, by the way, she showed never the faintest sign of recognition. I don't suppose she even noticed me that other November day when I was sitting at the far back of that Seahurst room. When the coffee cups had been drained and the last conversation made the two women announced that they were going shopping. We left them at the cloakroom.

"What a charming woman your wife is!" Cortin said.

You can't say much to a remark like that. I think I said it might be quite a good thing for both to have got acquainted. And I remembered something.

"I forgot to ask you, but it's all right about what you were hinting that afternoon at Tyefield?"

He didn't get me for a moment, and then he beamed. He said it was quite all right. Edward Cortin the Third was definitely on the way.

"That's grand," I said. "And she's keeping well?"

"Never better," he said. "She hasn't had a headache for weeks now."

After that lunch our two women occasionally met and did things together. Bernice still thought Helen Cortin one of the most charming women she'd ever met. Also—and don't take it as cattish—Bernice told me Helen still had a pull with Georges Pellot and got her clothes at a much reduced rate, a privilege which, I gathered, was being extended to Bernice herself. I guessed that the reduced rates of people like Pellot and Dior and Schiaparelli would be just about twice what Bernice had been used to paying elsewhere. But I didn't say so. Bernice has her own money. All I ever do in the matter of her clothes is dutifully admire.

I didn't see Cortin again for some time. He was a busy man, at least during the week, what with Coventry and the London office and various commitments abroad. It was not, in fact, till March that I did see him again. Why and where is quite another story.

PART III
MRS. CORTIN

7
TWO MEETINGS

A LOT of things were to happen in the course of the next few days, and if they're to be clearly followed they have to be put in some sort of order, even if there is occasionally an overlapping. It's best perhaps to begin with my next meeting with Edward Cortin. He'd rung me and suggested lunch. I said it was my turn, and we agreed to meet at my club.

I didn't think for a moment that any business would be talked, though I did notice something peculiar about his response to my enquiry about his wife. There was a slight frown as he said she was reasonably well. That qualifying adverb might have meant something to do with her pregnancy, so I didn't call attention to it. Then I asked about Henry Calvert.

"Henry's fine," he said. "That German trip modified his ideas considerably. I think for the first time he's begun to realise what a big thing that racing business is."

"On the Continent it's a matter of national prestige," I said. "Over here we assume we've got most of the prestige we need."

"Exactly. Foreign governments regard it as a necessity. Every kind of sport for that matter. And they're prepared to subsidise. I don't think Harry realised the sums involved. At any rate he's changed his ideas. And he's got himself a job. The Quentin Group are putting a new sports model on the market next year and he's going on their technical staff."

"You must feel pretty relieved," I said. "He's taking up the new job at once?"

"In about a month. It'll mean his being at Coventry, of course. If necessary I'll be able to keep an eye on him. I'm pretty sure, though, it won't be necessary."

We were having a sherry while he was telling me that, and if people hadn't begun moving towards the dining-room I know he'd have told me more. That morning he was a long way from the carefree country squire of Tyefield, and I had more than a suspicion there was something nagging at his mind. It was not till after the lunch and in the comparative quiet of the smoking-room corner that he told me a little more. I'd asked what he did with himself at Coventry. Did he live in an hotel or did he have a place there.

"I actually live at the works," he said. "I've got a small flat. Just a corner of the administrative offices. I never know how late I'll be working."

I think he remembered then what he'd been telling me about his brother-in-law. Something was on the tip of his tongue. He hesitated for a moment.

"I was telling you about Harry being at Coventry," he said and as if with a sudden resolution. "My wife has ideas about that. She wants me to quit the town flat and get a place near Coventry. She thinks it will be better for Harry and that I'm doing too much rushing backwards and forwards."

"But surely that won't mean your selling the Manor? Tyefield's a long way from Coventry."

"Yes," he said, and frowned at the glass he was holding. Then he set it down.

"Look," he said, "I'll be frank with you. I'm worried about the whole thing. I don't know what your experience has been, but mine is that you can be married to a woman and still not know all that much about her."

"I know," I said. "They always have to retain the seventh veil."

"Something in that," he said. "But tell me this. Would your wife be happy at renouncing London for—well, somewhere near Coventry?"

"She might pretend to like it, if it was part of some idea of mothering me, but I know that at heart she'd hate it. I don't say she'd ever admit it."

"It's quite unnecessary," he said. "Somehow I think it's something beyond just me and Harry. It's as if she'd suddenly begun to hate London."

Something stirred somewhere at the far back of my mind. What it was I didn't know. It was like some little ripple of cool air that puffs at you suddenly on a still, warm afternoon of July, so that you look up at the sky and think about thunderstorms.

"Does that include Tyefield?" was all I said.

"I don't know," he said. "At present I think not. She's spending most of her time there now, by the way. Perhaps your wife mentioned it."

"I believe she did."

He didn't say anything for a moment or two. I thought I'd suggest something.

"If I might be personal, has this sudden idea anything to do with the pregnancy? I've had no personal experience of such things, but it's supposed to be a part of common knowledge that women do get queer whims and fancies during pregnancy."

"I've thought of that," he said, "and I did mention it privately to her doctor. But I don't know."

Again there was a hesitation. He took a sip of the port and set the glass down.

"I'm not being a nuisance about all this?"

"Far from it," I told him. "I'm interested. And I'd like to help."

"Then I'll tell you something else. There's a different atmosphere at Tyefield, and ever since Harry's been back. I can't quite explain it. It's as if she'd rather shut herself off from me. There's something worrying her, something at the back of her mind, and I'm damned if I know what it is. I've asked her and she simply laughs at me. Nothing wrong at all. Just my imagination. But it isn't my imagination. I know it's there. And another thing: there's something between herself and Harry—something they're sharing and which I'm not supposed to know."

He waved his hands with a kind of helplessness. "I can't describe it. It's just a feeling. But it's there."

I was going to say something, but he cut me off.

"If you're going to suggest again it's to do with the pregnancy, then I'm sure you're wrong. This is something different. And she's begun having those headaches again. Her own doctor can't understand it."

"I'm sorry," I said. "It seems pretty baffling."

"Yes," he said, and then he looked up. "Look, Travers, you're an understanding sort. I'll tell you something else that worries me and I'm wondering how it ties up with all the rest. Let me explain."

Besides arranging a marriage settlement he'd also ensured that his wife should have an ample private income of her own. He didn't believe in charge accounts and preferred that she should have moneys entirely at her own disposal and unconnected with household accounts. Among the investments he'd made for her was a block of Denton, Rale—the Newcastle engineers. He'd had a tip about them which had been justified. A "one-for-one" bonus distribution had been made and the dividend declared later had meant a considerable rise in income.

"All her holdings are with the Sussex branch of the bank," he said, "and I had a confidential talk with the manager. I didn't quite know what my wife would be like when a biggish income was available. It was a novel experience for her, so I arranged for him to let me know privately if she should outrun the piper and then I'd sweeten the account. I didn't expect to, mind you, but I like to envisage possibilities. She might have launched out a bit too heavily to begin with."

"And did she?"

"Oh no. Something very different. I heard only this morning. She's instructed the bank to realise those Denton, Rale shares."

I'm afraid I stared.

"How many?"

"Two thousand. They're standing at just over fifty shillings."

"Five thousand pounds," I said. "That's a lot of money to want at your disposal? But wait a minute. You think it has something to do with your brother-in-law?"

"It can't have," he said. "Harry's own account is in good shape and he doesn't need any money in his new job. He told me so himself."

"Then you think your wife might be thinking of reinvesting it?"

"Don't know," he said. "I can't ask her. If I let her know about any collusion between that bank manager and myself it'd be as if I was spying on her. I will tell you this: I'm hoping for a chance to say something. She might let something fall which gives me an opening. Also, strictly between ourselves, I've arranged to be told just how she disposes of that five thousand when it's paid in."

"It must be worrying," I told him. "Still, let's hope it straightens itself out. Maybe there's some simple answer to everything. Let's hope there is."

"I hope to God there is!" He gave a dour shake of the head. "I hate things below the surface. I'm a direct sort of chap myself and this worrying about something you can't get to grips with isn't doing me any good. I'm sorry you had to hear all about it. It was unpardonable of me."

"Not a bit of it," I told him. "It'd be a hell of a world if there were no one worth telling our troubles to."

"Yes," he said, and smiled. I knew it was the first time he'd smiled since we came into that room. And then his hand went out and he was patting my shoulder.

"You're a good fellow, you know, Travers. I only wish we could see more of each other."

"Maybe we can," I said. "But what about another port?"

"Port?" he said, and as if he were getting back from quite another world. "Sorry, no. It's good of you but I've got to be running along."

The next event, and only a couple of days later, was an unexpected meeting. It came about like this. I wouldn't like you to shrug it off as yet one more coincidence.

I have always an eye open for antique shops, and the smaller the better. We have some quite good stuff at the flat, and I've long since been warned not to add to it and make the place still more of a museum. Not that there's much chance nowadays of picking up bargains. People know too much. The old days have long since gone, even if one still hopes.

And, paradoxically, the best place to strike a bargain is in a suburban or provincial antique shop—provided you're a specialist in something. A dealer's interests have to be so widespread that he simply can't have specialised knowledge about everything, and he may know far less than you about your own particular branch. Suppose, for instance, you spot in a shop a porcelain Nymphenburg figure—one of those stock characters of the Italian Commedia dell'Arte, a Pantaloon or a Columbine or Scaramouche. It might be by Franz Anton Bustelli, and, if so, and it was in perfect condition, it might be worth up to four thousand pounds. The dealer might merely know it was good and he might ask a hundred for it. But you have that specialised knowledge. You get the price down to eighty guineas, say, and you buy.

That may be an extreme example, but it's the kind of thing that's always happening. And I'd seen in a small antique shop near Notting Hill a smallish rococo figure, carved in what I thought was walnut, of a boy playing with a dog. What I'd gone in to see was a cup and saucer that looked to me like Chelsea but which was priced at only two guineas. It turned out to be a fake, hot from the kiln, as they say, but I'd noticed that figure and had naturally not asked about it. What I did do that particular afternoon was to go to the Victoria and Albert to have another look at their carved wood figures, hoping to refresh my own specialised knowledge and then go back to that antique shop and have a thorough inspection of the figure I'd seen.

I didn't learn a lot, except that if it were genuine eighteenth-century Austrian or Bavarian, then it was unlikely to be walnut. It was a dry, brisk afternoon and I decided to walk just beyond Harrod's and then take a bus. Inquisitive as I am, I had a look in every shop window that I passed. At some I stopped. But I wouldn't have stopped at what I'd call a woman's high-class shop if it hadn't been for something I saw. It wasn't a large place. Just two smallish premises that had been made into one, and with the two display windows. In one was millinery and things like gloves and scarves, probably to match, but the other window was being re-dressed. A chic-looking blonde of twenty or so was doing the job and an older woman was supervising. Not all that older. She had her back to me and it was purely by chance that I saw her as she turned. I glanced up at the name above the shop—MARLENE.

I'd gone by the door, but I turned back and went in. The older woman stepped down from the window.

"Yes, sir?"

The smile froze on her face. She gaped. She looked back at the window.

"Just a moment," she told me, and had a quick word with the window-dresser.

"Come through here," she told me, and I followed her through to a largish back room which was evidently the office. She turned to face me.

"My word, you gave me a shock!" she said. "Have you come about anything special?"

"Not at all," I said. "I just happened to catch sight of you and thought it'd be nice and friendly to have a word. What are you doing here, by the way?"

"Sit down," she said. "I'll make a cup of tea. I was due for one, in any case."

The little kettle seemed to be filled. She lighted the gas-ring and began getting things out of the cupboard.

"You knew the house at Harringay was in my name?" she said. "I sold it as soon as I knew Andy was dead and then I ran across Marlene Fryer who used to be buyer where I was. She had this place and wanted to expand. Had a chance of leasing the next-door premises, see, so I put some money in and came in as a partner."

"And how's it going?"

She smiled.

"Touch wood, but we're doing pretty well. There's a nice clientèle all round here and Marlene's awfully clever. She's a wonderful way with her. I do the millinery side principally. You know I was always good at that."

"I know," I said. "A shape, a twist of ribbon and some gewgaw or other and there's ten guineas."

She laughed.

"How you do talk! It isn't so bad as that. I won't say, though, there isn't a profit. But you've got to be good."

"You're slimmer," I said, and she was. She was in what I'd call business clothes, but she looked an even more attractive woman. And ten years younger than when I'd first clapped eyes on her in our office one November morning.

There was the sound of a buzzer.

"Someone Grace wants me to see in the shop," she told me. "Look after the kettle and make the tea."

A quick look in the mirror, a pat of the hair and she was out. I gently reopened the door just an inch and did some listening. I couldn't help smiling. I couldn't see the customer but she seemed to be an old and valued one. As for Doris Bosford—she'd ceased to exist. I was listening to a new voice—a very precious voice: that of Marlene Fryer's partner. She said 'Madame' not 'Modom'. She even had a kind of languorous Mayfair laugh. I gently closed the door.

I'd made the tea by the time she was back—as Doris Bosford.

"That was Mrs. So-and-so," she told me. "She's an awfully good customer. We can kid her now that we give her special terms."

"Don't tell me," I said. "You put the price specially up so that you can bring it specially down."

She wasn't a bit abashed.

"Yes," she said. "Isn't it dreadful! What about your tea? Milk and sugar? Oh, and I'd better take one to Grace. She's learning the business—partly."

It was snug enough in that room, but it wasn't intimate. Doris was the same pert character I'd known months since, but now there was a difference. Her troubles had gone and life was quite an enjoyment, and yet every now and again I caught a glance that had something about it both wary and watchful. It was as if she'd done something and was putting on an act as a kind of camouflage. It might have been, of course, the knowledge that I'd known her under different circumstances in the old Harringay days and the wonder if I was really being impressed by the front she was putting up.

"Where's your partner this afternoon?" I asked her.

"At a dress show," she said.

"You don't mean copying other people's ideas?"

"Of course not!" she said, and I almost expected her to wink. "But we do have our workroom on the other floor, and it does help. Most of our stuff we get from the wholesalers, but we do make our own models." Then she gave me one of those wary looks. "But about Marlene. If you ever should meet her, don't say anything about you know what."

"I'd never dream of it," I told her. "Not that I'm ever likely to meet her. But talking about that, I understand you definitely identified your husband's body. I don't want to remind you of what must have been a most unpleasant experience, but I thought identification would be almost impossible. How were you so certain?"

"I just knew," she said. "And there were the clothes, and so on."

She passed me the chocolate biscuits, but I wouldn't have another one, or a second cup of tea. I said I'd have to be going.

"Where do you live now?"

"Marline and I share a flat in Vickers Street. That's just short of Ladbroke Grove, on the right."

"And you really like it here?"

"It's fine," she said. "You're your own boss for one thing, and what you do you're doing for yourself."

"And you've never thought of marrying again?"

"What, me?" She laughed. "Once bitten, twice shy—that's me. Not that I don't think I could, mind you."

"And who is he?"

"Well, I oughtn't to say," she said, voice lowering. "I can't be sure, but I have my ideas. He's the representative of a firm we buy quite a lot from. The last time he was here he took me out to ever such a posh place for dinner and dancing. He's not half bad."

"I'm sure he isn't," I told her.

I was just getting up to go, and then I sat down again.

"Look, all that business you saw us about is long since over, but tell me something. Just between ourselves. I saw that man Marler when he was dead but I never saw him alive. Just what was he like?"

Her look had been warier than ever. Maybe she was totting up what she might gain and what she might lose. Maybe I mightn't keep my word about that partner of hers and spill something of which she'd been kept in ignorance.

"Well, I never knew him—not really. But he was about thirty-five and fairly tall and dark. There was a sort of foreign look about him."

"And one other thing: he had a queer sort of tattooing on his chest—like an eagle with its wings outspread and holding something like a ball in its talons. It struck me as most extraordinary. You ever hear him mention it?"

Her face had flushed.

"Of course not," she said. "He wouldn't have mentioned anything like that to me."

"Still, I thought I'd ask," I said. "I've seen a lot of tattooing in my time and all of it seemed pretty stereotyped. This was unusual and I wondered if there was a story attached to it."

We went out the way we'd come, past a stand of coats and a display cabinet of feminine knick-knacks. I was expecting her to say some sort of goodbye, but she didn't. She had an eye for the girl who was still dressing that window even while she was opening the door, and before I could utter any sort of goodbye myself she was closing the door after me, and all I caught was a smile and a surreptitious wave of the hand.

I thought a whole lot about her as I walked on and while I was on the bus. What I knew, for all the on-the-surface pleasure my call appeared to have given her, was that if she never saw me again it would still be too soon. When I had left that room, for instance, she hadn't asked me to bring my wife along as a prospective customer and shown me some fripperies or other, quoting prices as an added inducement. And she'd never been really comfortable with me. That tea hadn't been for my benefit but for hers—to know what I knew and hear what I might have to say.

I never had liked that business of the identification of her husband. My information had been that there'd been virtually nothing to identify—a rag, perhaps, a hank of hair and a bone. But she wanted him to be dead—legally dead. Luckily for her that Harringay house had been in her name, and there'd been no legal difficulties about selling it. Nor would there be about what furniture she hadn't wanted at the new flat. Bosford, I guessed, hadn't had a banking account. His transactions had been in cash and beyond the scrutiny of inspectors of taxes. All there'd been was that box under the bed.

I couldn't help telling myself again that Doris Bosford had been uncommonly lucky. Everything had dovetailed exquisitely in. In her way she was an excellent actress and I'd have liked to be present at that identification of her husband's body. In fact, if I'd been asked to bet one way or the other, I'd have put quite a reasonable sum on Bosford's still being alive. Something *told* me he was alive, and it was something that I'd never be able to prove. And then, thinking back to the quarter of an hour I'd just spent in Doris Bosford's company, I felt I could go even farther. I practically knew he was still alive. Only one thing kept me from being absolutely sure—that same old thing to which I had gone back again and again while I was still involved in the Case: that matter of a box under a bed.

But, assuming he were alive, what was happening? Was he in communication with her and was his disappearance part of a clever scheme? Would she join him or would he reappear under another name? Or was it that she had no real proof of his death and had contrived a reality out of a wish? Was she prepared to give him an account of her stewardship if he did come back? What she'd done with the moneys from that box, for instance?

Or did everything go deeper than that? Had Bosford become aware of an intrigue between his wife and Marler, and had he planned Marler's drowning? Was Doris Bosford afraid of that? Did that account for the wariness in her attitude that afternoon? Was that hint of a lovelorn representative of a wholesale firm intended as an additional proof that her husband was definitely dead? So much so that she could with impunity marry again?

I could have gone on like that, finding new hypotheses as quickly as the seconds passed, but the bus was at Charing Cross and I got off. As I walked home I could tell myself that as an intellectual exercise it had been quite good fun. As for fretting that hypotheses weren't facts, that was the last thing I intended to do. Doris Bosford would have no reason to fear another sight of me for the very simple reason that I had not the least intention of seeing her again.

Or that's what I thought.

8

THIRD MEETING

THE day after my meeting with Doris Bosford my wife went off for one of her periodic visits to her only relative—an aged and practically bedridden aunt. I'm an old campaigner myself, and such absences don't leave me altogether helpless. And ours are service flats. In some ways there's an advantage in being occasionally alone. Even at my age you like to know that the bachelor in you hasn't altogether gone. It's rather like Wordsworth's *Ode on Intimations of Immortality* in reverse.

Bernice left in the early afternoon. That evening I thought I'd dine out somewhere for an absolute change, which means that I wanted neither the club nor any other accustomed haunt. And I'd remembered that a new place had been recommended to me by a man I knew. I'd also seen a couple of puff paragraphs about the same place in two different newspapers. One was only that morning and I looked it up. It wasn't gushing. It just quietly—almost confidentially—recommended the Restaurant Club

Antoine Dupont in Osbert Street. Like Jurgen, I'm prepared to try any drink once, so I decided to give it a trial.

I had a good idea where Osbert Street was, even if it's off the beaten track which I usually take to the club. I ought to have known the quickest way to it because it's right in the heart of the West End, but I did know it was in easy walking distance from the flat, so I didn't bother about a taxi. If I hit Jermyn Street I guessed I'd be right, and it lay a bit farther along towards St. James's.

I didn't actually get lost—you can't do that in streets so short and if you've got a tongue in your head. What I did was get involved somewhere off Lower Regent Street. Then I saw a short passage of about fifty or so yards, with bright lights at the far end, so I thought I'd cut through and get new bearings. The passage itself wasn't too well lighted and it was rather wider than most. I had my eyes, I fear, on the lighted street towards which I was walking and that was why I practically stumbled over a man.

"Sorry," I said, and then I saw he was stooping over another man. That man was on the hard ground, leaning against the walls, and the one I'd stumbled over was trying to support him.

"What's up?" I said. "An accident?"

"Smells to me like a drunk," he said. "He was sprawling here and I nearly trod on him."

He was a youngish man, whom I guessed to be a clerk of some kind. I squatted down to have a look at the man against the wall, and the first thing of which I was aware was a reek of whisky. Then I must have given a gasp.

"Good God! I know him. He's a friend of mine."

It was Harry Calvert. I had to think quickly.

"I don't think it's all drink. He's an epileptic. I'll try and get him to his feet. Would you be a good fellow and see if you can get a taxi at the end of the street there?"

He shot off at once, and I hoped it wasn't to rid himself of the whole affair. I tried to hoist Calvert up, but he slid back on me, and he was a pretty good weight in spite of his slimness. And that game leg of his didn't help. Then at last I did get him up, and it was then that he opened his eyes. He was snapping them as if they were out of focus, and then they closed again and it was a job to support his weight against that wall.

His jacket and overcoat were opened, and as I tried to button them up against the cold I knew that his waistcoat was wet. That was where the reek of whisky was coming from. I deliberately took a whiff of his breath, and it didn't seem alcoholic to me. As I was trying to work that out his eyes opened again. He tried to take his own weight.

"Easy," I said. "You're not in very good shape."

He didn't know me from Adam. He didn't even resent the fact that I had an arm round his waist. All he did was try to take a step, and then I heard a call from along the passage.

"A taxi here. Can I lend you a hand?"

We got Calvert between us and took most of his weight while he shuffled towards the lights.

"Got far to go?" the Good Samaritan said.

"Only to my place, St. Martin's."

We got him into the taxi. I explained to the driver about the epilepsy. The Good Samaritan got in, too.

"You might want some help at the other end."

I said that was very good of him, though I wondered if he were trying to enquire into my bona fides. I told him my name. His was Walters. He said he worked in a bank in the suburbs and was spending a casual evening in town. By then we were practically home, and it was then that Calvert really roused himself. He was between us, and it was as if he were trying to make a bolt.

"Steady, Calvert," I said. "You're in good hands. You know me? I'm Travers."

"Travers?" The voice was slurred.

"Yes, Travers. We met at Tyefield, your brother-in-law's place."

The taxi was drawing up outside the flats. Calvert still couldn't get out under his own steam. The night porter came out to lend a hand. I paid off the taxi-driver.

"It's all right, Tom," I said. "Mr. Calvert here has had a bit of an accident. What about you, Mr. Walters? Won't you come up for a drink?"

He wouldn't. He wouldn't even let Tom get him another taxi. Calvert was trying to follow him through the swing-doors, but he just couldn't make it. But he managed with help to get to the lift, and he seemed even steadier when we went into the flat. I switched on the light, got him into a chair, and then had the electric fire going. I was watching him. In that light he was looking in pretty bad shape. In the deathly pallor of his face the dark eyes looked more deeply sunken than ever.

"You're Travers," he said, and the voice was less thick. "I remember you now." He squinted up at me as I rose. "What happened?"

Before I could tell him he was trying to get to his feet, and his hand was at his mouth. I got him to the bathroom, and I could hear him retching as I closed the door. It must have been a good ten minutes before the door opened again. He was looking better. There was a bit of colour in his cheeks, but he was still not too steady on his pins. I'd made some coffee, most of it milk. I don't think he'd have sat down if I hadn't virtually made him.

"Drink this," I told him. "It'll help ease the stomach."

He gave me a queer look, but he took a drink of the coffee, all the same.

"Like to tell me what happened?" I said.

"Guess I was tight," he said. "How'd you happen to find me?"

I told him just what had happened.

"A good thing we can keep it in the family," I said.

"The family?"

"Yes," I said. "Cortin's a personal friend, and your sister and my wife are pretty friendly, too. That makes you a friend."

"Yes," he said. "Sounds as if it does. You were certainly a friend tonight. Who was the other chap?"

"The one I was telling you about. The one who actually found you. What about your pockets, by the way?"

"Nothing taken," he said, and began getting to his feet again. "Guess I'm all right now. Think I'll get home between the sheets."

"Where's home?" I said. "The town flat?"

"That's it," he said. "I had some business in town. Helen and Ted are in Coventry." He tried to make the smile rueful. "Must have met some pals and had one too many."

"You're not fooling me," I said. "That whisky sloshed over your waistcoat is an old trick. It was something else that put you out."

His eyes narrowed.

"I ought to know. And it's my business, isn't it?"

"Not altogether," I told him. "Otherwise you wouldn't be in this flat."

The eyes narrowed again. The smile, when it came, was just a bit lame.

"Guess you're right. Don't believe I'm not grateful."

"I'm not looking for gratitude," I said. "I'm just far too curious. You're still sure you wouldn't like to tell me what happened?"

"Perhaps I don't remember it at all myself."

I left it like that. I did ask him if he'd rather stay at my flat for the night. If he felt like eating I could ring down for something. He said he was grateful and it was more than good of me, but he'd better get home.

"I'm fine now," he told me at the door. "No need to come down with me."

"I'd better," I said. "I explained you away to the hall porter as an epileptic. Might be as well to go through with it."

"An epileptic," he said slowly. "That was pretty thoughtful of you."

I said not at all. Wasn't it all in the family? Then we went down the one floor and Tom fetched a taxi. I didn't know if Calvert were really going home. All I knew was that he'd told the driver to take him to Morniment Mansions. Just round the corner he might be giving that driver different instructions. Not that it was any of my business. Or was it?

On his account I'd had no dinner and it was latish now to have any. And hadn't I said that Calvert was one of the family?

I told Tom to have sandwiches sent up. Over them and a bottle of beer I began trying to think things out. I found that I liked Harry Calvert a whole lot better now he'd become a kind of personality and no longer the shadowy kind of figure of a quarter-of-an-hour's acquaintance at Tyefield. He spoke quite well, as I knew. There are flying officers and flying officers, and he was the good type. He had a good background. And so, I thought, did his sister. She might have described herself as a mannequin, but she was more than that. I thought I'd like to know far more about the Calvert history. Some day I'd wheedle it out of Cortin.

But that was really only the dim back-cloth against which had been the play of very different thoughts. So I went to the bathroom. It was normal, and the only scent was a faint one of Bernice's bath salts. Calvert had made a good job of tidying it up. Some trace of dirt on the floor showed that he had brushed his clothes, and the damp towel said he had washed his face. I closed the door, put on my overcoat again and went out.

As I've said, I'm an inquisitive soul. I like to know the ins and outs of things. I even like learning. If I watch a navvy using a road drill it's because I like to watch anyone who knows his job. That's the jackdaw in me—storing up all sorts of knowledge because one day it might come in handy. As a detective I've only one asset: that same inquisitiveness. With my six-feet-three of leanness and horn-rims, and a face which a reporter once described at patrician—he was probably tight at the time—I'm the kind who, once seen, can hardly be forgotten. I'd be about as much good on a criminal trail as a Dalmatian with pink and green spots. But I am a sticker. I'll gnaw away at an unsolved problem till it drives me practically frantic, and after a breather I'll start all over again.

That was why I went back to that passage. It took me quite a time to find it, and then I discovered that the lighted end of it was actually Osbert Street. I'd been far too busy in that taxi to notice it or enquire. As for the passage, it seemed to be useless as a back entry. It wasn't nearly wide enough to admit more than a small delivery van. High walls ran each side of it, and there were doors—three of them—and curtained windows through which one could see lights. That passage, in fact, told me nothing. I decided to look at Osbert Street.

And right on the corner was that restaurant for which I'd been looking. It had long, twin windows. I looked up from the opposite pavement and read the words in their brave new paint:

RESTAURANT CLUB ANTOINE DUPONT

The windows had what I'd call an extraordinary decor. It consisted of receding black curtains in which were framed a large-scale menu. I gave my glasses a clean and had a look at it. The paper was spotlessly white and the lettering in embossed gold. It was very high-class. It gave me the impression that there was a restaurant whose primary concern was food. A *bonne table*, as they say. And then I gave my glasses another and quite unnecessary polish. Somewhere I'd seen windows like that before, and for the life of me I couldn't remember where. Dim recollections went tantalisingly across my mind, but that's how they stayed. Somewhere before I'd seen windows with just that framing of a menu, but exactly where was altogether beyond me to recall.

I went back to the passage. That very first door, about twenty feet along, would be an entry to the restaurant. It was about another twenty feet beyond that, and well short of the second door, that Calvert had been lying. I went back to the restaurant door. I listened, but could hear nothing. I gently eased the door open. It was a small kind of kitchen annexe, piled with boxes of tinned goods and spare kitchen ware. There was an overwhelming and mouth-watering smell of food—the smell of a French kitchen with its unmistakable garlic. A man was talking near by, but I didn't listen. I closed the door, stood just beyond it for a moment, and then went back to Osbert Street. I went into that restaurant.

I went straight into a small foyer, just off which was the cloakroom. A kind of glorified waiter was on me at once.

"May I take your hat and coat, sir?"

"Thank you, no," I said. "I'd like a word with the proprietor or manager."

His eyebrows lifted slightly, and fell.

"I'll see, sir. Would you be so good as to wait here, sir? And your name, sir?"

I waited. A couple of diners came through, and I had a momentary view of a dining-room beyond. It seemed pretty full, latish though it was, and it gave that same impression of class. Then my man was back.

"M'sieur Simon, the manager, will see you, sir. Will you come this way?"

We went by the cloakroom to some stairs. We went up to a largish landing. My man tapped at a door and looked in. Then he was out again and asking once more for my name. I gave him a private card and he went in again with—"Just a moment, sir." In less than no time he was back and ushering me in.

"Mr. Travers, sir."

I was in the manager's office. He was a small, dapper sort of man of about fifty, wearing a moustache and a small imperial. As he rose from behind his desk he was holding that card of mine.

"You wish to see me, Mr. Travers? Will you sit, please."

His accent and intonation were as phoney as a certain Chelsea cup.

"Thank you," I said. "I speak French, by the way, if it's any help to you."

"But no," he said, and the smile was expansive. "I speak English, as you hear. It may not be so good as your French, but—" He broke off with what was meant to be a disarming gesture. "And what is it that you wish to see me about?"

I told him I'd been a purely disinterested party in a certain affair, and it was only an inherent nosiness that had prompted me to make enquiries. I proceeded in that roundabout way because I wanted to see if he was immediately interested. For all the show of bewilderment, he definitely was.

I said I didn't know the man I'd happened to find lying in the passage. He'd just managed to say, when I got him into a taxi, that he lived somewhere in Kensington, but I'd not caught the name of the road. Then, just as the taxi was moving off, he'd said something about the restaurant.

"I'll almost certainly never see the man again," I said. "But it made me wonder. Unpardonable of me, perhaps, to bother you like this, but I was interested. He seemed a superior sort of chap to me."

"Yes," he said slowly. "I think something was said about it. Wait a moment, will you? I'll find someone who will know more perhaps. Will you drink something?"

"Very good of you, but I won't. I've only just finished dinner and my usual ration of drinks."

"A liqueur, perhaps?" He smiled when I didn't show an immediate reluctance. "A Grand Marnier? Kümmel? Almost anything you wish."

"That's good of you," I said. "A Grand Marnier, if I may."

There was a large corner cupboard that looked half-filled with bottles. He poured me a generous tot. He said he'd not keep me more than a moment or two. The liqueur was good and I didn't stir. There was nothing, in any case, that I wanted to see more closely in that room. But he was away longer than his few moments. I'd drained the liqueur glass by the time he came back. He was all smiles and affability.

"Your friend, he was drunk—"

"Pardon me, not my friend," I reminded him. "He was a perfect stranger."

"Of course, yes. But he was drunk. He said he had seen a man he wanted to see. Some friend of his, perhaps, and he wanted to come up here. He said he had seen that friend come up here. He was in the foyer at the time. They tried to restrain him, if that is the word, but he forced his way up here. Then he collapsed. He was very drunk, so we simply ejected him. He was taken where he was found. I assure you it was all very—what you say?—discreet. We thought the fresh air would revive him. Afterwards, when one of the kitchen staff looked out, he had gone." He shrugged his shoulders. "That was the last we expected to hear about it."

I got up at once. I held out my hand.

"I guessed something of the kind had happened. May I congratulate you on handling things so well."

"You are too good," he said. "It was nothing really. It was the kind of thing one has always to expect."

I turned at the door.

"I'd like to ask you something, in quite a different context," I smiled. "I know there's only one answer, but this restaurant is good?"

He looked almost startled.

"It is more than that, m'sieur. Here you will eat as good food as anywhere in London. Also the cellar is superb. Here you eat in France itself. And you drink in France. The only difference is that one pays much less."

"That's fine," I said. "I dine out a lot. I must try you out."

"Ah!" he said, and smiled and spread his neat little palms. "You eat at the Antoine Dupont and afterwards you will come many times. And you will bring your friends."

He came with me to the foyer. He said an effusive good-bye. Then, at the outer doors, he had a last word.

"This man, this drunk, if you should happen to hear of him again you will let me know?"

"If I do," I said. "But I can't see how there's one chance of that in a million."

As I walked home the warmth of that liqueur was still in my stomach. I felt good. The Bright Boy of St. Martin's, as George Wharton had once ironically alluded to me, had put in an admirable half-hour at that restaurant. And something was telling him that in the morning he might find out considerably more.

The first thing I thought of when I woke the next morning was the layout of the twin windows of that restaurant. Few good restaurants have a garish front—most have merely a name in lights. But not one that I knew of in London had a specialised front like the Antoine Dupont, and what kept nagging away at me was the knowledge that somewhere or other I had seen just that kind of layout before—the simple black curtains framing an enlarged menu.

But it's no use chasing memories or dreams. Dreams are gone for ever, but memories come back, and when you least expect them. They're secretive things that resent probing: that's why they pop up at unexpected moments. At any time—while I was having breakfast or later in the morning some association of ideas would make that memory pop out of its hole like a rabbit with a ferret on its tail. Besides, I had plenty of other things to do.

I thought I'd be early and make sure that Harry Calvert would be in, so I was ringing the bell of the flat door just after nine o'clock. I rang three times before the door opened. Calvert blinked at me, recognised me, gave a sheepish kind of grin.

"Ah," he said. "The Good Samaritan."

"Not quite," I told him as he drew back to let me enter. "The other fellow was the Good Samaritan. I was the Levite, just passing by on the other side. But how are you this morning?"

"Me? I'm fine," he said. "Just having breakfast sent up. Will you join me?"

He wasn't looking all that fine. There were dark pouches under the dark eyes and his cheeks still hadn't even the colour they'd had at Tyefield. But there was a peculiar toughness about him. For all his height, he couldn't have weighed ten stone, but what there was of him was bone and sheer muscle.

I said I'd have a cup of coffee.

"Might as well have it here," he said, and switched on the electric fire. "Make yourself comfortable."

He didn't take long ringing down for that breakfast. It came almost at once. There was plenty of coffee but no bacon and eggs—just grapefruit and a little buttered toast and marmalade.

"My stomach's not too happy yet," he told me, and tried that grin again. "I don't say I've a hangover, but that certainly was a heavy night."

I let him get away with it. A sip of the scalding coffee and I put the cup down on the low table.

"A nice place, the Antoine Dupont," I said reflectively.

"The what?"

"The Restaurant Antoine Dupont," I said. "The one you were carried out of last night."

I did wish he wouldn't narrow his eyes. One couldn't tell if it were incredulity or menace.

"Who says I was carried out of it?"

"The manager. A little dapper sort of fellow. Calls himself Simon: pronounced Simon. Supposed to be French, of course. The waiter who took me to him pronounced it that way."

He didn't know what to make of me. He finished his grapefruit before he spoke.

"What's the idea of all this?"

"Just a wish to see the whole thing out," I said. "I know you're absolutely helpless. You can't bring a charge. It'd be your word against the manager's and a couple of other fellows'. You feel like telling me about it? Who the friend was, for instance, whom you followed up the stairs?"

"My God!" he said. "You get around!"

"All free service," I told him. "All in the family."

"But what's the idea?"

"Sheer inquisitiveness," I said airily. "The wonder, perhaps, if I might help. Also I can keep a very still tongue in my head. And, as you've said, I get around."

"All right then," he said. "It was just nothing. I was going in that place to have a meal when I saw this chap I particularly wanted to have a word with. He was inside, if you get me. I was in the foyer. He caught sight of me and he went out at the far end. I had an idea I could catch up with him if I slipped round by the cloakroom, only there happened to be stairs. I went up and another chap—a waiter sort of chap—stopped me. I went to hit him one, but he got his in first. Knocked me out cold. Then I reckon they carted me out after spilling some whisky on me to give the idea I was tight and cooked up that yarn accordingly." He looked up from his plate. "Satisfied?"

"Good lord, no!" I said. "I had a good look at you last night while you were out. There wasn't a mark on you. I even had a look at your solar plexus. Nobody knocked you out. What knocked you out was a Mickey. Chloral-hydrate in whatever you drank. You hadn't been drinking. I doubt if you ever do much drinking. It was what I said. That's what made you puke your soul out. That's why you've got those bags under your eyes."

"I see." He pushed the plate back and took out his cigarette-case. He passed it to me. "Anything else you know?"

"A lot more," I said. "But it'll keep. Depends on what you're prepared to tell me."

"You'll keep it strictly to yourself?"

"Haven't I said so?"

"Right," he said. "This is the truth, the whole truth and nothing but the truth. I ran up against a tout not too long ago in the bar of the—well, the name doesn't matter. I was in the mood for a gamble and I went in a taxi with another chap to a certain private house. Don't ask me where. I don't know. All I think is that it was in the south-west district. I had a fairish stake, but I lost it, and a couple of thousand or so as well. I saw this fellow there— the one I was after last night. He didn't play himself. He rather struck me afterwards as being one of the organizers. I don't think I was supposed to see him. Just happened to see him—and he saw me—through a door that happened to be opened."

"What were you playing?"

"Just roulette. There were about a dozen of us there. Afterwards I happened to read an article about that sort of thing somewhere and I knew that wheel had been crooked. It was too late to do anything about it then. In strict confidence I can tell you that I made a clean breast of it to Ted Cortin and he honoured the I.O.U.s. But that's why I thought I'd like to meet that particular man."

"And he was the one you saw last night?"

"The very one. A biggish, florid sort of man with a neat little beard and wearing glasses. Horn-rims, something like your own. Everything else was what you guessed. I was stopped on that landing and I told the chap I was after a crook. I described him and he told me to wait there and he'd make enquiries. Then another chap—that manager, I guess—came out and asked me if meanwhile I'd like a drink. He brought me a whisky and soda. That's about all I know. I reckon I passed out before I'd time to know it. Next thing I remember was being in a taxi."

"You didn't handle things too well," I said.

"I know," he told me ruefully. "I went at it like a bull at a gate. I wanted my money back or else I was going to raise a hell of a stink. I wanted to give Ted back his cheque."

"Well, there it is," I said. "Everyone was too clever for you and now you can't do a thing about it. But I can. If you'd like me to."

"Let it go," he said. "I made a fool of myself. I'm not likely to do so again—not in the same way."

"Is that fair?" I said. "What about the other fools who're going to fall for the same racket."

"But you yourself said there was nothing I could do."

I told him what influence I had and how, with no mention of names, I could pass on a strong tip to the police. "They'll know what to do," I said. "But this man you saw last night. Was he a diner or connected with the restaurant?"

"To tell you the truth," he said, "at the time I thought he was a diner, bolting out to the lavatory or some place when he saw me. But now I've had time to think it over I'm pretty sure he must either be connected with the place or else a man who spends packets of money there. That'd be why they had to cover up for him."

"Right," I said. "Leave it to me. I'll soon find that out."

"But won't you be recognised if you go there again?"

"I'm not going," I said. "That's the kind of thing I employ other people to do."

"Look," he said. "If you're going to spend any money, then I'm going to pay. Which reminds me, I already owe you for a taxi."

"On the contrary. You saved me a reasonably expensive dinner. I was just going to feed in that restaurant myself. As for the other thing, it'll just go on the expense account."

I'd got to my feet and he went with me to the door. I could almost feel his uneasiness behind my back. But it wasn't quite that.

"I don't like it," he said. "I'd like to pay."

"Right," I said. "One of these days you'll get a bill. But do I take it we're not friends?"

He gave that sheepish but attractive grin. It gave him more than a look of his sister.

"Reckon we are," he said, and held out his hand.

In our job we use all sorts of operatives, and if we happen to be short of a specialist we can get him from some other reputable agency with whom we have a working agreement. I didn't use an outside man; I wanted this kept "in the family".

Our man might be described as our man-about-town. We hadn't had him long, but he was good—a man of about forty, Willis by name, who'd worked for Intelligence in his time and could put up the snootiest of fronts. The next evening he had dinner at the Antoine Dupont and he came to the flat later to give me a personal report.

Calvert's man was no other than Antoine Dupont, the proprietor. He appeared to be genuinely French and he'd apparently adopted the custom of all really intimate French restaurateurs of visiting tables and having a word with his guests. His description was little different from Calvert's: a biggish, florid man with a neatly clipped moustache and imperial and his age about the early forties.

"You had a good meal?"

He said it was fine, even if it had set the agency back a matter of fifty shillings. The whole place had class, he said. Antoine Dupont had class. He even wore white gloves: a kind of *de rigueur* if he courteously filled a guest's glass.

"How long was he there?"

"Only between half-past seven and nine," he said. "The main rush of diners, I'd say. I didn't see him after that."

I told him he'd got just what I wanted. In the morning I went round to the Yard and had a long talk with someone who wasn't George Wharton. The someone said he'd keep me informed.

9

ANOTHER BODY

IT WAS the very next morning when George Wharton rang me. It was early, about half-past seven, and I was having my early morning cup of tea in bed and smoking a cigarette. I hooked off the extension receiver.

"That you, Travers? George Wharton here."

"You're pretty early, George," I said. "Guilty conscience, or what?"

"It's what," he said. "You busy?"

"Far from it."

"Right," he said. "A man's body has just been discovered near Fallgate golf course and I'm going along for a look-see. You might as well come. In ten minutes?"

I told him to make it a quarter of an hour, and even at that I was a minute or two late and badly shaved. A police car was standing by and we were off at once. It was a grand morning, the sun shining and a nice early nip in the air—the sort of morning that makes you determined to get up early every morning and see some more like it.

George and I were at the back, and for once he wasn't wearing that old navy-blue overcoat of his with the worn velvet collar. He had on a grey suit I'd seen once or twice before, and his bulk had stretched it a bit at the seams. He did have on his old bowler and not a hat to match.

"Fallgate golf course," I said—that isn't its real name, by the way. "In a wood, did you say?"

"Don't pump me," he said. "I know little more than I've told you. It's the body of a middle-aged man and there're some tricky things about it. How's Bernice?"

I know when I'm being edged away. This time I didn't think it meant much, even if usually he likes to keep a lot up his sleeve. I told him about Bernice and the car kept rolling north-west. The streets were fairly clear at that hour, but it was a long ride, clean to the outer suburbs. We came into the town and went through it and left to a common. But that wasn't it. We turned again into a Links Road, on each side of which were detached houses of good, fairly modern types. We went for a half-mile past the last of them, and I could see that that road had a dead end. To the left was the golf course, and then, each side of the road, a fairly narrow stretch of wood—oaks, mostly, and with quite a bit of undergrowth. The hedges on each side were badly gapped.

At the far end were two cars and we drew in behind. An old friend—Chief Inspector Jewle—was there, and the local inspector with him, a man called Andrews. Jewle gave me a nod and a smile. Wharton came bustling up from his side of the car.

"The body's just in here, sir."

"Right," Wharton said, and followed Jewle through the gap.

"And who's that?" he said with a look ahead.

"The one who found the body," Jewle said. "I thought you might like his story at first-hand."

We went only about thirty yards into that wood. The body was in the middle of one of the few clumps of scrub beech. I saw only a bare foot and then Wharton was obscuring my view. I daren't walk round for fear of obliterating foot-prints.

Wharton had a real good look. He even got down on one knee.

"What was that medical report again?"

"It's only sketchy," Jewle said. "They'll know more when they've worked on him. Been dead about two days. Manual strangulation."

"Right," Wharton said, and got to his feet. "What're the burns? Acid?"

"Yes, sir—acid. And poured on him here. We've taken some soil for analysis."

Wharton grunted. He drew back and let me have a look. There wasn't all that to see, unless you got down to it as Wharton had done. And, as you know, I'm not too much at home with corpses. But I could see that the man was stark naked; that he was lying sideways, and that the side of his face that was upwards was badly disfigured. I could see, too, that he was bald, and I was mentally agreeing that his age would be around fifty.

The youngish fellow who'd found the body was standing a bit away with one of Andrews's men. Wharton beckoned him over. He looked a bit scared.

"Don't be afraid," Wharton told him genially. "Nothing to get alarmed about. You're doing us a favour, not the other way about."

He pointed to the body. "You know him, by any chance?"

"No, sir. Never saw him in my life."

"How do you know he wasn't a club member?"

"Well," he said, "if he'd been a member I'd have known him. I know all the members, or practically all."

"Make up your mind," Wharton told him, still genially. "Why practically all?"

"Well, sir, some don't play all that often. Or it might be a new member you haven't seen yet."

"Right," Wharton said. "Let's make a fresh start, at the beginning. Tell us your name and who you are and all about it."

His name was Aston, and he was one of the almost extinct tribe of caddies. His age was twenty and he'd been at the club ever since he'd left school. He'd got up early that morning to look for balls. With balls at three-and-six, he sometimes had quite a profitable hunt, and that wood was always worth a search. A lot of people sliced into it from the seventh fairway. The seventh was a dog-legged hole, bogey four, but the tigers often got trapped in it when trying to carry it and be just short of the green in one.

That was how he'd come to find the body. He'd at once run to the club-house and told the steward, who'd rung the police. And that was all he knew.

"When was the last time you were in here?"

"About a week ago," he said.

"Any ideas as to why some golfer who'd seen his ball come in here didn't find the body?"

Jewle broke in there. The body had been well hidden, he said. They had to pull back the undergrowth to uncover it. Aston had ideas, too. After the week-end the course was always rather empty. He'd been looking for a tiger's ball. The tigers used the best balls. Also a long-handicap man could never slice so far into the wood.

There was some more talk, but I wasn't paying too much attention. Wharton was merely skimming the surface of things, as it were, before dismissing a witness. I was thinking, as I always did, of what some might take to be a callousness in the presence of death. That was what used to horrify me in my earliest days with George Wharton and till sheer routine made me see things from his angle. That body in the beech clump, for instance, wasn't even a body. It was merely a problem. It was an immediate source of possible clues. Beyond that it had no value—except, maybe, to those of whose lives it had once been a living part. But the living thing, to George Wharton and Jewle, was a murderer. He was the vital thing. That thing in the beech clump had no value beyond the help it would give to the finding of that murderer.

Aston was allowed to go. The photographers arrived and the ambulance. Jewle was nominally in charge and George and I walked on towards the light that showed through the far trees. Through another gap we stepped out to the golf course. We checked up on what Aston had told us about that seventh fairway. It was warm out there in the open, but where the morning shadows still held the heavy dew we could see where Aston had left the wood and how he had been running, and then three sets of feet for the return—Aston's again, and those of Andrews and his man.

"No importance in all this, is there, George?" I said.

"Just a check-up," he told me. "No use cluttering up that wood."

The wood wasn't cluttered when we got back. The photographs had been taken and the body had gone to the local morgue. Anders, our own man, would be there by now, and it wouldn't be long before we knew a whole lot more about that body.

"What're you going to do?" Wharton asked Jewle.

Jewle said Andrews was sending another couple of men and the area of the body would be searched. Wharton nodded approvingly.

"I don't think we'll get a lot out of any footprints in here," Jewle said. "Looks as if all sorts of people have been in from time to time, from boys to courting couples. No identifiable car marks on the road outside. It's hard metal. What might help is to canvass the houses just up the road and try to find out if anyone heard a car down here, and when."

"Fine," Wharton said. "I'll be along later. If you should happen to want me I'll be at the club-house and then at the local station."

We went to the club-house in the car, passing the common again and then turning in at a drive. The club-house had once been a large private house whose grounds were now a part of the course. The steward had little to tell us beyond verifying Aston's story. He asked us if we'd like some coffee. George said we would.

There was a fire in the dining-room and we had our coffee there. We'd hardly sat down when George was asking me what I thought about things.

That's his way. I think it's a hangover from the very old days when I was a kind of apprentice—the master using his own adaptations of the Socratic method to find out just how far the pupil has progressed. But nowadays there's one big difference. There may be an impish wish to trip me up. Or George himself may be genuinely at a loss. But that wasn't the case that morning. Everything was almost too obvious for words.

"The immediate problem is identification," I said. "I think it's even the main problem."

"How do you mean?" George asked blandly.

Once I used to get angry with George, but that was long since. Now, if he hectors me, I hector back. If he cajoles, I find out why. If he pretends an ignorance, I know he already has just what he wants to know.

"You tell me," I said. "I'm not even in the case officially—as yet."

That took him out of his stride. He shot me a look from under his beetling eyebrows.

"Well, he has to be identified, hasn't he? Someone took an awful lot of pains to see he wasn't. His clothes removed so there shouldn't be a clue in 'em. And that acid poured over his face. And the body dumped in that clump. If it hadn't been found for a week or two identification would have been harder."

"Exactly," I said. "If the body can't be identified, then you'll get no further."

"We haven't even started yet," he told me snappishly. "There'll be Anders's report. And we can get a good look at him when he's on the slab. And if he meant anything to anybody, he'll be a Missing Person, won't he?"

"No harm in a little anticipation, though," I said. "For instance, can we assume that the murderer knew just where to dump him? Looks like it to me. The dead end of a road, and hard metal right up to the edge of the wood, and plenty of gaps and a fair amount of undergrowth."

"You think it's a local affair?"

"Not necessarily," I said. "I do think he was dumped by someone who either lives here or once lived here, or who played sufficiently on the course to remember the possibilities of that wood."

"Yes," he said, and licked the last drops of coffee from his moustache. "That struck me, too. Maybe we can fit it in with what we pick up later."

He went out to ring the station, and Anders. He came back to say it was no use going along for at least an hour. The steward had given him a couple of morning papers and we sat on the veranda in comfortable wicker-chairs, with the first tee almost under our noses. It was fine there in the spring sun. The first players arrived—a couple of ladies. A men's foursome was next, and I could watch them as far as the third tee. I thought it was a grand way to spend a morning. I'm not much of a golfer myself nowadays, so there's a kick in seeing the other fellows make mistakes.

George looked at his watch and got to his feet. It was after eleven o'clock and we went back along the common to the town and the police station. A uniformed sergeant took us along to the morgue. Anders and the local surgeon were both there.

Anders is a hard nut. He gave me a quick nod and a grin and turned an ironic eye on Wharton. The body on the slab was covered with a waterproof sheet and on the long porcelain-topped side table were various jars. I didn't look that way.

"In a bit of a hurry, aren't you?" Anders said.

George shrugged his shoulders. Anders is one of the people out of whom he can never get much change.

"You mentioned an hour. It's over an hour and a quarter."

"He's in no hurry," Anders told him, and waved a hand at the sheet. "I doubt if he'll run away. And, to save you asking, he's been dead for about sixty hours. He was probably killed on Sunday night. Work it out for yourself."

"Seems all right by my kind of arithmetic," George said. "And what killed him? Manual strangulation?"

"Ah!" said Anders ghoulishly. "I'd like you to have a look."

He drew back the sheet. I took one quick look and turned away. It was a horrible sight. One side of the face was heavily burnt and whatever had caused the burning had seeped to the other side so that there were dark patches and one long furrow that ran down to the neck. The body itself had a kind of luminous whiteness, and for some queer reason it seemed to associate itself with the stench of disinfectant.

"Only one side burnt," Wharton said. "How do you work that out?"

"The acid was poured only on one side," Anders told him dryly.

"In the wood?"

"In the wood. The soil sample proves it."

Wharton grunted.

"A queer business. What d'you make of it?"

The question had been put to me. I shrugged my shoulders.

"It could be all sorts of things. The body was brought to that wood by car. If it had been poured over the face at the site of the actual killing, then there might have been some signs of corrosion in the car. Doing the job in the wood was safer. What the pourer forgot was that the wood would be very dark and he daren't use a torch, and he'd put the body down so that it lay on one side. That's one explanation."

"Not a bad one either," George said. "But what actually killed him? Manual strangulation after being coshed out?"

"Look for yourself," Anders said. "There's no trace of injury to the skull."

"You're right," George said. "Then he was attacked from behind and just strangled. That means whoever did it ought to have some lacerations. This chap looks big enough to've put up a fight."

"He didn't," Anders said.

Wharton stared. He let himself smile.

"All right. You've got something up your sleeve. Why not give us a clue."

The other surgeon—his name was Watson—turned round from his table and slipped the gauze from his mouth.

"As a matter of fact he died from cyanide poisoning."

"Good God!" Then he was frowning. "But what about those bruises on the neck?"

"That's up to you," Anders told him. "We can only tell you the facts. Those bruises are fakes. They were made after death!"

"But why? Dammit, you must have some idea!"

Anders had ideas. He had to have ideas. When you've spent some thirty years at his job you've learned a whole lot about the jobs of other people. I've often thought that if Anders had been switched to pure investigation he'd have made a remarkably fine hand of it. I think that Wharton had that idea, too. He'd never been above picking the old police-surgeon's brains.

"All right," Anders said, "but don't quote me. The bruises might have been a kind of false trail. That's what you've already guessed yourself. Mr. Travers here wants something more imaginative. Maybe he's thinking of hate complexes and all that. Even when the man was dead the other man just got a bit of extra hate off his chest with a squeeze or two."

"That mayn't be so funny after all," Wharton said grimly. "I had a case like that years ago." He turned an accusing eye on

Anders. "You were in it yourself. That Brecknock Road affair." He whipped round on Watson. "What was the cyanide in?"

"Whisky."

Wharton grunted.

"The nature of the stomach content give you any ideas as to the time?"

"I'm working on it now," he said. "More of a bowel content. He took that whisky on virtually an empty stomach." He gave Anders a look. "I doubt if we shall learn much more than that."

Wharton nodded heavily.

"No offence meant, but we're not getting very far."

"Wait a minute," Anders told him. "There's a whole lot more yet. Take another look at the face."

Wharton shot him a look, took his glass out and bent down. He gave a grunt as he straightened himself again.

"See what you mean. He had a moustache but it was shaved off after death."

Anders was indicating something with a finger.

"See there? Just above and slightly round the mouth corners? Tells you the very kind of moustache he had. Not a canopy like yours, George, but a pretty straggling one. Dark, with quite a bit of grey in it."

George gave himself a nod.

"Now we're beginning to get places. Looks as if we might manage a reconstruction. Think you two could get me out a detailed description?"

"If you give us time," Anders said. "What about coming back in another hour?"

I was glad to get out of that morgue. Watson had told us of a place for lunch and we went there. It was as good a way as any of passing away Anders's hour, and in our job you never know when another meal's likely to arrive. It wasn't a bad lunch, and the beer was good. We talked about the case, but it didn't get us any further. Before we left the hotel George did some telephoning. He was away quite a time.

"A couple of the back-room boys are coming along," he told me. "They're going to try to get that face back to where it was, then we can circulate photographs. Good job we spotted that moustache business."

I nearly laughed at that *we*. You'd have thought Anders hadn't had a thing to do with it. But that's George to the life. He doesn't mean to snatch credit—it's just that he wants to be plumb in the middle of things. As I've said before, he fires questions at me and expects immediate answers. Well, I can usually give answers because I have that kind of mind. But if a propounded theory turns out to be wrong, then that theory was mine. If it has a certain rewarding merit, then it's ours. If it happens to be a winner—and I admit that's rare—then it's George's own.

We went back to that morgue. Watson had gone and Anders had a description ready. It was pretty comprehensive. The man was Jewish by birth. Age—the late forties. Hair a greying black. Moustache the same colour, and straggly, but no beard. Dome bald. Height, five feet ten inches approximately. General condition good except for slightly arthritic knees. No distinguishing marks except a small mole under the right shoulder-blade.

That was the gist of it. Wharton said the back-room boys might make some additions, but that night's *Police Gazette* would be printing it. Anders, washing his hands at the porcelain sink, said he was getting some lunch and later he'd be back. There were one or two things still to clear up. Nothing important, he said. Just enough to satisfy those whom he called the red-tape merchants.

Wharton and I went back to that wood. Jewle had found nothing that the murderer had dropped and nothing that could be thought of as a clue. But he had had luck at one of the houses— the last but one, nearer the wood, on the right, about a hundred and fifty yards from the hedge gap that had probably been used.

The woman there—her husband, a stockbroker, was now in town—had heard a car driving away from that dead-end just after midnight on that vital night. She and her husband had gone to bed late—friends had been in for bridge—and they'd both heard the car start up.

"I asked if they'd seen the lights," Jewle said, "but she said they hadn't. Their bedroom is at the front, so there wouldn't have been any strong light coming through even if the headlights had been on. I think there were only the side-lights, and maybe not even those till he got well along the road. And one other thing, sir. There was nothing about hearing the car go *down* the road, only coming back. And you see why? The road's downhill from that far lamp-post right to here. He could have coasted down, right to where he stopped. And, by the way, there wasn't a moon that night, as you know. It was overcast, and towards morning there was a little rain."

"You're doing fine," Wharton told him. "Everything's beginning to fit. Drop in on me tonight when you get back."

A word about the back-room boys and we were off again, and this time back to town.

"No point in you coming up," George told me when we got out at the Yard. "To tell you the honest-to-God truth, I don't see at the moment where you can help. Do you?"

I agreed. It might take quite a time to identify that body and that wasn't my kind of job. And I had an idea that once the body was identified the rest would be what one calls open and shut.

George thought so, too. Jewle was a good man, he said, and he might have the luck to see the whole thing through.

"I'll see you don't lose your morning," he told me as he put out a hand. "The labourer is worthy of his hire."

I said I wasn't worrying about that. What I did wish was that he'd let me know of any spectacular developments. I added that if by any chance he then wanted me—well, like that body on the slab, I wasn't likely to be far away. It was then nearer four o'clock than three. What George had alluded to as a morning had virtually been a day.

10

FOLLOW THE LADY

I TOOK a taxi to Broad Street. Bertha hailed me as I was going through to the office.

"There was a Coventry call for you, sir. A Mr. Cortin. He said he'd ring again. That was just after two o'clock."

"Any idea what he wanted, Bertha?"

"Only that he wanted you and not the office."

"Right," I said. "I'll be here for quite a time. If he doesn't ring before, you might see the call's put through to the flat."

I don't think I'd said more than a word or two to Norris—I still had my hat on—when the buzzer went. It was for me—Cortin on the line.

"Glad to get hold of you, Travers," he said. "I've just got in from Coventry. Flew down. Could you see me here for a few minutes?"

"Where's here?" I said.

"Sorry. At the flat. I'm just collecting a few things and flying to America tonight."

I said I'd be along at the double. A clock was striking five as I got out of a taxi at Morniment Mansions. I just rang the flat bell once and the door was opened almost before my hand had time to draw back.

"Come in," Cortin said. "Come through here. Sorry to be in such a hurry."

We went through to the drawing-room. He waved me to a chair. Everything was rather jerky—if you know what I mean. He seemed to be having an attack of nerves.

"Have you had tea? Shall I ring down for some?"

"No, no," I said. "Not worth the bother."

"A drink?"

"Too early. I'd rather hear what's on your mind."

"So you spotted that," he said wryly.

He didn't take a chair. He stood there by the empty fireplace, hands behind him as if there were really a fire.

"I'm flying to New York tonight," he said. "It's most important and I can't put it off. That's why I'm so worried."

"Your wife again?"

"Yes," he said. "And much worse. I'm worried because she's worried. I'm definitely afraid of a nervous breakdown." His hands went helplessly up. "And I can't do anything about it. The doctor can't understand it. And I asked her myself. I begged of her to tell me what was on her mind. You know what she said?"

"That it was nothing; it was all your imagination."

"Don't know how you knew," he said, "but that was what she did say. She even laughed when I asked if the baby was worrying her. So what could I do? You can't look your own wife in the face and tell her she's a liar."

"Tell me some more."

"Oh, there's plenty more," he told me grimly. "There's that hole-and-corner work going on between her and Harry. He knows more than I do. And that's the hell of it. She can make a confidant of him but not of me. But that's nothing. Remember that five thousand pounds I was telling you about from the sale of those Denton, Rale shares? Well, the bank manager was asked over the telephone a most peculiar question. Could he have available for her four thousand in pound notes—used pound notes."

He didn't add to it. He just stood there looking at me.

"I see," I said. "You'd like me to try to explain things."

"You think you can?"

"If you're prepared to face up to what I tell you."

"Speak your mind," he said. "I'm no child."

It wasn't like him to snap like that. Had I been in a querulous mood myself I might have snapped back. But it was straight talking, it seemed to me, that was going to do him most good.

"The whole thing's simple," I said. "Considering my job, if you know what I mean. Yours is a case that's always happening—the kind of thing we're constantly handling. Your wife's being blackmailed."

He stared. He couldn't believe his ears. *His* wife! Edward Cortin's wife!

"The whole thing's fixed for after your departure tonight," I said. "Your brother-in-law's—well, in the know. The blackmailer'll get that money soon after you're in New York."

"No, no," he said. "It can't be. It must be something else."

"Very well," I said. "You asked my opinion and I've given it. Now what?"

"No, no, no! Don't go." His hands moved helplessly again, and then he was going across to the cabinet by the Sheraton table. He poured himself a drink.

"You'll change your mind and have something?"

"Thanks, no."

There was a quick squirt of the siphon. He drank. What was in the glass when he came back looked pretty strong.

"Let's say you're right," he told me. "What're we going to do about it?"

"We?" I said. "You're making this your affair. I'm not doing a thing. Unless you can imagine yourself an ordinary client sitting in my office at the agency and me putting the questions and getting the answers—the right answers."

"What sort of questions?"

"Look," I said. "Let's take it easy. Sit down and let's talk it over calmly. And don't tell me it's easy for *me* to be calm."

He took the chair that faced me.

"Very well," he said. "Fire your questions."

"I'll put them in a roundabout way," I said. "To me this case is as hackneyed as a score of others we've handled. Someone's dug up something from your wife's past life—something that might considerably upset her relations with you if it got to your ears. She's trying in her way to keep it from your ears. Very well then. If I'm going to have anything whatever to do with the business you're going to tell me everything you know about your wife."

He gave a grunt. He licked his lips. He looked down at the glass, emptied it and set it by him on the floor.

"Very well," he said. "I'll tell you. Her grandfather was the Dean of Stowminster. Her father was a missionary in China, and he and his wife were murdered there by the early Communists. My wife and her brother were being educated in England and their home was at Stowminster. The dean died when she was twenty and her brother two years older. He wasn't a wealthy man. Helen got about four thousand and she came to town and invested it in a hat shop. She always had a liking for that sort of thing. It wasn't a success, and she lost practically all her money. Harry was in the Air Force, as I think I told you.

"Then Helen got in touch somehow with Georges Pellot and became a mannequin. She was good at it and became a kind of receptionist and also did some designing. Then she met that man Marler. I think you've heard about him."

"Yes," I said. "But you give me your opinion of him."

"He was a specious devil," he said. "Good-looking in a way. A German-Jew in origin, I'd say. He ran a restaurant place—showy and shady, if you know what I mean. Helen didn't take long to know she'd made a hell of a mistake. She was still at her job and she left him. Then I came along. That'd be about three years ago. I wanted her to get a divorce, but Marler wouldn't hear of it."

"You saw him yourself?"

"Oh yes, it wasn't a job for a woman. He told me perfectly frankly that he'd divorce her in his own time, and perhaps not at all. And he said he was taking care to give her no chance to divorce him."

"He was still sore about her leaving him?"

"I thought so then, but I changed my mind later."

He rose from the chair and stood by the fireplace again. He seemed to be wrestling with a problem.

"I shan't need to warn you how confidential this is," was what he said, "but I had a communication from him about a fortnight before his death. I met him at a certain bar and he told me he was now ready for a divorce. The price was five thousand pounds."

It didn't surprise me. I merely asked if he'd paid it.

"Yes," he said. "I didn't argue or try to beat him down. That'd have been like squabbling over Helen herself. I gave him a cheque and I made him sign a document. In it he admitted adultery and gave details, and agreed not to contest the proceedings. I post-dated the cheque so that I could verify the facts before he could cash it. A few days later he was dead. That saved the hell of a lot of trouble. And that's virtually all I know about him."

"It's all I want," I said. "May I see the document he signed?"

"But I burnt it. There seemed no need to keep it after his death. And Helen didn't know everything. About the five thousand, for instance. I didn't want her to see what was agreed on. I simply told her that I'd got Marler to agree to a divorce."

"Well, what's burnt is burnt," I said. "You've given me the facts and all I want to know is what I'm to do. Am I to handle this just as I would for any other client?"

He hesitated. He glanced at his watch, and the shrug of the shoulders was like one of despair.

"Yes," he said. "But for God's sake be discreet. One false move and the devil knows what might happen."

"Take it easy," I said, and got to my feet. "This is just routine to us. There'll be no false moves. Perhaps I already know more than you think I do."

"Oh?"

"Leave it," I said. "And what about yourself? Where do we get in touch with you if it should happen to be necessary? I don't anticipate that it will be. It ought to be all cleared up by the time you're back."

He gave me the name of his New York hotel and its number. He said he'd make a point of being there at nine o'clock each night, New York time, in case we wanted to ring him.

"Right," I said, "but don't ring us. If you hear nothing, it means that everything is going smoothly. Don't pester us. Let us get on with the job."

"That's fine," he said, and for the first time he sounded more like his old self. "You've taken a devil of a load off my mind. But you will be careful?"

"No more so than usual. If we weren't competent to handle such things we'd have a pretty poor reputation. Where's your wife now, by the way? At Tyefield?"

"Yes," he said. "Harry's there, too. I said goodbye this morning and flew to Coventry and back this afternoon."

"Right," I said, and held out my hand. "Have a good trip and stop worrying. And you've still got time to change your mind."

"I'm happier already," he said. "Maybe you can't understand me, but what I hate is this dirty underhanded side of it—this having to spy on my wife. Call it what you like, but that's what it amounts to."

"Whenever you think that," I said, "ask yourself one simple question. Who began it? She refuses to trust you, so how can you trust her."

He was going to prolong the argument, but I was making for the door. Thad it open before he got there.

"Goodbye again," I told him from the corridor. "And don't forget, everything's under control."

There was no sign of him when I glanced back just before the stairs. I'd rather expected him to be there. And just as I was waiting for a taxi I remembered that nothing had been said about a contract. Maybe it was unnecessary with everything, as it were, in the family. But that was why I didn't go back to the office. I preferred to let Norris have at least an idea. That's why I rang him at once. He'd left the office, but I got him at his private address.

"Can't tell you about it over the telephone, but there's a rather important job turned up," I said. "Is Hallows available, by any chance?"

He said he was on a job, but it wasn't so important that someone couldn't take his place.

"Then call him off," I said. "Wherever he is I must have him here at the flat tonight. Doesn't matter how late he is. I'll be up."

A year or two back we'd had a disastrous experience with an operative who'd taken advantage of what he knew about a case to try blackmail on the clients. It's something that has always to be guarded against, and there're two ways of doing it. One is to let the operative have only so much information and no more, and the other to use on ticklish cases only men in whom you have come to have implicit trust. Hallows was such a man. Had he ever turned blackmailer he could have made a little fortune— till we or the police caught up with him.

But maybe you think you know just what I meant when I let fall to Cortin—I admit it was inadvertently—that I knew far more about things than he could possibly have guessed. I think you'd be wrong.

To save going over the same ground twice, you can assume that what I tell you now is what I told Hallows when he turned up that night soon after nine o'clock. I did know a lot, and the knowledge had grown miraculously in that half-hour or so I'd just spent with Edward Cortin. The way I argued (and Hallows agreed with me; he's no sycophant, and if he'd disagreed he'd have spoken his mind) was this:

Marler had gone as far with that smuggling racket as he dared, and he was intending to get out of it. I think he was intending to go to France with Bosford to start some new racket operating from over there. That's why he wanted Cortin's five thousand pounds and why he also sold his car, and why the Sharman House office had been given up.

That's where Bosford came in. I'd long since begun to think of him in quite a different way—not as a singing moron who was over-fond of his wife but as someone who had infinitely more brains than I and that wife had given him credit for. I thought he'd been putting on a very elaborate act. I even suspected that of him and Marler his was the more cunningly deceptive brain.

Very well then: Marler had put the new idea up to him. Ana Marler had money—at least six thousand pounds in cash. So Marler was killed. His death and all that boat business was faked and it was Bosford who went alone to France. But what of that box beneath the bed? Wouldn't he have taken its contents with him?

To that there were various answers, all satisfying. There mightn't have been much in that box compared with Marler's six thousand pounds. Or the decision to kill Marler might have come suddenly, down at the Happton bungalow, when Bosford had to set off what was in the box against what Marler had. And Bosford could tell himself that in any case he could later return to England under a different name if it so pleased him and get surreptitiously into touch with his wife.

And everything was telling me that that was what he had done. That curious attitude towards me of Doris Bosford when I was in that room behind the shop told me she had a secret. That's what that secret was. I didn't say that she knew precisely where her husband was, but she knew he was alive. Remember the supposed lovelorn salesman she had thrown at me? Very well then. Bosford was alive: it was he who was blackmailing Helen Cortin.

But how? What did he know? It was a question I couldn't answer, but the theories had presented themselves. He had been very close to Marler, and so obviously there had been a something else in her past life that Cortin didn't know about, and Bosford had learned of it from Marler. Maybe Marler had been intending to do a spot of blackmail himself. What that something was I couldn't possibly conceive—not that it mattered. I'd have liked to know, but I wasn't too anxious to find out.

And why didn't it matter? For this overriding reason: if everything was reduced, as I thought it now was, to the fact that Helen Cortin was about to hand over blackmail money to Bosford, then our job was simply to follow her till she led us to Bosford, and then the whole game would be up. As soon as Bosford was spotted, then we'd hold him—even if we had to use force—and bring in the police. They'd handle the blackmail side of things with discretion. What they'd want Bosford for would be the murder of Marler. Maybe they wouldn't be able to prove immediately that there had been a murder, but they'd have more than enough for a holding charge while they went back and dug down. Quite a lot might be gathered from the French side, too; but, whatever happened, Helen Cortin would be mentally free. Maybe she'd even own up to her husband whatever it was on which the blackmail had been based. My idea was that after she'd left Marler, and before she met Cortin, she'd been involved with some other man, and Marler had had ample proof of it. I could even whisper to myself that man might have been Georges Pellot himself.

"So there we are," I said to Hallows. "You see what we've got to do. How do you propose setting about it?"

"I'll have to have another man," he said. "I'll get hold of Laurie Peters of Private Enquiries. He might have one. And he needn't know too much. Soon as possible we can replace him with a man of our own."

"And then?"

"Well, we'll keep Tyefield Manor under our eye. If the lady goes to town in that Rolls, then we'll follow it. If she goes to town by train, then I'll be on the train. I'll get the other chap to ring you at the agency and say what train and to where and then you can have a car there ready to follow her if she takes a taxi."

That sounded all right to me. I said that I'd manage somehow to bring a man with me in the car. Hallows said it might be dangerous for me to show up at all, since the lady knew me.

"You don't mind me saying so," he said, "but you're not exactly anyone who can melt into a background."

"You leave it to me," I said. "I told Cortin there wouldn't be any slip-up, and there won't. So let's leave it like that. By seven o'clock in the morning you're to be near Tyefield Manor. It sounds a bit early, but we can't take a chance. I'll be at the office at eight."

It wasn't far short of midnight and I was just falling asleep when Hallows rang me again. He'd thought it over, he said, and he hadn't been happy about an outside operative, so he'd got into touch with Norris. Norris was sparing one of our old hands, a chap named Davis.

I hate alarm clocks and their ticking away in a bedroom. In any case I don't need one. I've even been known to boast that I can wake at practically any time I like. That morning proved the truth of the boast, as it had often done before. I woke in the small hours knowing it would be later, and from then on had half hours of sleep between periods of waking. When six o'clock came I decided to have no more of it and I began getting up.

I supposed it showed the measure of my interest in what I had hoped that day would produce, even if it showed the lack of control that might make wakeful, say, the night of a schoolboy who the next day is making his first appearance in the first eleven. And I was still resolved to be a kind of Johnny-on-the-Spot. Hallows had made a big mistake in thinking I'd keep in the background. Not that I wasn't going to take every precaution. I'd told Cortin there would be no slip-up, and that was something by which I was still prepared to stand.

After breakfast I looked at my newspapers. Both had an account of the finding of the body of an unknown man in that Fallgate wood, and printed the description that Wharton had issued. It didn't differ from the one Anders had outlined except that there was something about the teeth. Dentures had been removed and what natural teeth were left were in none too good condition. They, and the dead man's fingers, said he was probably a chain-smoker of cigarettes. There was no photograph.

But what I'd really been looking for was a possible air-crash or the turning back of a transatlantic plane to its port of departure. That sort of thing rarely happens, and apparently it hadn't happened that night. Edward Cortin might be presumed to be as good as at New York. Naturally there was no mention of his name. Cortin might be the wealthy chairman of an air concern, but he didn't rank so high as news. If he'd wanted that kind of publicity, then he'd chosen the wrong line—he should have been a crooner or a diplomat, or one of the pets of Portland Place.

I was at Broad Street well before eight o'clock and the man on duty had nothing to report. That was when I knew I'd been a bit too precipitate that previous afternoon. I ought to have induced Cortin to give me a special letter of introduction to that bank manager, so as to have been given the tip when Helen Cortin actually drew that four thousand in notes. Maybe it would be a day or two before she did collect it, which would mean that much suspense and a couple of men hanging about in the neighbourhood of Tyefield Manor. And then—it shows the state of suspense I was in myself—I knew that Cortin could never have given me such a letter. That bank manager had stuck out his neck a very long way in giving Cortin those confidential tips about his wife's account. It had all been highly irregular and the kind of risk a manager might be prepared to run only for a particularly valuable and trusted customer.

Bertha arrived, and then Norris. He at least made someone to talk to, though I was to think that to his sane, unadventurous mind we were being highly optimistic about the whole thing. I don't think he changed his mind even after my telephone call came, and that was at a quarter-past nine.

"Davis here, sir. The car took a certain party to the main-line station. The train just left. It doesn't stop at London Bridge, so she may be getting out at either Waterloo or Charing Cross. Time of arrival ten twenty-five."

"Right," I said. "Was the lady alone?"

I hadn't prepared him or Hallows for that. All he could say was that there'd been no one in that Rolls but the chauffeur and the lady. She carried the usual handbag and also a smallish attaché-case. I told him he'd done fine and he was to report back with Hallows's car at the office.

I took a taxi to the garage and got out my own car. I drew just inside the yard at Charing Cross Station and I hoped the police wouldn't move me on. If that train was on time, then I had only a couple of minutes to wait. So, sheltered behind a newspaper, I sat in the car and waited.

11

NEAR MISS

THE train was dead on time. Three minutes after its arrival Helen Cortin emerged from the station, but only as far as the queue of taxis not six feet from the exit. I swung into the taxi queue, and as I did so I saw Hallows. He glanced back, but my car was hidden and he took another taxi. I moved out and followed him. All three of us were held up by the traffic coming down the Strand. The first taxi then went left towards Trafalgar Square, where the lights were against us. That gave us both a chance to edge nearer.

After that there wasn't any great difficulty, and by the time we were in Victoria Street it was plain that Helen Cortin was going to Morniment Mansions. Hallows had guessed that, too. As her taxi drew in, his went slowly past. I stopped about twenty yards short, and I could see Helen Cortin go in by the main entrance. I got out of the car so that Hallows could spot me. I got back as he neared, and he slid in alongside me. Her taxi had been dismissed and so had his own.

"What's the idea of her coming here?" he wanted to know.

"Probably she's having to pass that money over later," I said. "She might even be coming here to get telephoned instructions as to when and where to deliver it. I take it the money was in that attaché-case she was holding on to so firmly?"

He thought it was. Forty packets, each of a hundred one-pound notes, wouldn't require very much space.

"What'd we better do?" he said. "Watch from here?"

It seemed the only thing to do. It might be far too suspicious to loiter in a corridor, so we sat on. I'd brought newspapers with me and we took turns at reading them. It was about twenty-past eleven when Helen Cortin appeared again, and just when we'd wondered if we might have to arrange about staggered lunches. She was still carrying that handbag and the attaché-case, and when I put my glasses on it and her I saw that it now had a label attached.

She crossed the road and went away from us. But it was only to a bus-stop. Hallows got out. As she looked towards the way a bus would be coming, he too crossed the road. Then a bus came in sight and he had to quicken his pace. A couple of minutes and the bus had passed me. The road was fairly clear. I turned into the car park, swung round and got into position about a hundred yards behind that bus.

It made its leisurely way almost due north. A couple of cars had overtaken me, but it was easy to keep that bus in full view and to see who dismounted at the stops. It came out near Hyde Park Corner and went on. Now another bus was between me and it, and there was a press of traffic. Just short of Piccadilly Circus I had some luck. Maybe that bus was getting behind schedule, but it swung out just as the traffic lights were with it and rounded the Circus and pulled up just along Regent Street.

I hugged the kerb and gave a stop signal. Helen Cortin was one of the first to get off. Hallows was just behind her.

I let traffic regulations go hang, locked the car, pocketed the keys, and, when the traffic stopped, I was not too far behind the couple as they crossed the street. Helen Cortin gave never a look back. In two or three minutes she was going through the swing-doors of the Great Metropolitan Hotel.

Luckily for me there were plenty of people in that huge foyer. I moved straight over to the lifts and stood there back to the wall and a paper before my eyes. Helen Cortin was at the enquiry desk and almost at the head of the queue. Hallows was immediately behind her. I couldn't see what was happening because of another queue that straggled from the main desk. People were booking out just before the hour line of noon.

Another two minutes and Helen Cortin emerged from that queue and she was carrying only her handbag. Hallows appeared, too. But he didn't stir far. He just stood there, watching her as far as the swing-doors. I circled quickly round and let him see me, then took a risk and went through the swing-doors myself. The commissionaire was just seeing Helen Cortin into a taxi and I drew back till it had moved away.

I got a pound note from my wallet and the Agency identification card and I came quietly alongside that commissionaire. I let him see the note and gave him a quick glimpse of the card. I rather think he took it for a Yard warrant card—there isn't all that difference.

"That lady you just saw into that taxi, where was she going?"

He gave me a quick look, then his hand closed over the note. It was so deft that I thought he had palmed it.

"Didn't quite catch it, sir. Some Mansions or other."

"Morniment Mansions?"

"That was it, sir—Morniment Mansions."

"Thanks," I said. "That's all."

I nipped back through the swing-doors. Hallows was still near that enquiry desk. I drew in alongside him. If everything hadn't been so tense it would have been almost amusingly conspiratorial.

"All clear," I said. "She's on her way back to Morniment Mansions. Did you manage to read what was on that label?"

"Never a hope," he said. "She just handed the case in at the desk there and said something I didn't hear. All we can hope for is that someone will call for it."

"I've got a pull here with the manager," I said. "I was with Wharton here on a murder case a year or so ago. I think I could work the bluff that I'm here on Yard business."

"Don't try it yet," he said. "Let's wait and see what happens."

We waited. The queues gradually thinned. It was well after noon and the exit rush was over. Soon that enquiry desk was clear. The woman on duty moved a few steps and picked up that attaché-case. She read the label. She peered across the foyer, caught someone's eye, and beckoned. A man who might have been a liftman came up.

"Roberts, take this to Room 337 and see it's handed over personally to Mr. Foster."

I was so close, behind my newspaper, that I heard each word as if it'd been to me she was speaking.

"O.K.," Roberts said, and went towards the lifts.

There were ten people in that lift, and Hallows and I were almost the last. When we got out, Hallows went ahead and I kept just in sight of him and that attaché-case. We went along corridors, and then Hallows flattened himself against a wall just by the right-angled turn. I still kept back. Another minute or two and Hallows moved on. Roberts came in sight on his return journey. Hallows went straight on past the door of 337 as far as a left-angled turn. He went round and again flattened himself against the wall. I slowed as I neared him.

"See anything?"

"Only that Roberts went in and out again, and came out without the case."

"Let me take over here," I said. "Bosford has never seen me. It's ten to one he'll grab a taxi outside so you move my car round to near the hotel and then wait in sight of the lifts and pick me up there. We must follow Bosford at all costs."

I couldn't do any wall-flattening business. I merely hung around, and when anyone came along I made as if I was waiting for someone, but always with an eye on the door of 337. A shortish man—rather stout and with a muffler round his neck—emerged from the door of 339. He hadn't any luggage and he walked away from me towards the lifts. My heart had given a sudden leap till I'd realised he'd come out of the wrong room. Just after he'd disappeared round the corner, another man emerged from somewhere about room 320. I noticed him because I had to wonder if he were coming my way.

I waited till I was tired of waiting. It had just gone one o'clock when a chambermaid came into sight. I decided to take a risk.

"Pardon me," I said, "but I'm supposed to see a man in room 337 and I can't make anyone hear."

"Perhaps he's out."

"He can't be," I said. "He said he'd definitely be in his room before one o'clock. It's too important for him to break his word."

I gave a smart rap at the door while she stood by. Luckily for me there was never a sound. If Bosford had opened that door I was going to pretend I'd made a mistake about the number. It should have been three-five-seven. But there was no need. I rapped again.

"You've got your key," I said. "Think you could look in?"

She brought out her key, gave a rap of her own, and opened the door. I went in. That room was as bare of occupants as my palm is of hair. I moved quickly to the window. There was no fire escape that ran anywhere near. From that window was a sheer fall to a concrete yard two storeys down.

I saw a door on the left and tried the handle. The door was locked, or bolted from the other side. I looked in the wardrobe.

"Extraordinary," I said. And then a cold sweat was on my forehead.

"Where's that door lead to?"

"A bathroom," she said. "It's a kind of suite. People take both bedrooms."

"Then he may be in 339," I said. "Do you mind if we try there?"

I knocked and listened, and all the time I knew it was useless. She opened the door. That room, too, had no occupant. I asked her to look in the bathroom, and as soon as she was through the door I was looking in the wardrobe, and when she came back I was looking under the bed. I came out with an attaché-case. The lock had been forced and there was no label.

"You see?" I said. "He's been here. This is my attaché-case. I lent it to him only last night."

"Oh, but you mustn't take it," she told me. "I have to hand it in. If he's booked out, that is."

"Look," I said. "There's the telephone. Ring down and ask the manager to come up here. My name's Travers—T-R-A-V-E-R-S—Travers. Tell him he knows me and say it's most urgent."

I laid my hat on the table under the window and sat in the one easy-chair. A minute and she was saying the manager would be coming up.

"You'd better wait till he's here," I said, "then you can go."

I gave her a couple of half-crowns—about all the loose change I had. She hardly had time to thank me before Ardly, the manager, was coming into the room. He remembered me.

"Hallo, sir. Not more trouble, I hope?"

The chambermaid slipped out of the room. I told him we were after a certain confidence trickster and he'd been traced to Room 337 at the hotel.

"Name of Foster, *alias* several other things," I said. "I wanted to pay a surprise visit, but he appears to have given me the slip. He left only this empty attaché-case, which I'd like to take and check for finger-prints. But could you find out for me straight away if he booked both this room and 337?"

"He'd have to," he said. "We don't book these rooms separately."

"That settles that, then," I said. "While we were watching 337 he slipped out of that door. There's a man of yours named Roberts who collected this case from the enquiry desk and brought it up here to Foster, as he was calling himself. Could you get Roberts up here?"

Roberts came up. He looked a bit alarmed at the sight of the manager and me.

"Nothing to get alarmed about," Ardly told him. "You brought this case up here at about midday. It had something in it then and it had a label on it."

"That's right, sir. It said Personal. To be handed to Mr. Foster in room 337."

"And what happened when you handed it in?"

"Well, sir, I just knocked at the door and was told to come in. The gentleman was in the bathroom there. He said who was I and I told him, and he said to leave the case on the bed. So that's what I did."

"You never actually saw him?" I said.

"No, sir. I didn't worry about it not being him."

"It was him all right," I said. "What sort of voice had he?"

"Well, a kind of thick voice, sir. As if he'd got a bad cold."

That was no help. Ardly fetched that chambermaid I'd already seen. She'd never clapped eyes on Foster.

"Which bed had been slept in?"

"This one, sir. The other was just as I made it."

So that was that. It was worse still when I thought of something else as Ardly and I were walking towards the lifts.

"I wonder if you'd do something for me?" I said. "This room here—322. Could you let me know who took it, and when?"

I left him at his office, and the attaché-case with him. The one who had pulled off that coup was far too clever to have left prints. Hallows—I had to look round for him—was in a chair in the sun-room with both stairs and lifts well in sight.

"Anything happen?" he said.

"Everything."

I told him about that double-bed suite. He'd never anticipated anything of the kind either.

"But wait a minute," he said. "Would you mind describing to me once more what Mrs. C.'s brother is like?"

I didn't know why he was asking but I gave a description.

"Then it *was* him," he said. "Except that he was wearing dark glasses. I caught sight of him about twenty minutes ago. I couldn't get too good a look because he was on the move."

"Where'd he go?"

"Through the main doors."

"Try to think back," I said. "Did you also happen to catch sight of a man with a white muffler round his neck? A shortish man with a bit of a belly? He had a grey overcoat on."

"Wait a minute," he said. "I think I can remember something."

Hallows has a different mind from mine. His is a photographic one, and when he wants to remember anything it's as if he winds a film backwards till he comes to the picture he wants.

"You stay here," I said. "I've got to see the manager again."

Ardly had what I wanted about room 322. It had been taken up that morning by a James Taylor, who'd given his address as 40 Colchester Road, Chelmsford.

"The receptionist doesn't remember him, not well enough to give a description. The room's empty, by the way. That fibre case was in it. A few bricks wrapped in newspaper to give it weight."

"I know who he was," I said. "He's another confederate. And we know where he regularly hangs out."

"We've got an excellent description of the woman who handed in that attaché-case at the enquiry desk."

I laughed.

"Weepy Mary—that's the name we know her by. She's the third member of the gang."

I held out my hand and thanked him. He said it was he who ought to thank me. It was horrifying to think of a trio like that in an hotel like his. Anything might have happened.

"You'll never see them again," I told him. "Keep it well under your hat, though. This is a very confidential job and we don't want it even whispered."

I motioned to Hallows as I went by, and he followed me out. He'd parked my car in Willow Street, about forty yards from the hotel, and we sat there for quite a time talking things over.

"About Harry Calvert," I said. "I didn't get a good look at him. He only had to cross the corridor and I wasn't interested in anyone coming from the other side. But about the man in the muffler: have you thought of anything?"

"It's all very hazy," he said. "I must have had practically hundreds of people under my eye, but I do remember that white muffler. Also I have the vague idea he had a beard. There was something dark under his lower lip and just above the muffler. That's the best I can do."

"It could hardly have been a false beard. If it had, he'd surely not have needed the muffler. But stay here. I've got an idea."

I went back to the hotel and that commissionaire. I had another pound note ready.

"I'm interested now in a man with a white muffler round his neck who came through these swing-doors at just after one o'clock," I said, and then added a little more description. "Did you see him?"

He'd seen him. That was his job, to cast an eye over everyone who entered and left.

"Did he take a taxi?"

"No," he said. "He just walked straight on across the street there and that's all I saw of him. I wouldn't have remembered that if it hadn't been for the muffler."

"You didn't notice if he had a beard?"

"I wouldn't have noticed if he had," he said. "He had his overcoat collar turned up and that muffler right round his mouth." He looked up reflectively. "I'd say he was a man of about my own age—fifty. He had a moustache—I know that. Just a bit grey, it was."

He did another palming act with the pound note, and I went back to the car.

"We'll go to the flat," I said. "I don't feel at the moment like going to the office."

I left the car at the garage. It'd be handy enough if we wanted it again, but what I wanted was to use their telephone. I rang Morniment Mansions and asked to be put through to Mrs. Cortin. I gave my name as Franklin, slipped a handkerchief between my teeth and waited. A minute or so and Helen Cortin herself was on the line.

"This is Franklin of Quentin Motors," I said. "May I speak to Mr. Calvert?"

"I'm sorry," she said, "but he isn't here."

"Can you tell me where I can find him? It's rather urgent."

"You might possibly try Tyefield Manor later," she said, and repeated the name and gave me the number. "I'm his sister, Mrs. Cortin—"

"Much obliged to you, Mrs. Cortin."

"Not at all," she said. "I ought to warn you that he doesn't keep me advised of his movements. I might not see him for quite a time."

I thanked her and rang off. As I told Hallows on the way to the flat, the key word seemed *later*. That presupposed some knowledge of his whereabouts. Not that we particularly needed that.

At the flat we talked the whole thing over. Our reconstruction was broadly this: Helen Cortin had been instructed to have that money available. She had pleaded that she couldn't do anything about it till a certain date—when her husband was in America. Then her instructions had been to be at the Morniment Mansions flat at a certain time.

There she had been rung and told exactly how to hand in that money at the hotel. She hadn't been left a lot of time; not that Bosford's agent had worried about her communicating with the police. In any case he had taken his own precautions. He had been in the bathroom when the case arrived, and if there'd been anything suspicious he'd have gone out at once by the door of 339, bolting the communicating door behind him.

Calvert hadn't been seen at Tyefield that morning because he was already at the town flat awaiting the arrival of his sister. He, of course, was in her confidence. As soon as the instructions came through he went at once to the hotel and booked a room as near as possible to 337. He almost certainly had had a taxi waiting at the flats. I hoped to heaven he hadn't seen me, though almost certainly he'd seen Hallows. Not that that mattered.

His job wasn't to follow Roberts into that room but to trail whoever it was who had taken the money. And that's what he'd done. And that could mean only one thing—that Helen Cortin didn't know who the actual blackmailer was. It was doubtful if she'd ever clapped eyes on Bosford, so Calvert, whose own scheme the whole thing doubtless was—would trail the unknown Foster. Once he'd traced him to his hangout, then further action might be taken.

"Wonder what sort of action?" Hallows wanted to know.

"Don't know," I said. "His first job is to discover whether Foster's the principal or only an agent. We know he's an agent. If Calvert thinks he's the principal, then I don't like the look of things."

"You mean Calvert'd kill him?"

"Why not? He thinks as most of us do, that a blackmailer's the lowest form of life. Also, if he's sure in his own mind that Foster's the principal, then killing him is a final way out. It'll ensure that his sister's not blackmailed again. But that wouldn't be the story he's told her. It's his own private solution, but if she happened to suspect anything later, then she'd never dream of giving him away. They're pretty close, those two."

"Tell me some more about Calvert," he said. "You never know. Something might give us a lead on him."

I told him all I knew—war record, artificial leg and all. I said he was an acquired taste. I'd found him quite odd at first but later I'd quite liked him. And then I decided to tell him about that queer affair of the Restaurant Antoine Dupont, and I hadn't quite finished the story when suddenly I stopped. My fingers went instinctively to my glasses—a nervous trick of mine when I think I've made a discovery. Then I smiled sheepishly.

"What is it?" Hallows said.

"Just an idea that isn't panning out right," I told him. "I merely wondered for a moment if our Mr. Foster mightn't be Simon, that fake French manager of the Antoine Dupont. But he was what I'd call a dapper sort of man."

"You wouldn't look dapper if you had forty packets of pound notes tucked under your belt," Hallows suggested dryly.

"You're right!" I said. "He had to get those notes out somehow. Why the devil didn't I think of it."

I got a sheet of paper from the desk.

"My drawing hand's like a fist, but I'll try and give a rough idea of what he looks like."

At the second attempt I got something that didn't dissatisfy me. Hallows had a good look at it. He said he'd know a whole lot more if he could get a look at Simon himself.

"Look," I said. "What about this? I'll ring Norris first and see if Davis is still standing by."

I rang the agency. The first thing Norris wanted to know was how things had gone.

"Everything's a bit more complex than we'd thought," I told him. "I'll tell you about it later. Is Davis there, by any chance?"

Davis came on the line.

"Listen to this carefully," I said. "You'd better take it down. You won't need the car. Hallows will be calling for it, but you're to go to the Restaurant Club Antoine Dupont in Osbert Street—that's near Jermyn Street—and keep an eye on the place."

I described Simon and said that if he left the restaurant he was to be followed. What was wanted was his private address. If he didn't leave, then Hallows in any case would be along at about seven o'clock and would make contact and give any further instructions.

"You heard that," I said to Hallows, "so what about this. You collect your car and go home and doll yourself up a bit. Then you go to the restaurant and ask to see the manager. You don't know his name. Your wife was dining there the other night and thinks it's there that she lost a valuable ring or something. Fill in the details to suit yourself, but get a good look at Simon."

"Sounds all right to me," he said. "And where do I report?"

"Outside that restaurant," I said. "I as good as promised to have a few meals there. I think I'll start tonight."

12

DEAD END

I wasn't too pleased with myself—we'd been too near to disaster for that. All the same, we still had a chance. At half-past one that afternoon there hadn't been the vestige of a chance. Now we had at least something tenuous on which to work.

I knew also that I had to get moving if I was to be at that restaurant soon after seven o'clock. I rang the Yard at once and asked for X, to whom I'd given that tip about private gambling. When he came on the line I asked if he could be available if I got to the Yard in about ten minutes.

I saw him in his room. Everything was naturally in confidence, with my wanting to give as little as possible away. I did say that information I might be able to hand him later made me more than ever convinced that Dupont himself was in the gambling racket.

"We've had our eye on him," he said. "We've even got his prints, only to find he hasn't got a record. He hasn't a record in France, either."

"I'm not surprised," I said. "I think everything's done through an agent. You know where he lives?"

"In a small flat he's had adapted on the top floor of that restaurant. The floor below it is a sort of club restaurant and dance floor."

"The club strictly legal?"

"Subscription purely nominal. You know how it is. More or less a front for the sale of drinks. Nothing we can quarrel with."

"What about the actual gambling? My client was taken to a private house. He doesn't know where. He went in a taxi—probably specially hired—and went back to the West End in a similar taxi."

"Even if Dupont did have a private address he wouldn't be such a fool as to have gambling there," he told me. "But that's easy. He has his touts, and he has his own place, and there's no end of characters who'd be glad to give the loan of a private house for a night—for considerations."

He leaned forward.

"You know what's worried me about this Dupont? Where'd his money come from? Not long after he took over the place he completely transmogrified it. From an almost down-at-heel sort of place he's made it into something special. Neat but not gaudy, if you know what I mean. It must have cost him a packet, and he did it off his own bat. He has a ten-year lease, by the way, with an option of renewal. We reckon he spent the best part of eight thousand himself. Where'd it come from? And our information is he's going to spend more."

I thought I knew, but I didn't say so. What I did say was that since his whole history wasn't known, then he might have had money—honest money. He shrugged his shoulders.

"Well, there we are," he said. "Dupont's just one cog in our general machine. Rest assured, all the same, that we'll have our eyes on him till we're dead sure about him. Glad to have anything at any time, of course, that you're able to pass on."

That was all. I didn't mention Simon. I thought if I did he might pop a man round there at once and that might interfere with the work we had in hand. I thanked him, promised to pass on anything we found out, and then went back to the flat. I thought about putting on a black tie, then changed my mind. I put on a grey suit with a black polka-dot bow instead. I looked so distinguished that when I took a peek at myself in the glass I almost cocked a snook at what I saw.

I'd booked a table and in my own name. I'd already given that name to the manager, but it didn't worry me. After all, there are at least sixty of us in the London Telephone Directory where I appear as just an unobtrusive Travers, L. Also I'd given Simon the impression that I mightn't be from London at all. Even if Simon had an interest in me I doubted if he'd be able to run me down.

It was about a quarter-past seven when I walked into the restaurant foyer. The same man wasn't on duty there and a much older man took my hat and coat and escorted me to the cloakroom.

"You've booked a table, sir? Right, sir. You'll see the head waiter just inside the door there."

He ushered me through to the ground-floor restaurant. It was a larger room than I'd thought. It had what Doris Bosford would have called "chick". There were no murals—just a simple wall decoration in off-white and gold. The tables weren't too closely spaced. The linen looked spotless and the silver lustrous. As yet there weren't more than twenty diners.

The head waiter—who looked rather like a young Forbes-Robertson—checked my name and beckoned to a waiter. He conducted me to the far end of the room. I had the choice of two seats, and I chose the one facing the wall. I didn't want to be conspicuous and besides, that far wall was mirrored and I could see everything that went on behind my back. I was given the menu and chose the table-d'hôte dinner. I said I'd choose a wine later.

There were double swing-doors to the kitchens. My waiter, a man of about forty, whom I guessed to be Swiss, didn't go through to the kitchens but back to the head waiter. There was a brief whispering. The head waiter went into the foyer and my waiter made his way back through the swing-doors. Almost at once the head waiter came back to his post. It was all highly suspicious. It even looked as if the staff had been warned to look out for someone of my name and description, and word of my arrival had been sent upstairs to Simon. I was hoping that it had.

The meal began. The table-d'hôte dinner at a guinea had given something of a choice. I'd ordered Crème Soubise, Truites au Vin Rouge, Gigot Braisé à l'Armagnac with Mokatine à la Chantilly as dessert. For wine I'd a Tavel Rosé. I didn't think they'd have it, but they did.

The soup was very good. By the time I'd emptied the plate the restaurant was filling up. By the time I'd eaten the fish it was virtually full. Surreptitious glances in the mirror showed no one whom I knew. The main dish arrived and then something happened. In the corner to my left was a space where the small trolleys stood for hors-d'oeuvres and desserts, and behind and across was a three-fold screen. Behind that there must have been a door, for Antoine Dupont suddenly appeared in front of the screen and he stood there surveying the room.

He was a tallish man and rather broad. His cheeks were plump and carried the signs of good living. His hair was dark, with traces of grey at the temples. The neatly clipped, pointed beard gave the face a certain distinction. The lips were full, and but for the fact that the nose was straight there would have been much of Napoleon III about him. There was even something of a uniform about the white jacket he was wearing, and the white gloves. My horn-rims have become merely part of a face—his seemed to lend a kind of awareness. There was something almost avuncular in the way he slowly surveyed that room.

He moved forward to the table on my far left, and from then on I watched his progress round the tables. Each had a courteous bow. Some had only a few words, and some—old customers or friends—had a handshake and a minute or two of his time. Then at last he arrived at my table. The waiter had just cleared for the dessert and coffee.

"Everything is to your satisfaction, sir?"

His English was practically perfect, even if it hadn't been acquired in the highest circles. It wasn't unpleasant, but it lacked resonance and charm.

"Perfectly," I said. "In fact it's been as good a meal as I've eaten in London for years."

He gave me a little bow.

"M'sieur is generous. Not that we do not try always to please. The Rosé—it was good, too?"

"Excellent. I rather wish I'd had a whole bottle."

"It is a good wine," he said. "Might I ask where m'sieur made its acquaintance?"

"At Avignon," I said, "some years ago. I liked it enormously then and I've always tried to find it since."

His smile was really charming.

"M'sieur has already the makings of a connoisseur. Is it permitted to ask if you live in London?"

"At the moment—yes."

"Then perhaps we shall have the pleasure of seeing m'sieur again."

Another bow and he moved back towards the screen. He quietly surveyed the room again and then I heard the sound of a closing door. As I ate my Mokatine I was thinking he was my ideal of a restaurateur. He reminded me of the proprietor of a famous French provincial hotel at which I'd once stayed—quiet in manner, solicitous without being gushing, friendly with still the right trace of the formal; in other words, his hotel's best advertisement. And he had shown no special interest in myself. I had watched his progress round the tables, and he had spent on me no more than the average time.

It was another waiter who brought my coffee. I asked him what was the very faint sound of music I could hear.

"On the floor above, sir," he said. "There's another room there and a dance floor. You may go up if you wish, sir. But if you're not a member, then you can't get a drink after hours."

"I'm afraid my dancing days are over," I said. "And what time do you close down?"

"At midnight, sir. This is not a night club, sir. We don't keep late hours. Midnight suits our clientèle. A liqueur with the coffee, sir?"

I didn't want one. A liqueur Armagnac had been a constituent of the main course. I asked him to bring my bill.

Over that coffee and a cigarette I sat thinking about Dupont. His manner had been impeccable—so impeccable, in fact, that I was wondering uneasily if I hadn't been working on the wrong lines. Could it be possible that he was in no way concerned in the blackmailing? Was Simon the villain of the piece and was Dupont wholly unaware of it? After all, he had a little gold mine in the restaurant.

Then I pulled myself up short. When I'd hinted to X that I knew where Dupont had obtained the money he'd spent I'd had that illicit gambling in mind. But mightn't there be some other reason for the presence of Dupont in that house to which Harry Calvert had been taken? Was it Simon's house? I didn't know.

What I did know was that it had been Simon who had given Calvert that doped drink and had so fixed things that he was unable to bring a complaint.

My original waiter brought the bill. What with tip, cover charge, half-bottle and coffee, the simple table-d'hôte came to about forty-five shillings. But it had been a magnificent meal. I told the head waiter so when he courteously enquired while I was passing him on my way to the cloak-room. He, too, said he hoped I would come again. The lunch, he said, was equally good. And he didn't tout for membership of the club.

It wasn't far short of nine o'clock when I stepped out to Osbert Street. Across it a man was reading a newspaper in the light of a shop window behind him. It was Hallows. I crossed the road and went by him without speaking. There was no sign of Davis.

I walked on and into Jermyn Street, knowing that Hallows would be following me. The pavement was fairly clear, and soon I heard footsteps behind me. Hallows was overtaking me. He didn't turn his head as he passed.

"I think there's a man on your tail. You drop him and I'll tail him."

He disappeared ahead of me down a side turn. I walked on and came out at the Haymarket. The lights were at red and I saw a free taxi. I got into it just as the lights changed.

"Covent Garden via Long Acre," I told the driver, and settled back in the corner. The lights were with us at Leicester Square Tube Station, and when I looked back I could see no taxi on our heels.

"Get back the shortest way to the Strand," I said, "and drop me at Charing Cross Hospital."

I gave him a good tip and walked towards the flat. I stopped once or twice, but could see no one following me. I went to the garage, told them I shouldn't want the car again, and went out by the side door. A couple of minutes and I was home.

It was not till half an hour later that Hallows came in. He told me I'd shaken off my man. That taxi had taken him by surprise and there hadn't been another.

"He belonged to that restaurant?"

"That's right," he said. "He came out of the side passage and picked you up, and after he lost you he went back the same way. A youngish chap. Looked like a waiter."

"We'll talk about him later," I said. "What about Simon? You saw him?"

"Yes," he said. "Everything went as planned."

But he wasn't looking cheerful enough for my liking.

"You couldn't identify him?"

"No," he said. "Something tells me he was the man I saw at the Metropolitan, but I couldn't come anywhere near to swearing to it."

That was a nasty setback.

"You don't think you've enough confidence to work on?"

"Frankly, no," he said. "He fits what I saw, but I didn't see enough. But something else I did see. A man named Fincham. You wouldn't know him. Works for City Detection Limited. He was watching that restaurant, too. I saw him, but I took care he didn't see me. He and Davis don't know each other, by the way."

"That's queer news." My fingers went up to my glasses. "Wonder who's employing him?"

"No idea," he said. "And I don't see any means of finding out."

There *was* no means of finding out. No agency would break faith to that extent with a client.

"It's queer," I said, "and yet something tells me it's good news. You any ideas about it?"

"Well, yes," he said hesitantly. "It's a bit far-fetched. All I could think of was, it had something to do with Calvert. I wondered if we were on the right track after all."

He explained. Calvert, he thought, would not have trusted himself to follow Foster. He'd been in touch beforehand with City Detection—he'd see their name alongside ours in advertisements—and they'd had a man standing by. As soon as instructions about the money came to the Morniment Mansions

Flat, Calvert hurried to the Metropolitan, leaving his sister to warn City Detection. Calvert met Fincham at the hotel, and it was arranged that Calvert should take the room and pick up Foster. Fincham, in turn, should help cover Foster when he and Calvert come downstairs.

"But that's perfect!" I said. "If it's true, it clinches everything. Foster *is* Simon! He was followed to the restaurant and that's why it's now being watched."

He's a cautious fellow—Hallows.

"It seems a bit too pat for me," he said. "And what about that chap who tailed you tonight?"

"That's just what you might call an overhang from the original Calvert affair," I said. "After my visit Simon wanted to know more about me. If he's in the blackmail game he knows what he's in for in the event of a slip. He can't afford to take chances. You had any dinner, by the way?"

He hadn't. I had sandwiches sent up and brought some beer from the refrigerator. We went on talking. I told him about my evening, and how I was inclined to change my mind about Antoine Dupont. It all ended just where we knew it would—at a discussion of the next moves.

"I can't see anything," I said, "except watching Simon."

"What about Davis watching Fincham?" he said. "He might lead us back to Calvert, and then we'd feel more sure."

"Fincham will report back to his agency," I said. "If he does report direct to Calvert it'll be by telephone. No. What I think is that you should get back to Davis and tag Simon back to his home. The place shuts down at midnight. Ring me here, and then report at the agency in the morning if I don't tell you differently."

"And if Fincham should be tailing him, too?"

"Then don't risk it," I said. "Let Davis do the job alone. He can ring me here."

I went to bed at my usual time, and I must have been tired, for I was asleep almost at once. I'd put the extension on the near edge of the bedside table and I was dead to the wide, when the bell woke me. I switched on the light and hooked on my glasses.

"Davis here, sir. Our friend lives at—"

"Wait a moment. I'll write it down."

I had pencil and pad handy. Simon's address was 24 St. Peter's Road, Earls Court.

"What sort of place is it?"

"Detached," he said. "Old-fashioned three-storey affair. Quiet street. Hasn't gone all that badly down yet."

"And Fincham was on the job, too?"

"Yes," he said. "He quit as soon as he identified the place. I had a look round when he'd gone."

I told him to take the morning off and report at two and to pass the same word to Hallows. Then I switched off the light and got back to the warmth again. But I couldn't sleep. I was thinking about Calvert and how I had a duty towards him. Somehow, and I didn't know just how, I knew he was included in those last instructions that Cortin had given me. And now—maybe already, maybe in the morning—Calvert knew where Foster was, and that he was definitely Simon.

Would Calvert kill him? Surely not, in view of the fact that City Detection would at once have ideas about who'd done the killing. Would they be prepared to keep quiet about murder? I doubted it. But would Calvert doubt it? If he did doubt it, would it deter him? That was something that I doubted myself. Knowing even as little about Calvert as I did, I felt pretty sure he'd have no scruples about killing Simon, provided he was certain that it would bring the blackmail definitely to an end.

A few minutes later I switched on the light again, hooked on my glasses and went into my den. I found an old writing pad, put on gloves, tore out a middle page and began writing a letter in clumsy capitals:

MR. CALVERT,

SIR, DO NOT BE SO FOOLISH AS TO THINK ABOUT KILLING A CERTAIN SOMEONE. IT WOULD GET YOU NOWHERE, BELIEVE ME.

A FRIEND WHO'S ALSO IN THE KNOW.

I addressed the letter, using the same capitals, to Tyefield Manor. I slipped on a dressing-gown and went down the stairs.

The night-porter was dozing in his cubby-hole. I got him to slip out and post the letter which, I said, a friend had given me but I'd forgotten. I went back to bed. That letter would go by the earliest post and Calvert ought to receive it by the afternoon.

When I woke in the morning I knew the last place I wanted to see was the office. I was rather like a small boy who's played truant and knows the inexorable moment of return. Norris would know, even if he didn't say so, that we'd badly bungled the job. That's why I didn't turn up at Broad Street till about half-past nine.

Norris listened imperturbably.

"Well, say it," I said.

"Say what?"

"That we made a pretty bad hash of it."

"I don't know," he said. "I think you just had some bad luck. And you did have some good luck later."

I hadn't said a word, of course, about that anonymous letter, now on its way to Calvert.

"One thing I'm wondering, though," he went on, massive figure well back in the desk chair. "Let's suppose you get as far as being dead sure Foster was an *alias* for Simon. In other words, you know that Simon's the blackmailer. What're you going to do about it?"

That was the very question I'd been dodging. There was only one thing to do—throw the ball back.

"What would *you* do about it?"

"Damned if I know," he said, and frowned. "Unless it's this. We've tried it before, as you know, and once or twice it's come off. Make absolutely certain and get a few more facts if you can. Then try a bluff. Go to this Simon and say he was identified as Foster, and make him sign a document. If he tries his own bluff, say you're going straight to the police. Once he signs the docu-ment, then he'll have it hanging over his head. There'll be no more blackmail. You might even get the money back—or most of it."

"Yes," I said. "That's the very thing. What I'll do—"

The buzzer went. Bertha said there was a call for me.

"That you, Travers?" Wharton's usual opening. "Got some news for you. Something's come in about our friend who got lost in a wood. I'm just off to take it up if you'd like to come along."

I said I'd be along as fast as a taxi could get me there.

"No, no," he said. "I'll pick you up. We've got to go your way, in any case. See you at the traffic lights at the bottom of Cheapside."

That gave me time for a word with Norris.

"Don't know when I'll be back," I said, "but let Hallows take over if I'm not here by two o'clock. Tell him and Davis to dig up those additional facts you were talking about. Say he's to use his own judgment."

Ten minutes later the police car was drawing in just short of the traffic lights. I slid in alongside Wharton.

13

IDENTIFICATION

I ASKED Wharton just what was the news that was bringing him to the City.

"Further afield than that," he said. "Between Bethnal Green and Hackney. A Mallaby Street. Ever heard of it?"

I hadn't.

"It's simple really. That photograph was in the *Gazette* yesterday and it was seen by a man who was investigating a forcible entry. The local constable who reported it had seen the photograph, too, and they say the occupier of the shop concerned is our babe in the wood. A photographer of the name of Paynter. H. Paynter. Convey anything to you?"

It didn't mean a thing.

"Ah, well," Wharton said. "I took a chance and called you. Jewle's been there best part of an hour and he'll have everybody lined up."

"Got one of those photographs on you?" I asked.

He hadn't, but there'd be one at that shop. That was about all that was said. Wharton knew no more, in any case. Another five minutes and we came out at Mallaby Street, E.9. It was one of those High Street continuations—a kind of secondary shopping centre, its shops smaller and less garish than those of the High Street. The shop at which we stopped was really a photographer's studio. It had one large window in which individual photographs and groups were displayed. A notice, fixed to the window inside, said that enlargements were a speciality. I thought that window looked a cut above the neighbourhood. The photographs were good and tastefully set out. There was never a fly-blow on one of them.

Jewle appeared at the door as soon as the car stopped. We went in. There were three people there: the local detective-sergeant named Fry, a uniformed constable named Watts, and the occupier of the second-hand furniture store next door, a middle-aged man named Benstein. Jewle said there was an office at the back, so the six of us went there. Wharton took over.

The constable said he'd been informed by Mr. Benstein that he'd heard sounds in the studio at just about three o'clock in the morning after that same night when the body had been deposited in the wood. Wharton broke off to question Benstein. He said he'd just heard faint sounds which he took to mean that Paynter was moving about. It was the first time he'd ever heard such sounds. Then when Paynter didn't open the studio and nothing was seen of him for two or three days he mentioned the matter to the constable.

"You usually saw a lot of Paynter?"

"I would see him," Benstein said. "He would look out of the door there, and if I was also at my door we would speak. Then at one o'clock he would close the studio and go past my shop to Cohen's restaurant. Also I would see him coming back. And he has his entrance, like me, at the back, and the milkman left his milk and it wasn't taken in. He spoke to me and I tell him it is four days, perhaps, since I see him or hear him."

"He was a communicative man? He told you a lot about himself?"

"Never," he said. "He would say good-morning, or good-afternoon, but he would never stop to talk."

"Maybe he talked at Cohen's restaurant," Wharton said. "How long's he been here, by the way?"

"Just over a year."

"Only that long?" Wharton looked surprised. "How was the business doing?"

Benstein said that every indication was that it was doing well. Some of his own customers had patronised the studio and had been very satisfied.

"He took an interest in the business," he said. "For him it was everything. I think he was proud of himself. Sometimes he would stand out there and look in the window and seem pleased with himself."

"You don't know where he came from to here?"

Benstein had no idea.

"I take it he was of Jewish extraction, so doesn't it strike you, Mr. Benstein, that Paynter was a curious name?"

Benstein shrugged his shoulders. Paynter hadn't spoken English, he said, like a man born here. His own idea was that he was some sort of refugee. So maybe he'd changed his name. Often the new names were fancy ones which might look good for business.

"In this part of the world?" Wharton smiled dryly. "All right, Mr. Benstein. We're very grateful to you. If we should happen to want you again, then we know where you are."

The constable went on with his story. He'd examined the back premises and had found scratches on the lock of the door. The door itself was locked, so he got into touch with his station. Sergeant Fry took over. He said he'd made an entry with Watts and they'd found every sign of a burglary.

"That desk over there had been searched, sir. What was taken we didn't know. Upstairs had been gone through, too. The cameras and equipment hadn't been touched, though."

"What *was* in the desk?" Wharton asked Jewle. "Any private papers?"

"Nothing but receipts and a few bills," Jewle said. "No cheque-book, insurance policy—nothing. Not even the papers about the lease."

"And, of course, no prints."

"Only his own," Jewle said. "They tally, as you know, with the Fallgate body."

We went upstairs to quite a nice studio. There were two large cameras, headlights, side-lights and screens, and all the paraphernalia one might expect. There was a dark room, well fitted up. There was also a small bedroom, the bed still made.

"All this had been gone through," Jewle said. "We couldn't find anything of any help to us. No private papers. Nothing that could be useful as a clue. All we know is that he slept up here, used his office as a sitting-room and cooked his own meals in the small kitchen—those he didn't have at Cohen's."

We went down to the office again. Watts wasn't needed any longer, and there was more room for the four of us. Wharton gave the stand-at-ease by pulling out his pipe.

"What we've apparently got is this," he said. "Paynter was killed, but probably not here, by someone who gave him a drink with cyanide in it. His body was taken to where it was found and then the murderer came back here and went through the place with a small-toothed comb. He used Paynter's own keys. Those scratches are probably a blind. What he was looking for was anything that could give any news of Paynter beyond what the neighbourhood might have picked up about him. If so, he made a good job of it. If he'd made a better job of mutilating the face, then Paynter might never have been connected with where we are now. Any ideas, Jewle?"

"Don't know that I have, sir. I might say that Paynter himself seems to have been a secretive sort of man. We've already checked up at Cohen's and he gave nothing away about himself there."

"If he was secretive, and apparently he was," I said, "then he had something to be secretive about. Am I right in saying you have no record of him?"

"Never a thing."

"Mind if I have a look at that *Police Gazette* photograph?" I asked Jewle. "I'd like to see what he really looked like."

"I can do better than that," Jewle said, and produced a glossy photograph from his bag. "This is one the back-room boys took when they were satisfied."

I gave my glasses a polish and had a look at it. Almost at once I was staring.

"You know him?" Wharton said.

"Yes," I said. "I'm not dead sure but I think I do. And there's something else. Didn't he have arthritic knees?"

"He did. But what's that got to do with it?"

"A lot," I said. "The only time I saw Paynter was at Seahurst, that day of the inquest. He passed quite near me, and he had a dragging kind of walk."

"Just a minute," Wharton said. "Didn't you have some theory or other?"

"I'll put my cards on the table," I said, "though in this special context I'd like names kept out of it. I was at Seahurst representing a client. I had the idea the drowned man might be her husband, whom she was looking for. It wasn't. It was a man named Marler. The police down there seemed to take it for granted that this Marler and my client's husband had been engaged on a smuggling racket. Marler was the brains and the other man had a town office for receiving the goods. Then we reckoned there had to be a third man who'd get the stuff distributed to the customers. I thought the man was the one who'd tried to see—he actually did see—Marler's body in the mortuary. He was this man Paynter. He gave a false name and address down there and said he thought he knew Marler. I put a man on his heels back to town, but my man lost him in the Aldgate neighbourhood. That's the last we had to do with him. Some weeks later my client did identify the body of another drowned man as that of her husband."

Wharton let out a breath.

"Well, if that doesn't beat cock-fighting! I think I'd like to go into this further when we get back to the Yard. What's your programme, Jewle?"

Jewle had it ready. He'd try to find the dead man's bank. He'd interview the lessors and get details of how Paynter had come to take the studio. He might have let fall to them something of his antecedents. He'd have questions asked in the immediate neighbourhood to try to find out if Paynter had had visitors other than his customers. He'd question the tradesmen he'd dealt with.

"All right," Wharton said. "Ask for what men you want. Ring if you find anything."

He gave me a nod, and out we went to the car. A quarter of an hour later we were in his room at the Yard.

I'd never intended to open out in front of Fry. I wouldn't have minded with Jewle; and as for Wharton, there was no need to be secretive. He already knew that my client had been Doris Bosford, but in spite of that I had to repeat the events of that November morning.

"That theory of yours is all wrong," Wharton said. "That's why I wanted to hear the whole thing again."

I wondered what he was going to say. In no event was I going to betray any interest beyond what he already knew. The last thing I intended to tell him was that I virtually knew that Bosford was still alive.

"What theory?" I said.

"The one that made Paynter the third man."

"But why not?" I said. "Why else was he so anxious to see Marler's body and make sure he was dead?"

"I don't know," he told me impatiently. "Sometimes you can't see farther than your nose-end. Paynter wasn't the third man. He was the fourth man."

He was right. Paynter had been killed because of what he knew. It was also more plain why there'd been an attempt to hide his identity, both by that acid and the supposed burglary.

"There weren't three men in that gang," Wharton was telling me. "There were four, and the fourth man killed Paynter. He killed him so as to be the sole survivor. Now he's got nothing to worry about—or he thinks he hasn't. We shan't let out for the moment that we know the identity of the man in that wood."

"I think you're right—"

"I know I'm right."

"Very well then—you're right. But it makes it all the harder. What honest-to-God clue have we about the identity of that fourth man?"

"We'll get some leads," he told me confidently. "Jewle may unearth something. If it's there he'll find it. And we can reopen the Marler Case. We can start off again from the absolute beginning. We've had to dig far deeper than that in our time."

"You want me to do something."

"Almost a certainty," he said. "I'll have to talk things over at once with the Powers-that-Be. What I'll do is give you a ring. It mightn't be till the morning."

It was past my lunch-time and I decided to go to the club. Then I changed my mind. I went into a pub near the Haymarket and had some sandwiches and a pint. I didn't get any new ideas, but I wasn't displeased with those I already had. As I saw it, I'd be doing with Wharton what I should in any case have been doing for Edward Cortin—trying to prove that Bosford wasn't dead and trying then to get my hands on him. Instead of having to work with a meagre agency staff, I'd have the authority of the Yard, and I'd be paid for it. Edward Cortin and all that black-mail business could be kept well under cover till the last grand dénouement. Maybe they wouldn't have to be mentioned at all.

I admit, mind you, that something had been rankling—that failure of mine to see what Wharton had called the fourth man. Or maybe, I could tell myself, I'd been cleverer than I'd thought. Wharton's fourth man was still only the third man—*if Bosford were really still alive.* And that was something into which I proposed to make at once a minor kind of enquiry. That was why I took a bus for Knightsbridge. That was why I did some detective work, standing across the road from Doris Bosford's shop and watching it over the top of a newspaper. I had some luck, too. I hadn't been there long before Doris herself appeared at the shop door, ushering out a customer. I circled across and I spoke before she had the door closed again. She gave me that same startled look.

"Just something I wanted to tell you," I said. "No need for me to come in. Can you come outside for a moment? I shan't keep you longer."

She called back to the shop that she wouldn't be a minute. We walked on just a few yards.

"I thought it my duty to give you a tip," I said. "The police have discovered a man who used to be in a certain racket with Marler and your late husband. They're going to reopen the whole case. Keep that to yourself. It's highly confidential. Only I thought it my duty to a former client to give you the private tip that it's on the cards that the police will be questioning you again. This time it'll be Scotland Yard who're handling everything."

She'd been more and more perturbed.

"I've got nothing to conceal," she told me, almost defiantly. "You know that, Mr. Travers."

"Maybe so," I told her guardedly. "But I ought to warn you that they dig pretty deep. What are you going to say—if anything—about that famous box under the bed?"

"That," she said. "I don't see why I should tell them anything."

"That'll be for you to judge," I said. "But they'll know what you got for your house and they may check that against what you paid for a partnership in the shop. I don't say they will, but I ought to warn you."

She was licking her lips again. Then, for no reason that I could see, she suddenly brightened up.

"I think it was kind of you—really I do. And don't you worry about me. I'll have everything all ready."

"Fine," I said. "I'm sure you will."

Then I ventured on a smile.

"How's the handsome salesman coming along? The one you told me about. Any progress yet?"

She tittered.

"How you do talk! But funny you should ask me that. I'm actually seeing him tomorrow and he's going to take me out again."

"That's good," I said. "Keep the hooks well in."

Then I added a something else. It was just by way of making enough conversation prior to a graceful farewell.

"Doesn't he favour what you called 'posh' places?"

"Well, he isn't stingy with his money, if that's what you mean."

"Good," I said. "Here's another tip. Get him to take you to a place in Osbert Street—that's right against Jermyn Street. I had a marvellous dinner there the other night and there's a dance floor upstairs. All very high class. You'll love it there. The name's the Restaurant Antoine Dupont. Like me to write it down for you?"

"I'd like it ever so much. I like going to places like that." So I wrote the name for her and gave a little sketch map of how to get to it. As I said, it was all by way of a friendly farewell. Just what it was that I had hoped to get from her I naturally didn't know. Perhaps, like most people who're none too sure of their bearings, I'd merely been looking around and hoping that something would drop into my lap. But it hadn't. Or if it had, it had fallen with force enough to shatter one theory—the one about the fictitiousness of the lovelorn salesman. I was pretty certain now that there *was* such a person. Doris Bosford hadn't invented him in order to conceal any knowledge of her husband's being still alive.

I went to the office. Hallows, I was told, was still digging away at Simon. The only thing he had to report was that he was the owner of the Earls Court house and that a lean-to conservatory had been converted into a garage.

"Oh, and one other thing," Norris said, and produced an envelope from the safe. "Hallows got this newspaper from Simon's dust-bin. He thought it might have his prints."

When I left the office I took that newspaper straight to the Yard. I knew people in the finger-print department and I got one of them to vet that newspaper while I waited. Sometimes one hadn't to wait more than a few moments. Sometimes it was as long as half an hour. This time it was nearly an hour. Four sets of prints were on it: the newsagent's perhaps, the delivery boy's, the prints of a woman, and those of Simon himself.

He hadn't much of a record. His name was given as Arthur Simmonds; born at Camberwell in 1901; his profession, waiter. In 1937 he had done two years for peddling dope. In 1940 he had joined the Army, and in 1945 had become a sergeant in charge of an officers' mess. He then did three months for embezzlement of mess funds. He was next heard of as manager of a roadhouse in 1949, when he got another year for embezzlement. That was the last of him. But the thing that made my eyes pop open was the situation of that roadhouse—on the Fallgate-Harrow Road.

Naturally I was asked if I had any news of him. I could only say I might have and that if I unearthed anything I'd certainly pass the word on. But as soon as I got to the flat I rang Norris. Hallows happened to be in. He was given the Simon news and told to get out in the morning to the Fallgate area and dig up all he could.

I had an early meal and tried to do some thinking. I knew at once that I'd been over-optimistic in telling myself that through the discovery of Paynter's identity I would have the Yard virtually working for the agency. Edward Cortin would be back in under a week, and I'd been optimistic with him as well. Something was telling me now that he'd left with the impression that on his return everything would be cleared up. And now it looked to me as if the Yard and myself would be working in two separate compartments. They wanted to find who'd killed Paynter. I wanted to carry out what Cortin had entrusted to me and without giving the Yard the faintest idea of that blackmail business. My only hope was to find a kind of intermediate something that would serve as a liaison: something that would serve in some subtle way to help Wharton as well as myself.

Then almost at once I had it. He had spoken of going all the way back to Marler's inquest. Marler should be the connecting link.

Let me put it simply. It suddenly struck me that I might have been wrong in assuming that Helen Cortin was being blackmailed because of an association with a man other than Marler. Wasn't it far more likely that it was for something she had done while still living with Marler? Couldn't she have been tricked into, or taken unknowingly some part in, something highly illegal? That was the kind of thing that Marler would most likely have let fall to Bosford. And so, if Bosford was alive, he was being paid for keeping Helen Cortin out of the hands of the police.

And so I suddenly knew that I ought to know a whole lot more about Marler. It struck me, too, how very little I did know. I hadn't even a photograph. I'd had a description, but there was nothing I could really carry in my mind. It was a photograph that I badly wanted. I had to have something to show to those from whom I would make enquiries.

Then I had an idea. It was a long shot, but it might come off. Where I went was to the Pink Moon in Walling Street, the restaurant that Marler had once owned when it was called the Silver Boat. I asked to see the owner or manager. It was the owner I saw, a naturalised Italian named Pacelli.

He had been interested in Marler's death because it was from him that he had bought the restaurant. I said the police weren't altogether satisfied as to the cause of death and were still working at the case. The agency was working along the same lines on behalf of an interested client, and what I needed was a photograph.

It's curious how easily, when you have acquired the knack, you can blur an issue with words. He didn't suggest obvious ways—as from my clients—of obtaining such a photograph. He just shrugged his shoulders.

"I hoped he might have left some behind," I said. "Perhaps an old photograph of himself and the staff, for instance."

He shrugged his shoulders again. Then he remembered something. In an upstairs room was some junk he'd taken over. He seemed to remember some pictures. Maybe there'd be also a photograph.

We went up to a top-floor cubby-hole. Among the heaped junk there were some framed pictures—cheap coloured prints mostly. There were also three photographs in dusty frames, and the glass of two of them was broken. One was of the restaurant front, with a man whom I guessed to be Marler standing importantly at the open door. The second was the same front with a chef in full working clothes standing at that door. The third was of a staff of seven. The chef, still in his regalia, sat at Marler's right, and a youngish woman—probably in charge of the cash desk—was on his left. The others stood behind to form the group.

"I may have these two?" I said.

"Take them all," Pacelli told me. "Take everything. Maybe you make some money, perhaps. Me, I am too busy."

He wrapped up the photographs for me downstairs. There were questions I'd have liked to ask, but I knew I could always come back. I knew, too, that I'd been uncommonly lucky. I even thought I'd stretch my luck as far as having another quick look at the Restaurant Antoine Dupont.

But I didn't. I think I stopped for a moment in my tracks as I remembered something. It was something I'd forgotten. Pacelli and his restaurant had brought it back to my mind. But he hadn't brought an answer. What I now knew was that I thought I knew where I could find that answer.

As soon as I was in the flat I rang Bernice. I usually rang or wrote every day, and when she came on the line that night there wasn't a lot new to talk about. I did say I might be working almost at once with Wharton.

"I know what I wanted to ask you," I said, and I told her about that simple arrangement of the windows of Dupont's restaurant.

"I'm sure we saw windows like that somewhere in France," I said, "and I have an idea it was somewhere in Paris. We thought we'd have dinner there, and we did. A very good dinner indeed."

"It wasn't Paris," she said. "It was Dijon. Just opposite the Musée. Don't you remember, we'd been in the Musée and we saw this restaurant when we came out?"

"You're right," I said. "But that was a long time ago. Wasn't it just before the war?"

"Of course it was," she said. "In 1938. Let me see now. What was that restaurant called . . . Doré, or something like that."

"Wasn't it Doriot?"

"Why, yes—Doriot. You remember that perfectly exquisite Bordeaux we had? And the Gigot à l'Armagnac?"

I remembered that Bordeaux, but I'd forgotten the Gigot. But what Bernice had said had to be right. She didn't know about that Gigot à l'Armagnac I'd eaten at the Restaurant Antoine Dupont only the other night.

14

ALPHONSE DORIOT

IN THE morning I was stirring pretty early. I had a talk with Norris at his private address and then waited for Wharton to ring me. He rang at about eight o'clock—tried to pull my leg about my not being already at work, and finally wanted to know when I could be at the Yard.

I was there in a quarter of an hour, and I had those two important photographs with me. They'd been a bit chocolate-coloured from slight fading, but both were reasonably clear when I'd got them from their frames and cleaned them. I didn't let Wharton see them for the moment. They were only eight inches by twelve and just went into the inner pocket of my light overcoat.

"You've got any bright ideas?" Wharton began.

"Yes, and no," I said, and began filling my pipe. "I do have something I'd like to put up to you. For instance, am I right in assuming you're going to dig back into the Marler-Bosford business?"

"Didn't I tell you so? That's the only way to dig up the dirt about Paynter. And don't tell me you've changed your mind about him being the third man. That shop of his might have been partly a cover—if he was still at the same racket."

"I don't disagree at all," I told him. "I'm all with you. I think we've just got to know all we can about Marler. In fact, I was so anxious last night to get on with the job that I did a spot of work on my own."

His look was suspicious. Mine, I hoped, was honest and disarming.

"I don't know if I told you," I went on, "but I got to know through my client that Marler used to own a certain restaurant. I went there last night and happened to get hold of a couple of photographs Marler'd left behind with a lot of other junk. Like to see them?"

He saw them. He nodded so complacently that he might have found them himself. Then he picked up the receiver. "I'll get some prints made at once," he told me.

"Then make it quickly," I said. "I want those two originals back by eleven o'clock at the latest."

He gave his orders. The photographs were collected. I handed him a sheet of paper.

"Here are the few details, George, about the restaurant and so on. I don't think the proprietor knows anything that isn't written there. But he let fall something. He didn't know he was doing it, so I'd rather you didn't have him questioned. What he did let fall was something about Dijon. Don't ask me how I arrived at it, but I have an idea Marler once worked in a restaurant there. I might find tracks of him there. I'm prepared to bet it was before the war and, if so, we might get a whole lot about his history."

George pursed his lips. The moustache blew out like an awning.

"This isn't some idea you've got for a nice little Continental trip?"

He'd tried to make it sound like a joke. I preferred to take him seriously.

"Think what you like," I said. "I feel so strongly about it that if you don't give permission I'll have a few hours in Dijon at my own expense."

"I see." He leaned forward. "You haven't by any chance got some ideas you're keeping under your hat?"

"Some hopes!" I said. "This isn't an ultimatum. It's just my strong opinion on how to follow up a piece of information."

"I see. And how long would you be in Dijon?"

"I'd like to be there this late afternoon," I said. "If I can't dig up what I'm after by, say, twenty-four hours from now, then it won't be worth digging for."

He gave that knowing smile that's more of a leer.

"You're going to comb Dijon for an ex-waiter in a matter of hours?" He grunted. "All right. I'll buy it. What's the catch?"

"No catch," I said patiently. "It just happens that I have friends there whom I'm relying on to be in the know." While I was lying I thought I might as well be hung for a sheep as a lamb. "As a matter of fact, I've been in touch with them already."

That made him raise his eyebrows. We did do a little more talking, but the fact remained that I had those original photographs back well before eleven o'clock. With a warrant card in my breast pocket I was on the first Paris plane of that same afternoon.

My connection had been handy, and it was about five o'clock when my taxi dropped me near the Musée de Beaux Arts at Dijon. At once I began looking for the Restaurant Doriot. I spent half an hour wandering about and found no sign of it. A couple of people I'd questioned knew nothing of it and I decided to go to the Syndicat d'Initiative. They unearthed a Restaurant Doriot in the Rue Joffre and told me how to get there.

I asked there for the proprietor and he turned out to be a man of about fifty—a Henri Doriot. He told me that the Germans had used the original restaurant as a sub-headquarters and that after the Liberation his father had decided to open a new place. He himself had been working at Lyons. His younger brother, killed during the war, had worked at the original restaurant.

I'd shown him my warrant card, and then I let him see the photographs. They might have been photographs of some Kosey Kaff on the Brighton Road for all they conveyed to him. He'd never heard of anyone named Marler.

"It's possible that my father might know," he said.

"I can see him?"

"He retired about two years ago," he said. "He's over seventy and he had a bad time during the Occupation. He's at Courcey-Regnolles."

"And where's that?"

It was about twelve kilometres to the south-west. He said a taxi would get me there, and he drew for me a rough map of the village and the situation of his father's house.

"You couldn't telephone him to say that I'm coming?"

He said he would certainly telephone. I thanked him and went in search of an amenable taxi-driver.

In about half an hour I was at the door of a little villa perched on a bluff above a small river. It looked a charming spot. An elderly *bonne* or housekeeper admitted me. Before I'd given her my hat a man was looking out from a side door. He advanced on me, supporting himself with the aid of a heavy stick. He was rather stout and his grey hair was cut *en brosse.*

"You are M'sieur Travers?" He leaned over on the stick and held out a hand. "But come in. It is an experience to meet one of your English police, and from Scotland Yard." He stopped to give me a quizzical sort of look. "It *is* Scotland Yard? That is what you call it?"

We went into a living-room that had a fine view of the country beyond the bluff. I began apologising for my French. With an incredible courtesy he assured me that it was very good. He added what one would have expected, that he wished he had an English of the same perfection.

"An apéritif?" he said. "What would you prefer?"

I said that what suited him would certainly suit me. He thumped on the floor with his stick and the *bonne* appeared. Her name was Henriette. A minute or two and we were drinking an excellent Porto. Then Doriot remembered the taxi-driver and thumped the floor again. Henriette was told to take him to the kitchen. There would now be four places.

"But, M'sieur Doriot," I said. "I'm trespassing on your time. I can't possibly also eat your dinner. Also I haven't yet booked at an hotel."

"Don't fret yourself about an hotel," he said. "I can ring from here and at once you'll have a room. As for the dinner, it's just a simple meal. As soon as my son telephoned I had a chicken on the spit."

I liked old Doriot. He had that bluffness that often characterises the provincials, and a directness. You gathered that he was a man who always spoke his mind. He must have been a thorn in the flesh of the occupation authorities, even if he had had enough tact to keep himself out of the hands of the Gestapo.

"This business of yours first then," he said, "and after that we will eat."

I told him we were trying to trace the history of a man named Frank Marler. He stopped me at once to say that ever since his son had rung he'd been puzzling his wits and he could assure me that he had never known a man of that name. And what puzzled him still more was why we had come to Dijon, and himself, to trace the man.

"If you'll permit me," I said, "I'll arrive at it in a round-about way."

So I began at Dijon in 1938 and that interesting layout of his window and how it had attracted my wife and myself so much that we had dined at the Restaurant Doriot. I mentioned the Gigot à l'Armagnac and how, only a few hours past my wife was still remembering it. All the time he kept nodding and his dark eyes were sparkling with pleasure.

That brought me to the Restaurant Antoine Dupont, where, after many years, I saw windows like that of the Restaurant Doriot and where I also ate a superb Gigot à l'Armagnac. And as we had reason to connect Marler with that restaurant, I thought again of Dijon.

"He had been connected with the restaurant business himself," I said. "I wondered if by any chance he had once worked in your restaurant and, years later, when he had acquired a high-class place of his own, had borrowed some of your ideas."

I took the photographs from my small case and gave them to him.

"You will see him there, m'sieur. That is what he was like about two to three years ago."

He took his spectacles-case from his breast-pocket and began peering. I passed him my glass.

"Perhaps that will help you by making an enlargement."

He looked and frowned. Henriette suddenly appeared, announcing dinner. He waved her impatiently away.

"Un moment! Un moment!"

He frowned, nodded to himself, and gave me back the glass.

"M'sieur, you are fortunate. I know this man." He hoisted himself up with the help of his stick. "But let us eat. Then we can also talk."

It was equality and fraternity. We ate in the fairly spacious kitchen, with that chicken still slowly turning on its spit. Flaugeon, the taxi-driver, ate heartily. Henriette ate less and kept getting up to look to the pots and casseroles on the long range in the intervals of eating. It was a simple meal, but good: potage du pays, some local carp with a sharp sauce, then the chicken and salad, and cheese to end with. When Doriot asked me about wine I told him of that excellent Bordeaux my wife and I had drunk years ago, and a couple of bottles were fetched from the cellar.

And during the meal he was telling me about the man I knew as Frank Marler. He had known him as François Maille.

"That wasn't his name," he said. "It was the one under which he had made his way out of Germany. He was a Jew, and I have a weakness for Jews. My grandmother—do you remember her, Henriette?—was a Jewess, so when he came to me and applied for a job as a waiter I gave him a trial. He said his father had had a restaurant in Hamburg. He disappeared—doubtless the Gestapo. It was in 1935, when the persecution of the Jews was beginning to be serious. So this Maille managed to get away to France, he and his brother—"

"His stepbrother," Henriette, who had seemed not to be listening, suddenly broke in.

"Ah, yes—his stepbrother. I never saw him. I believe he went to Le Havre. He was a much older man. At any rate, I gave this

Maille his job. He was a good waiter—probably the best I ever had. He was ambitious, m'sieur. He saved his sous. One day he wanted his own restaurant, but that day never came—at least, not in France. When the real offensive began in 1940 and it was obvious that we had been betrayed by that *bande de voyoux*, he disappeared. Where he went I had no idea. Perhaps it was to that step-brother at Le Havre and so to England. But I don't know. I never heard a word from him. To me he was dead. And now, m'sieur, you have resurrected him." He gave a sad shake of the head. "And a world which will never come back."

"Maille had money with him?"

"Undoubtedly. I believe he had money when he first came to me, and, as I told you, he was ambitious. He never complained about work. He had the manner that produces good tips. He had that certain manner—the manner, if I may say so, of the born hôtelier."

"He was honest?"

He gave me a quick look. The dark eyes twinkled.

"M'sieur, in my restaurant one had to be honest. Maybe he made a few sous by this and that. Who knows?"

I had the idea that in that particular matter he wasn't telling me all he knew. And there seemed nothing else that he *could* tell me, and somehow the talk turned to the Occupation and to England and Churchill and the bombing, and we were still at it when we'd drunk the black coffee laced with rum and Doriot was asking about a liqueur. I glanced at my watch. It was after nine o'clock.

Flaugeon went, reluctantly, I thought, to see to the taxi. M. Doriot telephoned a hotel and fixed a room for me. I had to force a *pourboire* on Henriette, and then Doriot was coming with me to the door. We shook hands warmly. Flaugeon appeared to say a respectful goodbye.

"And how much will you charge my friend, M. Travers?" Doriot asked him sternly.

Flaugeon thought for a moment and mentioned fifteen hundred francs. Doriot shrugged his shoulders.

"Maybe it will be less by the time you arrive. It is necessary not to allow one's self to be plundered," he told me, not too seriously. We shook hands again. I begged him to let me know if ever he or his son came to London. The last I saw of him was as the taxi moved off and he was still standing there in the light of the open door.

It was about four o'clock the following afternoon when I walked into Wharton's room at the Yard. There had been something strange about that journey back and even the arrival at familiar scenes. France has always been a country that I've loved, and to me, at least, its people have always been *sympathiques*, and it was in some queer way like coming from something recaptured to a something almost unreal. I had also made a discovery—beyond what has already been told—and maybe there was a look of it on my face.

George's lower lip drooped a bit. His own French is far better than mine—his mother was French—and he hurled a bit of classical poetry at me: that line of du Bellay's about the happiness of a wanderer who returns, like Ulysses, from some great adventure—

Heureux qui, comme Ulysse, a fait un beau voyage.

"It was a *beau voyage*?"

"Couldn't have been better," I said. "I think I've picked up quite a lot."

He rang down for a tea-tray.

"Well, let's hear it. I knew something was pleasing you from that look on your face."

I had my story ready to the last word and appropriate gesture. I took my time over it. I made it like a detective story in miniature: the casting about in Dijon and at last a contact with a new Restaurant Doriot, and then that evening with Alphonse Doriot himself. George didn't say a word till that evening was over. Then he grunted.

"Started life as a waiter, did he? And came from Hamburg. Might have just slipped across here in the few days before

Dunkirk. And changed his name from Maille to Marler. He'd have had time for that before identity cards came in."

"There were thousands of refugees after Dunkirk," I said.

"They couldn't all be vetted. I know. It was my job, if you remember, during the war. Maille—or Marler—spoke excellent French, by the way. He also had some English. He used to try it out on occasional English visitors to the Restaurant Doriot. And the really strange thing is that he must have been there that night Bernice and I dined there."

"You weren't to know," he told me tritely. "Still, how's it all going to help?"

"Wait a minute," I said. "I haven't finished yet. What about that stepbrother of Marler's—the older man who was at Le Havre and who probably accompanied him to England?"

George stared.

"Yes," he said. "If that's right, then he was your third man! Marler, Bosford and this Maille—if that's what he was still calling himself."

He frowned.

"How the devil can we find out? God knows what name he took."

Then the light began to dawn. He stared again. It shifted to an almost accusatory look, and on me.

"We don't have to. Paynter's the man! That's why he went down to Seahurst. He said he thought he knew Marler! What he was doing was identifying his own brother!"

"I know," I said. "And we ought to have known it as soon as Paynter was identified."

For years I've had to watch George Wharton pulling rabbits out of hats, and I've always been expected to applaud. Now I was on the stage, sleeves rolled up and the hat in my hand.

"What d'you mean?" he said.

I shrugged my shoulders. I was going to savour my moment.

"What I say. We ought to have spotted it."

"God-dammit! Why can't you spit it out? What ought we to have spotted?"

"The two names," I said. "Notice anything about them? Any similarity?"

"Paynter and Marler," he said slowly. "Paynter and Marler." Then the light dawned again.

"Wait a minute. Isn't *Maler* the German for painter?"

"You've got it in one," I said. "The original name of those two was Maler. They were born as Maler in Hamburg. One changed his name in France to Francois Maille. Notice that he kept the initial of his Christian name. They often do. Maybe he was born Franz Maler; in England he became Frank Marler. What the other man—the stepbrother—called himself in France we don't know. He might have been born Hermann Maler. In England he became Herbert Paynter."

Another minute and that ruined tea-tray was placed on the side table and we were stoking our pipes and settling down. Wharton thought we ought to begin with Paynter.

It was a logical enough beginning. There was no coincidence about the association of those three men. All spoke French, and, since the smuggling racket that Marler had thought of was vitally concerned with France, they made a handy trio.

"But about Paynter," George said. "We haven't yet got a line on him before he took that photographer's studio. But he did take it, and after Marler's death. Something Jewle has picked up can throw a lot of light on that. Paynter didn't produce references when he signed the lease. He went one better and produced a year's rent in advance. That's the kind of reference that talks loudest with agents. Also, of course, fitting out that studio—it used to be a picture-framing business—must have cost him the very devil of a lot. So where'd the money come from?"

"Not from Marler," I said. "He was dead. And Paynter never came forward to claim any estate. I happen to know that."

"I don't know," George said. "Just before his death Marler was in possession of what he'd already made out of the racket and the proceeds of the sale of almost a new car." He frowned. "Wonder if Paynter was mixed up in that killing of Marler?"

He didn't answer his own question. He gave an exasperated click of the tongue.

"This is getting us nowhere. If Marler was dead and Bosford dead, then who killed Paynter? I tell you we've got to find an extra man."

"Not necessarily," I said, and told him just enough of my suspicions about Bosford. I reminded him that Doris Bosford's identification of her husband couldn't have been based on much more than very wishful thinking.

"All right then," he said. "Let's assume Bosford rigged up the whole thing and that he's still alive. Paynter was in it, too, and he got his share. Later he began blackmailing Bosford, and that was the end of him. All of which boils down to one fact: that we've got to find Bosford."

I agreed. It was my policy to agree and he'd played right into my hands.

"Right," he said. "Let's cut the cackle. From now on we'll work on the assumption that Bosford's alive. You write your report." He gave a chuckle. "The Powers-that-Be rather look down their noses at trips abroad. This'll make 'em snap their eyes. I might get a trip out of it myself."

So I got to work dictating that report. In it I managed what I thought was a very clever thing, even if I left it as a kind of vague recommendation. It was a way to get Wharton to discover the Restaurant Antoine Dupont for himself, and I did it by saying why I'd been attracted all those years ago by the Restaurant Doriot. I said, and admitted it was a very long shot, that when Marler had acquired a town restaurant he might have stolen something of Alphonse Doriot's ideas. If that didn't make someone spot the windows of the Restaurant Antoine Dupont, then, in Wharton's pet phrase, my name was Robinson.

15

NEW TRAGEDY

I WENT straight from the Yard to my flat. I rang down for a meal and, while I was waiting, got hold of Norris. I wanted to know if Hallows had unearthed anything while I was away.

"Nothing about Simon," he said. "That roadhouse has gone long since and he couldn't pick up any trail. But he did find something else. Up to the time he got hold of that restaurant in town Marler had owned a place in Fallgate."

"Good lord!" I said. "What sort of a place?"

"A restaurant in the High Street. Rather a superior kind of place. That's a high-class residential area, as you know. Hallows's information is that he was making a fair bit out of it. When he sold it, lock-stock-and-barrel, he got five thousand five hundred for it. It's gone down considerably since. A much cheaper sort of place."

That was something over which to think. Marler, it seemed, had at last acquired that restaurant which had been his ambition. It was only a *ballon d'essai*, and what he really wanted was the right foothold in town. But he built it up, and when a chance to buy the Silver Boat had presented itself he had sold up and reinvested. But the Silver Boat hadn't caught on. Even dance bands and crooners hadn't put it on its feet. So Marler knew he had to change again, and this time he'd need still more capital. Hence the smuggling sideline. Hence, still later, the agreeing to make a divorce possible and the taking of Cortin's five thousand pounds. But all he had found was a wet death. Bosford, who had been aware of all his plans for some fine new restaurant after a last remunerative trip to France, had simply stepped into his shoes and carried those plans on. And when that thought came to me I was suddenly gaping. It wasn't Bosford who had carried out those plans. *It was Simon.* Simon was the real owner of the Restaurant Antoine Dupont. Dupont himself was only a figure-head. He represented, and probably at a big salary, first-class publicity. It was he who gave the *cachet*.

It fitted in. Simon at that roadhouse near Fallgate and Marler in the town itself. The two must have got acquainted and to a mutual advantage. Simon had later become a member of that smuggling gang, and he and Marler were proposing to buy a promising restaurant in town. But it was Simon who bought it. Where Bosford came in I didn't at the moment know. But Paynter had to come in, and because Simon had had to kill him. It must have been Simon. Simon had known where to deposit the body.

It was when I'd got to that point that the telephone went.

I guessed it was either Norris or Wharton. It was neither—a woman's voice, an agitated voice.

"Oh, Mr. Travers, I've been trying to get you all evening. I'm worried. I don't know what to do."

"It's Mrs. Bosford, isn't it?"

"Yes. Doris Bosford. I've been trying to get you all evening. I'm frightened. I don't know what to do."

"Where are you?"

"Not far away. Can I come and see you?"

"Do," I said. "Come right away. I'll be here waiting for you. But you wouldn't like to tell me—"

The line was dead. I could only wonder what on earth had happened. Then I thought I knew. Her husband was alive and she'd suddenly discovered the fact. Maybe there'd been some threats on his part.

Still, in a few minutes I'd know far more. My tray had come up and I began bolting my meal. I needn't have been in such a hurry. The meal had gone and my door-bell hadn't yet rung. So I waited a minute or two and then took the tray downstairs myself. I told the porter I was expecting a caller and he was to send her straight up.

I went back to the flat and waited. Another ten minutes went by. Down I went again.

"No sign of your caller yet, sir."

"I know," I said. "I expected her long ago. If she should happen to come, just hold her here a minute, will you?"

I went out as I was and peered along the street. I went round the corner to the short cut that runs ultimately to my garage and on to Duncannon Street. About three-quarters of the way along it I could see people. A constable was there too, shepherding them away.

"Move along there, please. Move along. . . . Nothing to see now. . . . Move along. Move along, please."

Some premonition made me quicken my step. I was at the passage and before he turned.

"What's happened, officer?"

Maybe I'd put too much anxiety into the question. And there I was—hatless, coatless and a bit dishevelled. He gave me a queer look.

"Why, sir? You particularly interested?"

"If there's been an accident to a woman—yes."

I was feeling in my breast pocket. Luckily I had my warrant card on me. He had a look at it, then another look at me. I think he was pretty sure the whole thing was some kind of fake. There was a reluctance about giving the card back.

"As a matter of fact there *has* been an accident to a woman," he told me. "Badly coshed."

"You identified her?"

"Whoever's in charge hasn't. The one who coshed her took her bag—if she had a bag."

"Where is she now? I think I can identify her."

"Just taken to the hospital round the corner," he said. "Perhaps we ought to go along there—if what you say is correct."

Three minutes and we were there. In the hall of the accident reception annexe there were only two people—the reception orderly on duty and a man whom I thought I recognised. He spotted me at once.

"Hallo, sir. What're you doing here?"

It was a Detective-Sergeant Butt from the Yard. I told him about the call I'd had.

"You wait here, sir."

He had a word with the orderly and took the lift. It was five minutes before he was back. We rode the lift upstairs together.

"She's apparently in a bad way," he told me. "They're getting ready to operate at once."

A sister took us along the corridor to a small reception-room. It didn't take more than a glance to identify Doris Bosford as she lay there ready for removal to the operating theatre. There was no point in staying to watch that removal and we went down again. I asked Butt what he knew about it all.

She'd been found practically as soon as she'd been struck, he said. A man some distance behind her in that passage had seen her fall and he thought he had seen another man near her. A constable had been fetched and the Yard notified, and the hospital.

"There wasn't anything for me to do," Butt said, "except get the name and address of the witness. Not a sign of anything."

"What was she struck with?"

"That's asking," he said. "Something pretty hard, though. I gather there's a fracture of the skull. Oh, and something else. I wonder if you could throw any light on it. I bent over the stretcher just before they took her away and she was sort of mumbling to herself. You know, like as if she was delirious. And you know what I distinctly heard her say? 'He's here'—just like that. 'He's here.' She said it two or three times. What d'you make of that, sir?"

"Don't know," I said, "unless it was that she recognised the one who struck her. But that isn't right."

I thought for a moment.

"Tell me something. Just how did she say it? '*He's* here' or 'He's *here*.'"

"There wasn't any emphasis," he told me. "It was just what I said. 'He's here.'"

"Right," I said. "Strictly between ourselves, I think this is tied up with a case that I'm concerned with at the Yard at the moment. I'll get back to my flat and try to get hold of Inspector Jewle or Superintendent Wharton."

As I walked back I knew what those muttered words had meant. They could mean only one thing—that the *he* was Bosford. Doris Bosford had known her husband was back.

Whether or not it was he who had struck her down had yet to be proved. As for the taking of the bag, that might have been a blind, or because it held something that was badly wanted. Or it might have been simply an attempt to conceal her identity.

Jewle wasn't in, but Wharton was somewhere about. I said would they get him and I'd hold the line. In a couple of minutes he was speaking.

"Glad you rang," he said; and before I could get my word in, "You know that bit in your report about that Dijon restaurant? We've found one like it. Stumbled on it right away. A place called the Restaurant Antoine Dupont in Osbert Street."

"Quick work," I said. "But listen to this."

I told him about Doris Bosford.

"Good God!" he said. "Bosford's widow!"

"Or his wife."

He caught the implication of that.

"Right," he said. "I'll be along as soon as I can make it. See you at the flat."

I looked up the telephone directory and I found a Fryer, M. of 12a Vickers Road. I rang the number. Almost at once a woman was on the line.

"Mrs. Fryer?"

"Speaking."

She had a quick, brittle kind of voice. I told her who I was, but she'd never heard of me. Doris had certainly been secretive. So I said I was ringing from Scotland Yard. Her partner Mrs. Bosford had met with an accident and was just being operated on in hospital. I said it was no use ringing the hospital or the Yard at the moment. What I wanted her to do was come along at once to my flat.

"Ring the Yard first and make sure this isn't a trick to get you out of the house," I said. "Dial 999 and then mention my name. . . . No, I can't answer questions. It's all wasting time. We want you here at once."

I rang off. It was folly to conjecture. There was nothing to do but wait. So I lighted my pipe and waited. It was about forty minutes before Wharton arrived.

"Just dropped in at the hospital," he said. "She's still under the anaesthetic."

Before he could hang up his coat the door-bell went. It was Marlene Fryer. She was a tall, slim woman of about forty—smartly dressed and impeccably made up. I introduced George Wharton and got the two of them seated. I told her just what had happened. Her reactions were never more than an occasional moistening of the lips or a frown.

"Frankly," I said, "we don't think this is just an ordinary cosh attack. That's why we wanted you here, to see if you could throw any light on things."

"Well," she said, "I knew something was wrong. Doris was out last night with a friend, and she came home much earlier than I'd expected her. She said she wasn't feeling well and she went straight to bed. Then all today I could see she was worried about something. When I asked her, she said she had a headache. I wanted her to take some aspirins, but she wouldn't."

"And when did you see her last?"

"Well, at about half-past six tonight. We always have a kind of high tea when we get in, and then she said she had to go out again. I didn't ask her where. And she didn't tell me."

I caught Wharton's eye. He had no questions.

"Just something else, Mrs. Fryer," I said. "Is it Mrs. or Miss?"

"Mrs.," she said. "I divorced my husband some years ago."

"Sorry," I said, "I didn't mean to be inquisitive about your private business. What I wanted to ask was this: just how much did Doris Bosford pay for her partnership with you?"

She gave a little frown.

"Is that necessary?"

"We think so," I said. "I may tell you, by the way, that I've known Mrs. Bosford for quite a long time—in a private capacity, of course. I knew she'd bought the partnership."

"Well, it was actually four thousand pounds."

"A lot of money. Don't get me wrong. It was probably well worth it. It might have been worth even more. But any idea where she got the money?"

"She'd sold her house, for one thing. And her husband must have made quite a lot of money."

Wharton still had no questions. After all, he knew very little and had to feel his way.

"One other thing, Mrs. Fryer, and then I've finished. Do you know the name of the friend with whom she spent yesterday evening?"

She actually gave a little smile.

"Oh yes. He's a Mr. Halsey. Robert Halsey. He's the London representative of Longfield and Brown."

"The warehousemen of St. Paul's?"

"Yes," she said. "He's a very nice man. About my own age."

"Thirty-five?" Wharton asked. He always boasts of his way with a woman witness.

"Well"—she smiled with just a touch of irony—"somewhere about that."

"It was a serious affair?"

"On his part—yes. I'm not so sure about her."

I got to my feet. I said that was all for the moment. She was not to worry about Doris, who was in the best possible hands. She might ring the hospital for news in the morning. I thanked her for coming and said I'd see her into a taxi. Wharton, as I'd hoped, came with us to the flat door.

"Oh, just one last thing, Mrs. Fryer," I said. "Do you happen to know exactly where Doris went last night?"

"Oh yes," she said. "To a very superior restaurant in Osbert Street. What was the name, now? Dupont, or something like that."

I'd known, of course, where Doris Bosford had spent her evening, or, since I'd virtually sent her there, I could have made a good guess. But what I'd wanted was for Wharton to hear that name, and I'd had to manoeuvre things so that he could mull it over in the few minutes I was away. It was a long way from a surprise when he began throwing questions at me as soon as I was inside the door.

He said it beat cock-fighting. Why was it that as soon as the name of a restaurant had cropped up it should crop up again in the Doris Bosford attack? How did this new element—the restaurant—fit in? Why should she have been attacked at all? Did her money come from that smuggling racket? And so on and so on.

"No use being impatient," I told him. "Take that restaurant. This chap Halsey was in the habit of taking her out occasionally. They have gone to that restaurant by chance. We can only guess it was in any way connected."

"It must be connected," he told me. "She went there and she came home early. Whatever happened, happened there."

"You're rushing ahead," I said. "It might just have been a lovers' tiff. We'll know in the morning. If you like, I'll see this chap Halsey first thing and get his statement and bring it to the Yard."

He did a quick switch.

"Those words she kept muttering about someone—a he— being here. Who was the 'he' if it wasn't her husband?"

"I grant you," I said. "It's just possible she actually saw him there. But that doesn't alter the fact that we'll know a considerable deal more by the morning."

There was a lot more talking about it. It ended with his saying reluctantly that he'd expect me in the morning. Meanwhile, he'd slip along to the hospital again. If the doctor agreed he'd have a man sitting by her bedside in case she did any muttering again.

"Hope to God she doesn't pass out," he told me at the door. "Once we can get her statement the whole thing ought to be cleared up. It's getting beyond a joke. First Paynter and now this."

I wasn't too happy when he left. In order to protect the interests of Cortin and his wife, I'd had to steer an extremely tricky course. At any moment something might crop up and there'd be questions I'd no longer be able to avoid, let alone answer. But it didn't stop me from sleeping, even if the thought of Halsey woke me far earlier than usual.

Just before nine o'clock I rang his firm. He wasn't in, I was told, but he ought to be back at any minute. I'd given my name and I said the matter was extremely urgent. Would they tell him as soon as he did come in that I'd be along almost at once.

He was waiting for me. He was a tallish man of rather more than forty—quite well-spoken and good-looking in a virile way. He looked surprised when he saw my warrant card.

"What's wrong, Mr. Travers?"

"Nothing," I said. "Have you an office we can talk in?"

He did have an office. I told him about the attack on Doris Bosford. He was very upset. He was even talking of going to the hospital.

"No use doing that," I said. "If you like I'll ring them now."

I used his office telephone and was put through to the sister on duty. The operation had been so far successful, she said, but Mrs. Bosford's condition was still very critical.

"A bad business," I said to Halsey. "And, strictly between ourselves, we don't think it was one of those chance sort of coshings. We think it a deliberate attack for something far more than purse snatching."

He looked as if he couldn't believe it.

"Even if it isn't," I said, "it has to be enquired into, and thoroughly. Don't be offended about this, but even your own movements have to be gone into. For all we know, you might have had some cause to attack her."

"You can't believe that," he said. "Why, I'd have cut off my hand rather than anything like that should have happened."

"Maybe you would. But we've seen her partner Mrs. Fryer, and she told us that Doris came home very early. I wonder if you'd mind telling me just what happened the night before last?"

He made no bones about it. He'd asked Doris to make a choice of where to go, and she'd suggested the Restaurant Antoine Dupont, where there was also a dance floor. So they'd gone there. It was a smart-looking place and they'd had dinner downstairs. Then, in the middle of it, as near to eight o'clock as he could remember, she'd suddenly come over queer. He'd thought she was going to faint. She pulled herself together and went to the ladies' room. When she came out she was still looking very pale. She said it was nothing, just a sudden attack of something she couldn't explain. So he settled the bill for the unfinished meal and took her home to Vickers Street in a taxi. The next morning she rang him and apologised for making a silly of herself, as she put it. She said she was then feeling herself again.

"And that's all," he said. "As for where I was last night—" He broke off. "You haven't told me what time it was when this attack was made on her."

"You carry on," I said. "Then I'll tell you."

"Well, I rang her myself last night at about eight o'clock. I rang from here. I was working late, and my secretary was here, too. We didn't leave till a good half-hour later. Mrs. Fryer told me Doris was out and she didn't know when she'd be in."

I smiled.

"That seems good enough. Not that I ever suspected you of anything. It was just something for the records. But to get back to that restaurant. Can you fix—by anything that happened, say—the exact moment when Mrs. Bosford began to feel queer?"

He frowned. He moistened his lips.

"I can't," he said. "I do know it was after the proprietor had just made the rounds of the tables. That was it. He had a word or two with us. Asked if everything was to our liking and so on, and it was just after that. Perhaps I'd better explain about that."

"You needn't," I said. "I've dined at that restaurant and I know the procedure. What I want you to do now is to write down everything you've told me. Type it on that machine if you prefer. Regard it as entirely without prejudice. You'll be asked to make an authoritative statement later."

It was about three-quarters of an hour later when I went into Wharton's room. I told him the hospital news and he said he'd already had it. His hand went out for Halsey's statement.

He read it. He scowled at it and read it a second time.

"What d'you make of it yourself?"

"It's to the point—it's factual and it's genuine," I said.

"And this round of the tables business?"

It shouldn't have been necessary, but I explained that it was the kind of thing he must have come across many a time in France. Just a good restaurateur taking a personal interest in his clientèle.

"Yes," he said, and I don't honestly think he'd been listening. "And she felt queer soon afterwards. What d'you make of it?"

"What can one make?" I hedged. "That little chat at their table mightn't have had anything whatever to do with it. My guess—admittedly a wild one—is that her husband was dining in that restaurant and she saw him at that particular moment and recognised him."

"I see. And what grounds have you got for thinking that?"

"She rang me last night," I said. "She said she was scared to death and that she had been scared all day. The thing that would scare her most was the sight of a husband she'd virtually sworn to as dead. She was with another man, and doubtless they'd been having a happy time. And, if her husband were really alive, there might be accounts he'd want to settle. Don't ask me what accounts. I'm just ridding myself of ideas."

"All the same, I think we've got it," he said grimly. "What I don't like is this series of coincidences."

I reminded him that the very word *restaurant* was a connecting link. Marler had been mixed up with the restaurant business during most of his life. Bosford had first met Marler through singing in his restaurant. Bosford specialised in French *chansons*. Marler was French in a way. Maybe the proprietor of the Antoine Dupont had known Marler at one time. They might even have met years ago in Dijon.

"One could go on like that," I said. "I admit it doesn't get us very far."

He pressed the buzzer. He asked to be put through to the Restaurant Antoine Dupont in Osbert Street, and on no account was there to be a suspicion of where the call was coming from. Then he lighted his cold pipe again and waited. The call came through.

"Ah, yes," he said. "I take it you do lunches? . . . That's fine. Reserve me a table, will you? For one. . . . Just a moment. I'll see if my wife wants to come."

He cupped the receiver. I shook my head.

"Only one," he said. "At about one o'clock? . . . Oh yes. The name's Taylor, spelt with a 'y'."

There was a smirk on his face as he replaced the receiver and got to his feet.

"Well, nothing like having a personal look." Then he was whipping round. "What was the idea of not going with me?"

"Saving the taxpayers' money," I told him flippantly. "Lunch will probably cost a packet in a place like that. Also, if I'm not wanted too badly, I'd like to slip along to the agency."

"Nothing doing at the moment," he said. "Something might come in from Jewle. The last I heard from him was that he thought he might have a lead on Paynter."

So that, again, was that. Once more I'd managed to extricate myself pretty well. But as I waited for a bus to take me along the Embankment I knew somehow I couldn't go on wriggling clear for ever. Liars, as my old nurse used often to quote to me, ought to have good memories, and something was telling me that at any moment my memory might slip up.

16

FATAL NIGHT

HALLOWS had reported in that morning, Norris said. There was nothing else he could dig up about either Marler or Simon, so Norris had put him on another assignment. It wasn't so important that he couldn't be called off it again if I should badly want him.

I remember that day, until the evening and the sound of the buzzer in George's room, as being one of frustrations. I put in an hour with Norris at tax returns, and after that I was at a loose end. I went out to lunch too early and it was over too soon;

indeed, by the time I came out Wharton was probably entering the Restaurant Antoine Dupont all set for a regular blow-out— as he might have put it—at the taxpayers' expense. I went to the club so as to have a spot from which Wharton could ring me if he wanted me. By half-past two I judged that he must surely have finished that lunch of his, but I gave him another quarter of an hour and then rang the Yard myself. I was told he had come in and gone out. They thought he was with Jewle at Wapping. I left a message that I'd be at my flat.

What Wharton and Jewle were doing at Wapping was beyond me, till I remembered that Wharton had hinted that Jewle had picked up some tracks, somewhere or other, of Paynter. I thought that if Paynter had really come from dockland to Mallaby Road, E.9, then he'd come up a bit in the world. Still, I supposed I'd hear about it in Wharton's good time.

I'd bought an afternoon edition. There was a mention in it of that attack on Doris Bosford, name and address being given. It added that she had been successfully operated on and was expected to make a statement at any minute. That made me open my eyes. I wondered first of all if it were true and, if it weren't, what Wharton's idea had been in handing the story out. So I thought I'd have a quick minute or two at the hospital. They know me there, by the way. Bernice is still on their committee of management.

I found things difficult. I was passed on to a quite important person who had no first-hand knowledge of me, and I think he rang the Yard even after he'd seen my warrant card. Wharton had certainly made everything very hush-hush, but I was told that Doris Bosford was now considered to have a fifty-fifty chance, but that in the most optimistic circumstances it would be two or three days before she could be in any way questioned.

I asked if there were a man by her bed and was told there wasn't. But Wharton did have men on duty outside the room both by day and night. That cleared the whole thing up. Wharton had the idea that once the attacker knew that Doris Bosford was making a statement, then he might go to any extremes to keep her mouth still shut. Wharton, in other words, was trying a short cut. If the attacker tried by some pretext or other to enter that room, or if he even showed downstairs too great an interest, then he'd be held.

I went back to the flat, tackled a crossword puzzle and then spun out the time with tea. That made it five o'clock. At half-past I slipped out to the corner and bought later editions of the evening papers and by the time I'd read them it was six o'clock. I was getting annoyed at being kept on a string, so I rang the Yard. Wharton was in conference. What it was about I couldn't conjecture. In any case I'm far too unimportant a cog to be introduced into that kind of machinery.

Seven o'clock came at last and I rang down for dinner, and I told myself that even if Wharton did want me suddenly and urgently, then he could go on wanting till that meal was placidly over. You see how peevish I was getting. I needn't have been. The meal was finished, I'd lighted a pipe and read a few pages of a book when the telephone bell shrilled. Wharton was asking if I'd like to come along.

I took my time, and it was well after nine o'clock when I arrived. He was looking pleased with himself.

"Still feeling the effects of that lunch?" I asked a bit peevishly.

"And a good lunch it was," he said. "I don't know when I've eaten a better. A posh place, that."

"Did you see Dupont?"

"Oh yes," he said, and tried to make it off-hand. "We had a few words together—in French."

"Fine," I said. "And what's this I gather about Wapping?"

"Ah, that," he said. "We know where Paynter spent the last few years. He didn't spell his name with a 'y', by the way. Just the ordinary spelling. Suppose he thought he'd better posh himself up a bit when he moved to Mallaby Road."

That was as far as he got. *That was when the buzzer went.*

Wharton laid the receiver gently down, and he was still staring. I'd gathered so much and no more.

"If that doesn't beat cock-fighting! What d'you think's happened? That Antoine Dupont has shot himself!"

Before I could speak he was making for hat and overcoat. I grabbed my own and followed him down the stairs. A car was ready and we moved off. We went into Whitehall and were well along it before he spoke again.

"I didn't know a word about it," he said. "Apparently just the report of a suicide, and the usual. Then someone tied it up with various other things—Matthews, to be exact—and he thought I'd better be informed."

Matthews, like myself, had worked with Wharton for years. It was sheer luck that it had been he who'd gone to Osbert Street.

"What the devil Dupont did it for, I can't make out," Wharton was going on exasperatedly. Then he stopped, and in the light as we turned off the Mall I saw he was smiling to himself.

"Maybe it wasn't suicide."

I made no comment. To tell the truth, I'd been thinking of something else. It was only about a minute before the car stopped, and no sooner had he answered the question I put to him, than he was beginning to hoist himself out.

"About Paynter, George. What was he doing at Wapping?"

"Him?" he said. "Oh, he had a little chandler's shop. Did a little tattooing in his spare time."

It rang no bell. In any case I was getting out of the car. We went through the doors and into the foyer. Sergeant Matthews was waiting for us.

"This way, sir."

I'd like you to note the layout. As we went up, Matthews was telling Wharton that everything was being kept very quiet and the restaurant was functioning as usual. But first we had gone past the cloakroom. A little beyond it, to the left, was the men's wash-room and then the stairs. On the landing was Simon's room, facing the stairs—a room I'd already been in. Then came a choice of ways. To the right a very short but wide passage led to the door of the upper restaurant with its dance floor. The door had frosted glass, but you could hear the band playing. To the left was another short passage. Dupont's office was there, on another small landing from which stairs went down, and, as I subsequently discovered, to that door behind the screen from which Dupont was accustomed to emerge for his round of the tables.

We went into that office. Simon was there, standing just behind the door, and Anders. Dupont lay on the floor, and by his hand was a gun—a German Lüger. Matthews drew back to let Wharton move forward. There wasn't a lot of room between the four of us and the flat-topped desk.

Wharton's body hid Dupont from us. I turned slightly and found Simon looking at me. It was more of a petrified stare.

"Evening, Mr. Simmonds," I said quietly.

Then Wharton moved round and I saw Dupont again. Wharton was on one knee, lifting the head. There was a ghastly redness that covered most of the right temple, and a little blood had seeped along the cheek and down to the cropped beard. Wharton got to his feet.

"What about it, Anders?"

"Dead about half an hour," Anders said. "Looks open and shut to me. Everything consistent with suicide. Burn marks, as you see. Matthews says he was right-handed."

"That's what the manager here tells me," Matthews said. He looked around. "Hallo, where's he gone?"

"Don't worry about *him*," Wharton said testily. "You say he was right-handed. All right, then. What about prints?"

"They're there," Matthews said. "They'll have to be checked."

"Check 'em now," Wharton told him. "And shut that door, will you, Travers. There's the devil's own draught."

Matthews got the apparatus from his bag and got to work. I saw nothing but backs and I just stood there. A minute or two went by, and I began thinking of something else—that utter fright on Simon's face when he'd recognised me, and the even greater fright when I addressed him as Simmonds. At the first recognition he'd known I was connected with the police and might soon be divulging that Calvert affair, but that mention of his real name had absolutely terrified him. I wondered suddenly why he had slipped so quietly out of the room. I'd have mentioned it to

Wharton if I hadn't thought of something else—Paynter, and his little shop at Wapping, and the tattooing he did on the side.

And that was when something hit me. It was like that—an absolute shock of revelation. I think I must have stood there for a good minute, polishing my glasses and unaware that I was doing it. It was Wharton's voice that roused me.

"Well, that seems pretty conclusive. Try the paraffin test on him, just to make sure—not that I'm any great believer in it. Any particular point in keeping him, Anders?"

"Far as I'm concerned, you can't move him too soon," Anders said dryly.

"See to it, Matthews. And have the gun ready for testing against the bullet. I'll have a word with that manager. Why the devil did the fellow have to go out just when he was wanted. You find him, Matthews. Anders can ring here for the ambulance."

Matthews was pulling off his gloves as he went out of the door. Anders was dialling. I just stood there where I'd been practically from the beginning. There was something I ought to do, and I was almost dreading the doing of it. I held off till the last moment when Anders had replaced the receiver. My voice came so hoarse that I had to clear my throat.

"I've been thinking of something, George. Mind if I have a look at Dupont myself?"

"Why not?" George said, and waved a hand. "He's all yours, as they say."

Dupont was wearing that same white jacket, but his hands were ungloved. The white waistcoat was not fully buttoned, and beneath it was only a white linen shirt. It was unbuttoned too, except for the top, visible button. That gave me confidence.

"I'd like you to look, George," I said, and I pulled that shirt out and back till the chest was exposed. In the centre, visible against the map of black hairs, was a large circle of tattooing. It must have been a good nine inches in diameter. I took out my glass and had a look.

"Doc, have you got anything that'll remove all this hair?"

"I can clip it," he said, and got scissors from his bag. He got down on his knees. Wharton was peering closely.

"Fine chest on him," Anders said, clipping away. "Better collect this stuff, George. Your wife might want to stuff a cushion."

I looked through the glass again.

"See it, George. There's the original. Underneath is a bit of new tattooing, upside-down, to make the circle. All these little curlicues and things were meant to hide the original, and they almost do. But see here. There's the wings of the eagle making the top of the circle, and there's just a trace of the ball it was holding in its talons."

"My God, you're right!" He looked at me, almost stupefied. "It's Marler! That's who he is—Marler!"

I'd got to my feet and he was practically brushing me aside in order to get another and still closer look.

"We're right," he said. "Don't know how he did it, but he's Marler. And he knew his number was up."

"How do you mean?" Anders asked.

"Because he guessed we'd have a statement from Mrs. Bosford. She spotted him here in his own restaurant."

Then he was giving a queer, hesitating look.

"But how could she? She wouldn't see this chest of his?"

"There'd be something about him," I said. "Putting it bluntly, a woman doesn't sleep with a man and not get to have that queer sort of knowledge that'd make her spot him anywhere."

Wharton snorted.

"Dammit! I've seen his photos, haven't I? His own mother wouldn't have recognised him. And who told you she'd been sleeping with him?"

"Wait a minute, wait a minute," Anders said. "What about this?"

We looked as he twisted the head round towards us. There was a nick on the top of the right ear as if it had once been cut by something and had been allowed to set carelessly.

"That's it," I said. "That's what she spotted him by. He'd give that little bow of his at her table and that ear might have been right under her eye."

Then I was doing the staring.

"That's it, George!" I was telling him again. "That's what she was muttering to herself. 'His ear!'—not 'He's here'. *His ear—* the one she saw!"

"Yes," George said, and got to his feet again. "She spotted him and you bet your life he spotted her. And he knew she'd spotted him. That's why she was watched and then followed. By rights that blow on the skull should have killed her."

Matthews came in.

"Can't find that manager, sir. Looks as if he's bolted."

"Bolted?"

"Have a look at his room, sir."

We left Anders and hurried along the passage, past the sound of a band and the faint shuffle of feet, to that room I knew. The desk drawers weren't properly shut. One was half open. The door of a safe that stood on the floor in the corner was wide open.

"Right," Wharton said. "Get a man or two here. Go through this place with a small-toothed comb and then get the alarm out. Find out where he lives." He waved an impatient hand. "Get going. You don't want me to tell you what to do."

It was eleven o'clock when we got back to Wharton's room. Virtually everything seemed to be cleared up, he said, and pressed the buzzer for coffee to be sent up. But he'd like to hear my own version of things.

I said I'd probably be wrong about certain details, and that there'd be things we'd almost certainly never be able to prove, but how I saw it all was this. Things were getting a bit hot in that smuggling racket and, more important, Bosford was losing his nerve. His wife had told me he was a bit scared. So Marler decided to bolt, and to get rid of Bosford at the same time.

"That presupposes there were only the two of them in that racket," I said. "I think that'll turn out to be true. But what he did after he'd made all his preparations for getting money together was to have Bosford down at Happton. The reason might have been either a last coup or both of them skipping to France. And now come the sheer guesses. I think Marler got his stepbrother down there, too. Paynter arrived to find Bosford apparently asleep, but probably knocked out and doped. Marler might have pretended the whole thing was a joke—having an eagle like his own tattooed on Bosford's chest, I mean. He did very definitely offer quite a sum of money—the money with which Paynter bought that photographic apparatus and leased that studio. Then Bosford was taken to sea and the boat scuttled. Don't ask me how. Later the body came ashore. I should have said, of course, that Bosford had to be dressed in clothes of Marler's that would be recognised, and that Bosford's moustache was shaved off. The two men were not all that dissimilar, and after the sea had done its work that eagle on the chest would be the clinching thing. Also, Marler left plenty of clues about Bosford in that bungalow at Happton. And it was he, of course, who forged Bosford's name to the letter giving up the office at Sharman House, and who cleaned out that room.

"What happened then we may prove or we mayn't. In France Marler had his nose straightened and maybe a few other things done to change his identity. He also had that tattooing so added to as to obscure the original—just in case. Then he came back to England. The only other thing is that we know now just why Paynter went to that inquest at Seahurst. He had a lot of suspicions. He wanted to know exactly whose body it was. Later—and again don't ask me how—he either got into touch with the new Marler and tried to squeeze out a bit more money, or else Marler thought him too dangerous and got into touch with him."

"My own ideas exactly," George said. He pushed aside his empty cup and stretched his huge shoulders.

"It's getting pretty late," he said. "There'll be plenty of time to go into it all tomorrow. We may have a whole lot more news by then."

I left a few minutes later. George would have had me driven home, but I preferred to walk. As I came near the hospital I thought about Doris Bosford and how wrong my guesses about her had been. She'd been nervous with me for one reason only— because she knew she had lied in identifying a certain body as that of her husband. But I liked her, and I hoped—far beyond what recovery might tell us—that she would pull through. I thought she would; she wouldn't be one to lack fighting spirit.

Something else I was thinking about. Simon *alias* Simmonds had bolted, but Matthews had his finger-prints and someone might already be looking them up. I hoped it wasn't the one who'd recently looked up those finger-prints for me. I'd have a pretty hard job explaining to Wharton if it got to his ears. Still, that was a hurdle to try and clear when its turn came. Meanwhile I had plenty more to do. Wharton was going home to a nice cosy bed. I was going home to a restless one.

I'd already checked, in case of eventualities, New York times compared with our own. As soon as I got home I checked them again and then set the alarm clock for a quarter of an hour before the necessary time. Then I went to bed, wondering if I should get any sleep at all and if everything was right with the works of the clock. I did go to sleep, and when I woke it wasn't worth the trouble of trying to get off again. So I made myself a cup of tea, lighted a cigarette and then set about getting in good time that New York number that Cortin had given me.

There's always a sense of the miraculous to me when such a long-distance call at last comes through. This one came through amazingly clearly. I've had far worse reception in London itself.

"Is that you, Travers? Cortin here. I hope you've got no bad news for me."

"On the contrary," I said. "On two conditions—I repeat—on two conditions, I can have everything cleared up by midday tomorrow. I give you my word you'll never be troubled again."

"I see. What are the conditions?"

"That I tell your wife just as much as seems good to me, and that you yourself tell the police when you return. About that, I can see you here before you see them."

"And if I don't agree?"

"Then I wash my hands of the whole affair. Just hang up on me now and I'll know."

"My God, man, give me a second!"

"It's up to you," I said. "If you want to extend the call from your end. Yes or no?"

"Right," he said. "I'll trust you."

"You'll never regret it," I told him. "And just one other thing: whatever you're doing, arrange to ring your wife at Tyefield at midday tomorrow? You'll do that? Midday *our* time."

"If you think it advisable."

"I do," I said. "She'll be telling you some very good news."

I left it at that and rang off. I took that ticking clock into the bathroom and got back between the warm sheets.

17

JUST SUPPOSING

I GUESSED that Wharton would be in early, so I rang him at half-past eight. He was in high good humour. He didn't seem to mind in the least when I told him that important private business had turned up and I couldn't get to the Yard till after lunch.

"Not that you need me now, except for any statements," I added; and: "You didn't make too bad a hand of things, George."

"The Old Gent isn't done for yet," he told me complacently.

"Any more news of Mrs. Bosford?"

"Just finished ringing myself," he said. "She's out of the critical stage. Which reminds me: you know that a certain gentleman skipped last night? He turned out to have a bit of a record. Name of Simmonds."

I held my breath for a moment, but nothing happened. George had been too interested in Dupont's body, and I had spoken to Simmonds so quietly that he hadn't heard.

"But he won't get far," George was going on. "Funny thing he *should* bolt, when you come to think of it. We hadn't anything against him. All he's done is to draw attention to himself. He ought to make an interesting witness when we get hold of him."

"He certainly should," I said, and knew that I'd take good care not to be anywhere near. "What about the gun and so on?"

"Haven't got the ballistics report yet. The paraffin test was positive, though."

He knew I was about to ring off and he told me to wait a minute.

"Something else I wanted to ask you. Oh yes, here it is. Just jotted a few things down. That money question's been worrying me. Where did he get all that money to make a new place of that restaurant?"

"You certainly expect me to come up with some answers," I said. "But what about that racket he was in? Wasn't there plenty of money in that?"

"I know," he said. "I'd have liked something more positive. Question-marks don't look too good in a record. See you this afternoon, then."

"Fine," I said. "I'll be in about two."

So another bit of thin ice had been skated over, and if I handled that morning right, then there oughtn't to be a lot more to come.

I hadn't referred back, by the way, to that question of why no one had heard the shot. We'd gone into that the previous night and I think he'd been convinced by the fact that there was sound-proofing all along that floor. There had had to be; if not, the noise of the band upstairs would have been far too loud— that, and the feet of the dancers—and far too obtrusive for the staider clientèle who were dining downstairs.

And I'd also had the impression that, except for the records, Wharton wasn't worrying himself about the death of Marler. Marler was virtually a triple murderer, whose suicide had saved the state the costs of a trial. In a way he was no longer important except as something that cleared up Bosford's death and Paynter's. And, of course, the whole thing had been so sudden and spectacular, and to George himself the glory. Wasn't it that yarn he had handed to the Press about Doris Bosford's being about to make a statement that had driven Marler to suicide? Heaven forbid, of course, that I should even hint obscurely that George *wanted* a suicide. Maybe you have ideas about that yourself.

I waited till just after nine o'clock and then rang Tyefield Manor. It was Harry Calvert who answered.

"Hallo, Calvert," I said. "How nice to hear you. How're you keeping?"

"Can't grumble," he said. "And you?"

"To tell the truth, I'm just a bit worried. Do you think you could break some news to your sister?"

"Not about Ted!"

"Lord, no," I said. "He's fine, or so I gather. This is some very different news I don't think you're going to believe. It's about your sister's former husband Marler. I work sometimes with the Yard, and last night I was called to a restaurant that calls itself the Antoine Dupont in Osbert Street. A man had committed suicide and he turned out to be Marler. . . . No, don't argue. He *was* Marler. We have indisputable proof."

"I just can't believe it."

"You've got to believe it," I told him. "And you've got to break the news to your sister. Considering everything, she ought to be more than relieved."

"Right," he said. "I'll do it."

"One other thing. I ought to come down at once myself—unofficially, as a friend, I mean—and before I help to tie everything up with the police. I must have a chat with both yourself and your sister. You think you could see me at, say, half-past ten?"

"Yes," he said slowly. "That might do all the good in the world."

"Expect me then," I said. "No need to have me met at the station. I'll come by car."

It was a lovely morning of March. There wasn't a flush of green as yet along the thorn hedges, but the lilac buds in garden clumps were about to burst and there was everywhere an expectation of spring. It hadn't been too bad a winter, but all winters are best left behind when the sun shines on a still March morning. I'm no poet, but I didn't have to be to find something of a parallel in what would be going through the mind of Helen Cortin. Hers had been a winter she would never forget. As for her spring, it would be one she would always remember. Not that the winter hadn't been largely of her own making. Had she trusted her husband Marler's game would long since have been up. As it was, she had made pitfalls for herself, and even for me. She had had to be protected at whatever cost, and, but for some lucky breaks, the cost, even to myself, might have been disastrously heavy.

I drove quietly into the curving drive, but Calvert must have heard me or have been on the lookout, for he was waiting for me just outside the door.

"How'd the news go?" I asked him.

"A tremendous shock, of course," he said. "Lucky it was discovered in time. A bit of a shock to me, too, if it comes to that." He held the door wide for me. "You wouldn't like to give me a hint what it is you're going to talk about?"

"It's too complicated for a hint," I said, "but don't let it worry you."

We went into that lovely room where I had been once before. There was a fire in the grate and Helen Cortin's chair was facing it. A work-box was on the side table by her, but she laid the needlework aside as I came in, and she gave me a wan smile. Her face had a pallor, and the eyes were even more dark.

"How good of you to come," she said as I bent over her hand. "But what terrible news it was that you gave us."

"You're a real friend, Travers." That was Calvert. "It'd have been pretty grim if the news had reached us some other way."

"Please, Harry! Don't talk about it. Besides, here's the coffee. You *would* like some coffee?"

I said I'd love it. There were petits fours with it, too. But for what was in the air it might have been almost a reunion as we sat there chatting. I asked about her husband and she asked about Bernice, and then I asked Calvert when he was taking up his new post.

"As a matter of fact, I'm not," he said. "I suddenly realised I wouldn't like it a bit, so I'm going to Canada instead. Quentin Motors are opening a chain of agencies there. As a matter of fact I'm flying over the day after tomorrow."

I said I wished I was twenty years younger and able to see the world for a few years.

"But you're going to miss him?" I said to Helen Cortin.

"I shall," she said. "But I ought to tell you something. Harry's got quite fond of you, too. I'd been hoping you might be good friends."

"I hope we shall be," I said. "After all, your husband's already my very good friend; I think you and Bernice get on pretty well together, too."

"Isn't it getting a kind of mutual admiration society?" Calvert said dryly, and we all laughed. Helen Cortin actually laughed. It was a bit strained, but it was still a laugh.

Then coffee-drinking was over and the tray went out. The room held a moment's uneasiness. Calvert lighted a cigarette. I preferred my pipe. Helen Cortin sat almost primly in her chair, clasped hands on her lap. She was a long way now from that almost flaunting Carmen that hung on her dining-room wall.

"Well," I said, "I suppose we've got to get down to business some time. May I begin by telling you that I'm here on false pretences. Not officially, mind you—purely privately, but still on false pretences."

"Afraid I don't follow you," Calvert said.

"Let me explain," I told him. "What I say is going to come as an enormous surprise, but it's still unofficial. Just a little talk—a straight talk—among friends. Your husband, Mrs. Cortin, is, as I said, a friend of mine. For reasons of his own, he's convinced I'm someone he can absolutely trust—"

"I'm sure you are."

I caught her eye for a moment, but she looked away.

"Well, that's good of you. But just before he left for America we happened to be lunching together. He told me he was worried about you. He said there was something very serious on your mind and it was seriously affecting your health. He said you'd denied having anything on your mind. Then he asked me if I'd keep an eye on you while he was away."

"On me?"

"Wait a moment," I said. "I haven't fully explained. He could have asked that of me in two capacities—as a friend, and as the head of a detective agency. I said I'd prefer to combine the two. He refused. He said that while you were the one thing in the world who really mattered to him, he still wouldn't have you spied on. I convinced him otherwise but only after a protracted argument. My own point was that I also couldn't act as a spy. I could only handle the matter at a distance, as it were, and professionally. Also, as he would be my client, professional integrity would ensure that under no circumstances would anything that I discovered be communicated to anyone but himself. Everything would be as secret as between doctor and patient, or priest and penitent. And that was how things were left. My assignment was to discover what was worrying you."

Her face was even paler. The hands in her lap were no longer still.

"I set to work," I went on. "A labour of love for a friend, and with my own professional reputation also at stake. I had highly trained and trusted operatives at my disposal, but, all the same, I took good care that none of them should know too much. Whatever came to me I appraised and sorted and then gave new directions. I also did a considerable amount of work myself. Shall I tell you what I discovered?"

"Why not?" Calvert said evenly.

"Very well, then," I said. "I discovered a matter of four thousand pounds lying handy in a bank. I guessed that you, Mrs. Cortin, were being blackmailed. I and a man of mine were at a certain hotel when the blackmail money was handed in. I saw it delivered to Room 337, and later I saw you, Calvert, leave another room and follow the man who'd given his name as Foster. You followed that man and you led us to the Restaurant Antoine Dupont."

"I see," he said. "And what then?"

"Nothing," I said, "except that we identified the man Foster as a man whose name was actually Simmonds, the manager of that restaurant. But I'd like to go back a bit. Marler had been engaged in a smuggling racket with a man named Bosford, operating from a bungalow at Happton. Mrs. Bosford had come to the agency because her husband was missing, and we picked up a clue that took us to Seahurst. That was why I was at Seahurst the day of the inquest when you, Mrs. Cortin, identified a body as that of your husband Marler. The chief item in that identification was tattooing on his chest. Let me say at once that you were quite right to identify him. But the truth has turned out to be this: certain enquiries by Scotland Yard, in which I had a part, culminated in what happened last night. Marler, in short, had killed Bosford and passed off the body as his own. It was all very simple. Bosford had been drugged and Marler's stepbrother—a professional tattooist—reproduced the same design on Bosford's chest. Later we know that Marler killed that stepbrother in case he might talk.

"Then Marler went to France and employed a plastic surgeon. He came back to England with a face no one could ever recognise and used the money your husband had given him, Mrs. Cortin, to facilitate a divorce—five thousand pounds. And this is something that the police do not know, and I must ask for your implicit confidence. They think Marler simply rigged up everything because the police were on his track about that smuggling racket, and that he came back and started again in the restaurant business because that had always been his line. The real truth, of course, is this:

"You, Mrs. Cortin, were the one in his mind from the very start. The whole scheme was built round you. He knew a wealthy man was in love with you and would marry you as soon as the divorce was through. He chose a better way: he arranged his own death and you—after your new marriage—would be his income for life. Am I right?"

She couldn't answer.

"For God's sake get it over!" Calvert burst out. "What's the rest of it?"

"Bluntly—this," I said. "Marler made himself known. The shock must have been terrible. He had big commitments and he wanted big money—money neither of you had got. But if—I repeat *if*—a way out was found by letting him have a key to help himself to that jewellery at Morniment Mansions, then I would advise that a clean breast be made of it, Mrs. Cortin, to your husband. He'll almost certainly notify the insurance company that the jewels have been found and return their cheque. As for the four thousand, that also will have to be a confidential matter with your husband. The police are highly tactful. What estate Marler left is legally yours and your husband and the police and the lawyers can get everything settled up without anything getting through to the Press.

"And one other very important thing. The public have long forgotten—I doubt if they ever cared much in any case—that the supposedly drowned Marler had a widow. So you and your husband can get away for the statutory time and get legally married. That will make everything in order."

"No," she said. "No! There's no reason why Edward should know."

"Don't be foolish," her brother said. "You won't be mentioned if what Travers tells us is correct, but all this business will be spread across the newspapers. Ted's bound to see it."

"In any case, he knows something already," I said. "I rang him in the early hours of this morning. This is the actual conversation. . . ."

By the time I had finished she was crying gently to herself. I got to my feet.

"Don't forget," I said. "Not so many minutes now and your husband will be ringing you. You're all the world to him—don't forget that. It was he you were really trying to shield. So open your heart to him. Unless I'm very far wrong, he'll be back here in a very few hours."

She had turned aside in the chair and the tears were unashamedly coming. I gave a nod towards Calvert and we went quietly out.

"You're a good fellow, Travers," he told me, and he too seemed to have difficulty in finding words. "I don't know how we're going to repay you."

"Let that be my headache," I told him. "And, by the way, I've always wanted to see that garage-workshop of yours. Might I have a look?"

"Delighted to show you."

We went past the drawing-room and along the gravelled continuation round the house, and there the garage was. The Rolls was there, but no chauffeur. There was also a high-powered motor-bicycle. That, I thought, was how Calvert had got to Morniment Mansions or town when he wanted the matter kept secret.

It was a fine, large garage. It had a metal lathe, oxy-acetylene equipment and racks of tools of which I didn't even know the names. As I told him, it was a mechanic's dream.

"Sorry I can't get you to explain everything to me," I said, "but I ought to be getting back to town. Just one little thing I'd like to say, though. If you people are in any way worrying about Marler, then don't. Killing him was like treading on the head of a rattlesnake."

"Killing?" he said. "But he killed himself?"

"I know," I said.

There was an old box there, upturned and with a sack on it for cushion. I sat on it and began stoking my pipe.

"I'm a queer bird," I said, "and I often ask some damnably funny questions. For instance, do you ever find yourself asking if you're not two people?"

"Can't say I do," he said, and a bit uneasily.

"You are, you know. I certainly am. I'm a private citizen, for one thing—a chap who even broke the law occasionally during the war by buying this and that on the black market. Sometimes I have to be the law, which means that I have to look at things in a vastly different way. Now take Marler. Let's suppose he'd done to me what he did to you people. Do you know what I—the private citizen—might have done?"

"Don't know," he said. "You tell me."

"Well, I think I'd have gone about it this way. I'd have made up my mind to find Marler and then I'd have killed him, and with no more compunction than I'd have killed a rat. I mightn't have been as clever as you were in tracking his agent to that restaurant, but I'd have found means somehow. After that—maybe through a detection agency—I'd have got acquainted with the layout and the principals. I think I'd have arrived at a good idea that Dupont was Marler. Of course, I'd have ways of proving it.

It's true that I couldn't get him to bare his chest, but there was also that little nick on his ear. The agency I employed would find out about that for me. . . . You still interested?"

"Who couldn't be?"

"I don't know," I said. "After all, it's just supposing. But when everything was certain I'd have taken a gun I had, and in this shop I'd have made a silencing gadget for it. I'd also have contrived a kind of rubber seating, so that the silencer made no marks on the barrel. Then I'd have tried some very simple disguise—say a good false moustache and some dark glasses—and I'd have gone to that restaurant at about nine o'clock, just when Dupont had completed his rounds of the downstairs tables and would be in his room again.

"I'd leave an overcoat I didn't give a damn about—in case I had to go without it—at the cloakroom and I'd have gone to the wash-room and watched from there till people were going up the stairs to the restaurant. I'd have kept a bit behind them, and when they went on towards the restaurant I'd have slipped quickly along to Dupont's room, opened the door and gone in. One hand would have been pointing the gun at him and the other would have locked or bolted the door. I'd have told him to stand up and turn round. Before he knew it I'd have plugged him neatly by his right temple. I'd have taken from my pocket a fair-sized pad—one of those things you polish car windows with—and with the gun in his fingers I'd have fired a shot into that pad. I'd remove the silencer, rig the number of bullets, put the gun by his hand, take a quick look and then go downstairs again, removing my gloves. Then I'd tell the cloakroom girl I'd expected friends, take my coat and go out to look for them. And that'd be that. Except, of course, for one very vital thing: as soon as I'd shot Dupont I'd have naturally whipped open his shirt and verified that he had a tattoo mark. The original might have been disguised, but it'd still be there. And, in connection with that, just one other little thing. Keep it under your hat. The police don't know it. I took good care they wouldn't know it, but when I looked for that tattoo mark last night Dupont's shirt was still unbuttoned. *Someone had had a look at that tattoo mark before me.*"

He looked away. He didn't need to flick the ash from his cigarette. The hand was shaking enough already.

"You mean that you thought he hadn't committed suicide after all?"

"I knew he hadn't. For me it was just a question of which trust had to be betrayed—the semi-private one or the professional one. I kept my mouth shut. And so, Dupont committed suicide. Everything else tallies."

I looked at my watch and smiled.

"Sorry to have bored you with all this, but I thought you'd rather be out of the way while your sister was taking that telephone call. It ought to be pretty nearly over now."

He walked with me towards the car. Just at the angle with the drawing-room he suddenly stopped.

"This is just supposing: you ever going to tell anybody else what you've just told me?"

"Good lord, no!" I told him decisively. "I may be a couple of different persons, but neither of them's a big enough fool to bore people with his private opinions."

We moved on, and I got into the car.

"Well, good luck in Canada. It's a fine place to forget things."

"Yes," he said. "And to be forgotten."

"Something in that," I said. "Oh, and just one more thing: congratulations on your perspicacity."

He stared. My hand went to the gear lever. The car was already purring over.

"Just a matter of an anonymous letter," I said. "It tried to head you off that manager and tell you he wasn't the man. And possibly to stop you from killing him. Not that you'd have done it."

"Yes," he said. "That was the one thing I guessed right about. It bore your district postmark—W.C.2. That restaurant's S.W.1."

I didn't mind his having that last word. In fact, I'd moved the car on even before that last word had actually been spoken. At the drive gates I didn't take one backward look to see if he was still there.

I drove straight back to town, because I knew I'd have time at the flat for a service lunch and to get to the Yard by a just comfortable two o'clock. I didn't do much thinking about the spring as I drove. I was thinking about how narrow a squeak I'd had myself, and how I'd have to get word from Tyefield that evening of exactly when Edward Cortin was flying back, so that I could be at the airport to meet him. We'd have a lot to talk over before he saw his wife. And what I'd have to tell him I was already beginning to think out.

When I got into the London traffic I did no thinking at all, at least till I neared home and the hospital. Then I couldn't help thinking of Doris Bosford—the butterfly who'd been almost broken on a particularly nasty wheel. As soon as she left hospital, I told myself, I'd have to see her again. I think I smiled to myself or at myself, and that damnable inquisitiveness that always possessed me. Maybe, I was telling myself, I would really know at last just how much had been in that box beneath the bed.

THE END